SCOURGE

SCOURGE

THE KISS OF DEATH

a novel

TERRY WESTON MARSH

NEW YORK

LONDON • NASHVILLE • MELBOURNE • VANCOUVER

SCOURGE

The Kiss of Death, A Novel

Published in New York, New York, by Morgan James Publishing. Morgan James is a trademark of Morgan James, LLC. www.MorganJamesPublishing.com

ISBN 9781631953804 paperback
ISBN 9781631953811 eBook
Library of Congress Control Number: 2020948949

Cover Design by:
Megan Dillon

Interior Design by:
Melissa Farr
melissa@backporchcreative.com

Morgan James is a proud partner of Habitat for Humanity Peninsula and Greater Williamsburg. Partners in building since 2006.

Get involved today! Visit
MorganJamesPublishing.com/giving-back

PROLOGUE

In the long-ago land of Olde Earth . . .

PART ONE

CHAPTER I

Something shifted in the shadows of the midwinter moon. The Wild Dog moon, his mother called it, for the hungry packs that howled outside the nearby villages.

Geoffrey scratched frost from his window and peered out. Horses. *Bigger than Daddy's.* Men in steel helmets and leather armor, emerging from the edge of the woods.

The hairs prickled on Geoffrey's thin arms. He shivered then scampered away from the window. Strange that the pattering of his bare feet should sound like pounding hooves. He leaped into his bed, burrowed into the still-warm feather mattress, and tried to imagine himself an eagle, wings to the wind.

There was a sound like thunder; the ancient stone manor shuddered around him.

"Wellam, don't go down there!" Geoffrey sensed horror in his mother's voice, and—for the first time in his six short years—he was afraid.

Again the boom, and a splintering crash. Geoffrey tiptoed to his bedroom door and peered out into the dark hallway. His mother clung to his father. The man pulled free and charged down the grand staircase.

"Geoffrey." His mother propelled him backwards into his room. "Lock your door, don't come out."

In the dark behind the door, Geoffrey held his breath, tried to listen past the hammering of his heart. He heard his mother scream. He opened the door a finger crack, saw a soldier twist a fist into her hair and drag her down the stairs.

Geoffrey ran back to his bed, yanked a wooden box from underneath. His fingers combed through colored stones, pottery shards, a hawk's skull. *Where was it?* His small hand closed around the rusty dagger he had dug up in the woods last fall. He crept out to the landing, peered through the railing at the parlor below.

In shadowy torchlight, he saw his father swing a fireplace poker, strike one soldier, and whirl to face another.

Where was Mama?

A man on horseback stormed into the house through the wrecked front door, ducking his head to clear the lintel. He charged Geoffrey's father, swung a long club, and knocked him down with a blow to the chest.

Geoffrey shrank back, his stomach sick.

The horseman dismounted, grabbed the poker, and stirred the banked embers in the massive fireplace. "Where's the boy?"

Geoffrey raced back to his room, shut the door, and shot the bolt. Boots pounded the stairs, the landing, the hallway. The door handle rattled. He backed away, his dagger pointed at the door in two trembling hands.

There came the blow of a boot on the door. Another kick, and again. The dagger handle was slippery in Geoffrey's sweating palm. He shifted it to his other hand, then back.

"The battering ram." There was a soft bump against his door, as of a man leaning to rest. From downstairs, the smack of a fist on flesh, his mother's pleading sob. Geoffrey yanked the bolt, jerked the door open. A soldier lurched inward. Geoffrey ducked beneath him and ran down the stairs.

They were tying his mother to a chair, her hands behind her. She kicked. The horseman who had felled his father slapped her. Geoffrey charged the man, thrust his dagger with both hands, and felt it rip through fabric into flesh. A percussion of pain on his cheekbone downed him like a canary off a cat's paw.

"Curse you, poxed skellum."

Geoffrey rolled to his feet. A soldier seized him by the shoulders, jammed him into a chair beside his mother, and tied his hands behind his back.

The man whom Geoffrey had stabbed was short and stocky, with black eyes and a purple birthmark staining his forehead. He swore again as he jerked Geoffrey's dagger from his thigh.

Geoffrey's father was also trussed to a chair. A rope around his neck—tied beneath the seat—forced his chest against his lap. He craned his head sideways to address the man Geoffrey had stabbed.

"Bertraks," he said. "The Rebellion is over."

Bertraks stirred the contents of a bucket which hung over the fire then slung the thick black liquid onto Geoffrey's father and mother. Geoffrey, picking furiously at the knotted rope around his wrists, barely felt the hot pitch splashing onto his shoulders.

"Spare my family," Geoffrey's father said. "They have done nothing."

Bertraks yanked two torches from his saddlebags and lit them at the fireplace.

"Not our son," Geoffrey's mother pleaded. "Not the boy . . . please!"

Geoffrey strained with all his might, trying to yank his hands through the ropes. His skin shredded off, wrists burning and bleeding.

"Run, Geoffrey! Run, baby cricket, run!" his mother cried. Geoffrey bolted for the stairs.

Bertraks mounted his horse, tossed one of the torches to a soldier. "But not until they hear their son scream."

Geoffrey scampered up to the landing. Hoofbeats clattered behind him on the stairs.

Grandfather's sword . . .

He raced down the black corridor to the last door. He grabbed at the knob—locked. He slammed his little shoulder into the door, and again.

The hoofbeats stopped. The rider's boots stalked up to him, bearing a ball of fire.

Geoffrey stumbled backwards against the window at the end of the hallway. The torch hissed and snapped like a living beast. He felt the heat of it on his cheeks, saw the purple stain dance on the man's forehead. Bertraks touched the torch to the boy's pitch-covered shoulders. Geoffrey's breath caught at the back of his throat, erupted as an animal shriek, then blended with two terrible screams from the parlor below.

A few miles away, not far from another manor—grander than the one Geoffrey and his parents shared—a woman in a tattered nightdress leaned into a snowy wind as she stumbled through a field. She clutched a toddler in her arms.

Nighttime for the toddler had always meant drifting on a lullaby from drowse to dream as she merged into her mother's warmth. But now icy needles raked her naked little body, and her mother's skin was painfully clammy.

The woman fell again and hit the frozen ground so hard that the little girl spilled into the snow.

Her mother tried to rise but could not. She pulled the child into the curl of her body. Her stiff fingers brushed snow from the girl's long lashes.

"There, my baby, my—"

A coughing fit seized the woman, like the many the child had known since she was first jarred awake in the womb. A croupy bark, a gush of pink foam, moist warmth running down the toddler's neck.

Gradually, an awful solitude.

The cooling husk was not Mama, but a doughy length of wood next to which the little one lay. She touched what had been a face, tried to pull the mouth open, and finally wrapped her tiny fingers around the slender chain at the white throat. She tugged with both hands, as though she might pull a last bit of her mother into herself.

Just outside the smashed door of the stone manor where Geoffrey lived, a man on a great blue roan listened to the screams. Satisfied with the night's work, he turned his mount and set off into the stormy night.

He did not see the little boy, streaking yellow flames, plunge backwards out of the upstairs window.

In the instant after Bertraks's torch had ignited him, Geoffrey's fingers found the window latch behind his back. He shoved his little body backwards and the casement swung open.

Landing in the bushes below, Geoffrey rolled off and sprinted, still on fire, toward the woods. He tripped as he reached the first trees, tumbled down an embankment, and scrambled on hands and knees to the little brook where he had caught a crayfish last summer. He plunged his body into the icy stream.

Bertraks, on horseback, burst out of the front door and galloped to the end of the house. He jabbed the bushes with his sword, then circled the yard.

"Come out, fetid swine."

Hoofbeats, coming closer. As the torchlight splashed into the woods, Geoffrey forced himself out of the streambed and crawled up the opposite side of the ravine. At the top were the ragged remains of the tent fort he had built while playing soldier. He freed a blanket from a frozen sapling, wrapped it around himself, and stumbled out of the woods onto the road.

Out of the dark, a rider bearing down on him. "Off the road, beggar!"

Geoffrey fell as steel-shod hooves pounded the ground a hand's breadth from his little body. He watched the blue roan recede into the snowy darkness then willed himself to roll off the road into a field. He crawled until a violent chill shook him to the ground. Snowflakes drifted down and soon buried him.

———————

A gray light with cold orange streaks was growing on the horizon when Geoffrey heard a sound, like a mewing kitten.

In a snowdrift a few yards away lay a young woman.

Geoffrey dragged himself over to her. The woman's stiff arms cradled a little girl whose bright violet eyes regarded Geoffrey. As he lifted the toddler, the dead woman's necklace broke, so tightly was it clutched in the tiny fists.

Carrying the child, Geoffrey managed to stagger across a pasture before falling over a low rock wall. He had an overpowering urge to sleep forever as he sat with his back against the stones. He held the girl in his arms, trying to shield her from the cold.

He drifted off. Later, when a yelp floated to his ears on cotton and something licked his cheek, he tried to move but couldn't. It was like the nightmare of being paralyzed, brain and body struggling frantically to wake up.

"Tiberias."

Footsteps crunched through the snow. Geoffrey finally got his eyes open but still couldn't move. A man in a shabby chamois coat squatted and studied Geoffrey's face, so close that Geoffrey could see each white bristle on the man's sun-browned cheeks.

The last thing Geoffrey remembered before blackness fell was a strong arm, lifting the little girl and himself from the snow.

CHAPTER 2

Silas was indeed strong for a man who had seen some sixty winters. With Geoffrey and the girl in his arms, he tramped back through the snow to an old wagon. Covering the sides of the wagon was a peddler's collection of pots, kettles, and cans. A wisp of smoke curled from the pipe on the roof.

"We needed more trouble, Jenqy, and we got it." Silas's mare, tethered to a front wheel and munching a mound of hay, ignored him.

Silas climbed the steps at the back of the weathered wooden contraption and opened the door. The aroma of the bread he had baked earlier wafted out. He crossed the bearskin rug to the narrow bunk at the front of the wagon, where he laid the unconscious boy.

As he disentangled the toddler from the boy's arms, she began to cry.

"Muck head. Muck head." Silas's parrot, in a birdcage that swung from the ceiling, responded to the girl's outcry.

"Shut up, ya scraggly feather bag," Silas said.

The girl screamed louder.

"What a warbler, huh, Graycie? And the other one reeks like a chimney."

The boy was wrapped in a tattered blanket and smelled of pine tar. Puzzling, too, was the fact that the boy's left ankle was swollen and possibly broken. How had he walked, and from where? Except for a few country estates, the nearest houses were miles away.

"The purge continues, Graycie girl."

With the crying child on his hip, Silas put a teakettle on the little woodstove then opened the grate and tossed in some sticks.

"But they haven't got us yet, birdy bird."

He prepared porridge of millet and honey. The girl stopped crying after the first spoonful then slurped every bite like she couldn't get enough.

"Greedy little devil," Silas said.

"I think she's just hungry, sir."

Silas started. The young lad was watching him with calm serenity.

"Bet that boy's hungry too, Graycie—keep an eye on your birdseed."

"Is she going to be all right, sir?"

"I ask you, Graycie, dear bird, how should I know? I find Tiberias yesterday. What do I want with two more lost dogs?"

"We're not dogs."

"He has got pluck, Graycie. Has he got a name?"

"Geoffrey."

Silas settled the little girl onto a stuffed chair, the only sizable piece of furniture in the wagon, and tucked a coverlet around her. Her eyelids were drifting.

"Has this one a name?"

Geoffrey made no reply.

"Guess he doesn't know his own sister's name."

"She is not my sister, sir."

The girl's hand relaxed, revealing the remains of a chain with half a lover's locket attached.

Silas studied the talisman. No daughter of royalty would own such a cheap trinket. He looked again at the child. He reckoned that she was about three years old, maybe small for her age. With her large eyes, long lashes, and blonde ringlets, she was delicately beautiful, even as she slept.

Silas regarded Geoffrey. Who was this lad, perhaps not yet seven years old, who so favored his own lost son, and whose first concern had been, not for himself, but for the little girl—a child he apparently did not even know?

"Where do you strays come from?"

The boy looked into Silas's eyes but did not reply. His lips were blue and his face a cadaverous white.

As Geoffrey continued to gaze at him, quietude and compassion pooling in the wide brown eyes, Silas's memory intruded. That same serenity had been in his own son's eyes, when, dying of Scourge, he had awakened, looked up, and quietly told his father there was no need to cry anymore. A minute later the boy was dead, joining his young mother and leaving Silas utterly alone.

Silas retrieved a bottle of brandy and poured some on a cloth.

"Bite down." He jammed the cloth into Geoffrey's mouth. "Name's Silas. I'm gonna try not to hurt you."

He carefully unwrapped the blanket from Geoffrey's body—there must be injuries other than the ankle.

Not even the Battle of Shards, where Silas was witness to disembowelments, decapitations, and his best friend dying three days after an abdominal wound—agony increasing by the hour until at last his belly was so rigid that the slightest movement brought screams of pain—could have prepared Silas for what he saw next.

Waxy, charred sheets of skin slid off Geoffrey's shoulders as the coarse blanket came away. From the boy's neck to his navel and halfway down his back, much of his skin was burned off, leaving behind yellowish fat that was charred brownish-black. In some places muscle was exposed, black like burned meat. Some skin remained hanging, translucent, revealing clotted blood vessels underneath.

Silas knew from his war years that the one mercy accorded a severely burned person was the destruction of the skin's nerve endings. Not once did the boy cry out as Silas applied all the liniment he had. He wrapped the injured child in clean linen strips, which he tore from a shirt.

He cushioned Geoffrey as best he could by laying him on a sheepskin on the bunk and tucking it around him.

"Who did this to you, boy?"

Silas knelt beside Geoffrey and looked into his face. But the light in the boy's eyes had already clouded. His eyelids closed, even as the little body went limp and his breathing stopped. Silent moments passed.

A guttural cry burst forth from Silas. The parrot stopped picking at the salt stick in her cage as Silas tore off his clothes and threw himself on top of Geoffrey's still-warm body.

Twenty-five years had passed since Silas prayed for the life of his wife before she died. He had cried out, too, for the life of their only child, who had helped Silas nurse his beloved in the days before she died of Scourge, a virulent, plague-like illness. His dear child, of whom he thought, "the boy is stout like me, he will not sicken." But the boy died only an hour after falling ill.

When his son died, Silas had been unable to cry. Now his tears flowed onto the ashen cheeks of this child, a stranger.

Hours later, his body still racked with sporadic sobs, Silas heard something. The little girl was making a cooing sound, interrupting herself every few seconds with a hiccup.

That's when Silas noticed that Geoffrey was breathing.

CHAPTER 3

Geoffrey, riding piggyback, held onto the hard muscles of his father's shoulders and drank in the man's fragrance of leather and saddle oil. A soldier on horseback burst out of the woods, thundered straight at them, and hurled his spear. The point went all the way through his father's chest and jabbed into Geoffrey's stomach.

"Ho, on now."

Silas's voice jolted Geoffrey awake. He felt the wagon lurch forward. The cobweb strands of his nightmare floated away on the rhythmic creak of an axle.

From his bunk at the front of the swaying wagon, Geoffrey could see a square of sunlight as it travelled along the wall. He tried to turn his head to find the window, but his neck was encased in something like a cast. All else was as it had been: the stove, the yellow bird in its cage, the stuffed chair . . .

Where was the little girl? Geoffrey tried to get up, but his body would not bend. He managed to raise himself to an elbow before the pungent odor of camphor liniment started his head spinning.

"Halt," came a voice.

"Whoa, Jenquilla." Silas's voice. The wagon stopped swaying.

"Search it," the first voice said, creepily familiar.

"What reason?" Silas said.

"Business of the Order of Caerdon."

Bertraks! Geoffrey's face went clammy as bile came up the back of his throat. He felt the wagon shift as someone mounted the rear step. The door started to open.

"The boy's got Scourge," Silas said.

The door slammed shut.

Bertraks's voice again. "There's been no Scourge for years."

"Truth be, I ain't sure," Silas said. "Can you tell me if them dark marks and swelled neck be Scourge?"

"Shut up."

"That's why I keeps my girl outside."

The door opened again and a man holding a red cloth over his mouth and nose peered in.

Those black eyes. Geoffrey vomited. The man jerked back, must have fallen off the wagon into the snow. Geoffrey retched again then realized there had been no purple stain on the man's forehead.

A voice stammered that he'd never seen Scourge, but the boy in the wagon was awful sick.

"We'll just be a-gettin' on, then," Silas said.

"Soldier," Bertraks said. "How old is that boy?"

"He's about—"

"Just had his second birthday yesterday, same day as he took ill," Silas said.

"That seem right, soldier?"

There was a pause. "Uh, yes, sir."

"We seek Geoffrey Davenant," Bertraks said. "Six years old, brown hair, brown eyes. If you see him—"

"Caerdon now also hunts children?"

"Watch your tongue, old man," Bertraks said. "We just want him for safekeeping."

"Safekeeping?"

"He's an orphan. Parents were executed last night."

"What was their crime?"

"Wellam Lord Davenant gave aid to the Rebels near the end of the war," Bertraks said. "If someone finds the boy, they might harm him, as a Rebel sympathizer."

The sound of horse hooves faded.

Geoffrey sank back into the sheepskin and cried.

When Geoffrey saw Silas enter the wagon with the little girl, he fumbled for the end of the bandage—coming unwound from his neck—and dashed the tears from his eyes.

Silas settled the girl into the stuffed chair. "No one looking for you, little lass." He knelt beside Geoffrey. "Tell me what you know about this wee one, here."

It was hard to talk. Geoffrey's throat was raw and his lips were giant mushrooms.

"Was the dead woman wearing any other jewelry?"

Geoffrey tried to shake his head. His neck hurt.

The little girl—her eyes on Geoffrey—cooed at the parrot, who warbled back. She chortled as their conversation went back and forth, giggle-twerp-giggle-twerp.

Silas stirred a saucepan in its cradle on the stove. He put a spoon of cold millet porridge into the girl's mouth. She spat.

"No time to heat it up," Silas said. "We've got a long road."

He dipped another spoonful out of the pan. As it reached her mouth, her little arm sent the spoon clattering into the wall.

Silas growled, raised his hand.

Don't! Geoffrey lunged toward Silas. As he fell off the bunk, he saw that the man was only reaching to retrieve the spoon.

Silas chuckled and stirred the embers inside the little stove. "Just like my Cherissa. Things have to be a certain way, eh, Graycie?" He wiped a blob of porridge from his eye. "You hungry too?" Silas looked at Geoffrey on the floor. "Or just clumsy?"

Geoffrey's ankle throbbed with every heartbeat. He ached all over.

Silas picked him up and put him in a sitting position on the bunk. The bandages had slid down, exposing the burned flesh on Geoffrey's neck.

"This look like 'safekeeping' to you, Graycie?"

Silas adjusted the linen strips. "This was my only good shirt, boy. I'll see you work it off when you get well."

He handed Geoffrey a bowl of the porridge, now warm. Geoffrey drained it.

The girl started crying.

"I have scared her," Geoffrey said. Maybe he did look like a Scourge victim.

"Naw. She just doesn't want to be forgotten."

Silas gave her a bowl. She dipped into it and was soon covered in gray globs from her forearms to her forehead.

Geoffrey tipped over onto his side on the bunk and closed his eyes. Tiberias jumped up beside him, circled nose-to-tail, and nestled down at the boy's head.

"He's brought us real danger, Graycie." Silas poured some seed into a cup in the bird's cage. "As if you and me being fugitives ourselves isn't enough."

He wiped the porridge pan then stowed the bowls and spoons in a crate under the bunk.

"He's heir to lands and a title." Silas wiped the toddler's face. "But you . . ." He cupped her chin and looked into her eyes. "You're nothing but the daughter of a dead servant girl. For all you're so pretty."

A few moments later, Silas—the little girl bundled in his arms—stepped over Geoffrey and went out the front of the wagon. He sat on the box, picked up the reins.

"Ho, Jenqy." He turned the rig around. "We sure can't be going to Caerdontown to look for their kin, after all that."

The old wagon melted off into the fogged fields of snow.

CHAPTER 4

On a warm spring day a few months later, the wagon rolled along a rutted road through a meadow of wildflowers. Silas held the reins loosely, the little girl balanced on his arm.

Tiberias romped nearby, snapping at the occasional butterfly.

"Hey," Geoffrey called. He was walking behind the wagon, barely keeping pace.

"Not yet, boy."

Geoffrey stopped. He was out of breath and his ankle hurt.

I hate him.

He sat down in the grass beside the dirt road. Tiberias trotted up, put his paws on Geoffrey's chest, and licked his face. Geoffrey hugged the dog to him as they fell back in the grass.

Tiberias sprang at a cabbage butterfly, his claws digging into Geoffrey's chest.

"Ouch." Tender, thick scar tissue had begun to form on his body where the burns had been. He closed his eyes and felt the sun's red warmth flow through his eyelids. The creak of wagon wheels drifted away on a breeze of honeysuckle. Moments passed, or maybe hours.

"You're not building strength laying there on the ground." Geoffrey had noticed that Silas only used his country accent around strangers.

Geoffrey got up and limped after Silas; the wagon waited a hundred yards down the road. The fields, not yet plowed, were green with spring weeds and yellow with dandelions. He wandered over and picked one, rubbing it on his nose before he joined his guardian on the wagon.

Riding in silence beside Silas, Geoffrey watched as the mare tried to twitch a bumblebee away from her head. She whinnied when the bee disappeared into her ear, then bolted.

Silas fell backwards off the seat, lost the reins, and almost lost the girl.

Geoffrey grabbed the reins. "Whoa, girl!" The speeding wagon hit a rock; Geoffrey bounced into the air but kept his grip on the reins, regained his feet. He yanked the reins so hard he thought his wrists would break. "Whoa, Jenqy, whoa, now."

The mare slowed to a walk. Geoffrey sat down, his forearms on fire. Tiberias sprang onto the wagon and settled himself at Geoffrey's feet.

"Where'd a rich man's son learn to drive a horse and wagon?" Silas rubbed his knuckles into Geoffrey's scalp so hard it hurt. But there was a note of approval in that gruff voice.

"Jenquilla," Silas hollered at the mare. "You happy with this cabbagehead at the reins?"

Ask him now. "You did not tell me about the Rebellion," Geoffrey said. "Why Mama and Papa . . . and who—"

"Don't start your questions again."

"I need to know."

Silas gave an exasperated growl. "You said your father was a member of the House of Overlords."

Geoffrey nodded, rubbing his scalp—still tender from Silas's knuckles.

"I don't know why he would have supported the Rebellion," Silas said. "Higher ups like him already had everything. So someone must have falsely accused him of aiding the Rebels."

"Why?"

"So they could take his title and estate."

Geoffrey had a sudden, desperate need to remember his mother's face. She had that little mole above her lip—but which side?

"Best you don't think about 'em too much, son," Silas said. "But mind what I told you: don't ever tell anyone your full name."

They were driving past a farm, a repetition of the dozens they had seen that morning: a stone hut sulking in a muddy yard, a crumbling milking shed, a cow or two, the occasional pig or chicken.

"Who owns this land?" Geoffrey said.

Silas nodded toward a ragged man picking up stones and dropping them into a burlap bag. "Not him, that's for sure."

Geoffrey gave Silas the reins and took the little girl onto his lap. "She has a name." He smoothed the soft curls on her head, which always seemed to stick out in back.

"We don't know what it is," Silas said.

"She calls herself Dee."

"That isn't enough of a name for her."

"We can't just keep calling her 'girl.'"

"We'll call her Damaris. It was good enough for my grandmother." Silas settled the matter.

For a while, Geoffrey watched the blue smudges on the horizon. Mountains, secreting themselves behind clouds, in perpetual rearrangement.

"What happened to Damaris's family?" Geoffrey asked.

"I reckon same as what happened to yours."

"You mean her father—"

"Probably a member of the House of Overlords, like yours."

"But you said her mother was a servant."

"You're talking like your ears got burnt off too, boy," Silas said. "She's high-born; you can tell by looking at her."

The road was rougher now, the wagon creaking with every jolt. Tiberias leaped down and resumed his butterfly-chasing adventures.

"Where are we going?" Geoffrey asked.

Silas made no answer.

"My father told me about the New Land, across the Two Seas," Geoffrey said. "Can we go there?"

"Markarian? Not unless we can get this creaky old crate to float and teach Jenquilla to swim real good."

"I bet she could pull us across the Rockline between the Two Seas."

Damaris grabbed a double handful of Geoffrey's face and yanked on his cheeks.

"I bet *she* could pull us across the Rockline." Silas pinched Damaris's chubby arm. "Such a strong little whiffet."

Damaris chortled, and Silas laughed so loudly and with such abandon that Geoffrey, for the first time since the night of the attack, smiled a little.

"So here I am," Silas laughed. "Stuck with three lost puppies: one of 'em a furry four-foot, one of 'em a high-born maiden, and one of 'em a cabbagehead."

CHAPTER 5

O n a hot summer evening in a village square, a dragon roared.
"Louder," whispered nine-year-old Damaris to Geoffrey as
she swooped her unicorn marionette onto the stage of Silas's
wagon-turned-puppet theater.

But this was their fourth show that day; Geoffrey was dizzy and his throat hurt. He lifted his control bars over Damaris's blonde ringlets and charged his dragon at a marionette knight, operated by his other hand. His hoarse roar was drowned out by Damaris's higher pitched attempt.

"Shut up, I can do it," Geoffrey hissed. He bent his face to the back of his hand and wiped sweat from his eyes. Despite the heat, he wore a swatch of cloth around his neck.

"Watch out, Sir Knight," Damaris shouted, tapping the arm strings of her maiden in distress.

But the dragon attacked and the knight went down. Damaris's maiden leaped astride the unicorn.

"Charge!"

Silas—also behind the scrim—voiced hoofbeats and other sound effects as the galloping unicorn speared the dragon.

Geoffrey's dragon whipped its tail and slapped the maiden off the unicorn's back. He heard the usual stir in the audience when his knight caught the maiden in midair and killed the wounded dragon with his sword. Damaris voiced the dragon's dying wail, drowning out Geoffrey's attempt.

As the knight and maiden embraced, Damaris hissed at Geoffrey, "Say it. C'mon."

Geoffrey saw black spots where the marionettes had been. His parched lips peeled apart, but no sound came out.

"Your honor is avenged, milady," Damaris finally said, trying to make her voice sound like a knight.

Applause. The curtain fell. Damaris and Silas bounded from behind the scrim. Damaris pulled Geoffrey's arm and he stumbled out. Holding hands, the three bowed. The ground wobbled under Geoffrey's feet; he tried focusing on his toes in the dirt.

Damaris's hand wrenched free of his.

She doesn't want to touch me anymore . . .

He doffed his cap—wool with a short bill—and moved out among the dozen or so audience members. A runny-nosed little girl held out a coin. Geoffrey lowered his cap to the child's level.

It's because of what happened this morning. What that boy said about me.

They had stopped that morning outside Paynertown to water Jenquilla at a pond. The sun was barely above the horizon, but the air was already hot and humid.

Geoffrey stripped off his shirt and waded into the water up to his waist.

"C'mon, Dee." He slapped a plume at her. She sprang into the pond with a battle yell and piggybacked herself onto Geoffrey's shoulders, trying to dunk him. He yielded and she pulled him down.

As they scrambled to their feet, laughing and splashing each other, Geoffrey saw an unkempt little girl come down the hill to the pond's edge. She stooped, dipped a pail of water. Geoffrey felt her eyes on him, staring at his bare torso. The girl coughed, covered her mouth, and ran, her pail clanging to the ground.

"What's wrong with her?" Geoffrey wondered out loud.

"Probably ate at the Tongue-of-the-Boar Inn we passed this morning. Papa said they serve rotten meat." Damaris giggled. "More like *Dung*-of-the-Boar."

"Dee, Geoffrey," Silas called from the road. "Time to go, you lazy yam-sacks."

Geoffrey got out of the water and dried his face with his shirt.

A barefoot boy trotted up and retrieved the abandoned pail. "Whadda ya mean, scarin' my sister?" A few years older than Geoffrey, he wore a dirty shirt and breeches that were mostly patches.

"You oughta be in one of them shows, freak." The boy headed back the way he came.

Geoffrey pulled on his shirt. He rode inside the wagon—not his usual custom—the remaining distance to the village square. When he got out to help Silas set up their stage, a swatch of fabric was wrapped around his neck and his shirt was buttoned to his chin.

Now, standing there after their show holding his cap out to the runny-nosed little girl, his face burned like it had been rubbed in coals. After a dizzy minute, she opened her grubby fist, but her coin missed Geoffrey's cap and plopped into the dirt at the same instant Geoffrey's face did.

There was the gouge of fingers under his arms, then chafing on the tops of his feet as Silas and Damaris dragged him up the steps of the wagon. They got him into the wagon and onto the bunk; Silas dipped a cup of water from their pail.

"You gotta drink." Silas lifted Geoffrey's head off the pillow; Geoffrey turned away.

"Let me try, Papa." Damaris took the tin cup.

"Geffy," she said. "This is dragon nectar." He had once told her that dragon nectar, if you could ever find it, made you strong enough to fly.

Damaris's touch was gentle, the metal cup cool on his lips. He drank. She refilled the cup; he drained it again.

"What's wrong with him, Papa?"

"Heatstroke." Silas started to unwind the fabric that swathed Geoffrey's neck. "What were you thinking, boy? Wearing a scarf in this weather."

Geoffrey made a feeble attempt to remove Silas's hand.

"And ruining our tablecloth to do it." Silas removed the makeshift scarf then unbuttoned and removed the boy's shirt. "Dimwitted cabbagehead."

"Papa, Geoffrey's shirt is still dry," Damaris said. "But look how wet my shirt is. I'm sweating all over."

Geoffrey's face and arms were wet with perspiration; his hair was damp. But there was no moisture on the scarred skin of his neck and torso.

"Sweat glands got burned off and didn't grow back." Silas spread their shredded tablecloth over Geoffrey's chest and abdomen then dumped the pail of water onto him. "That's why Dr. Avery told us never let him get overheated."

Later that night, Geoffrey sat cross-legged on the floor while Silas massaged oil into his neck, shoulders, and torso. For although Geoffrey's burn injuries were long since healed, he had developed thick scar tissue over most of the burned areas.

These massive ridges of skin— fibrotic and tough, like gristle—were as thick as a man's hand in some places. They snaked and intertwined from his chin to his waist in angry shades of purple and pink. Most of the scar tissue had an irregular texture, like the braided surface of a large rope, but some areas were hard and smooth. Of the landmarks normally seen—nipples, naval, the outline of pectoral and other muscles—there were none, all obliterated by the mushrooming scar tissue. Similar heaps of scar tissue cascaded down Geoffrey's back from his shoulders almost to his waist.

The webbed growths encasing Geoffrey's neck caused pain if he turned his head too quickly or too far. So the strong hands of Silas worked on Geoffrey each night after supper, using every type of liniment, salve, and unguent they had been able to acquire during their travels.

"Why won't this go away?" Geoffrey asked Silas.

"Why can't you remember what Doc Avery told you?"

Geoffrey, of course, knew Dr. Avery's words by heart. "When burn injuries are deep, a person may heal with too much scar tissue." Geoffrey remembered the doctor's gentle voice, so unlike the growl of Silas.

"Doc said always remember one thing, boy." Silas kneaded the gnarled webs of scar tissue at Geoffrey's throat. "It's a miracle you're even alive."

This part of the therapy hurt the worst—Silas's fingers seemed to cause a toothache kind of pain that spiked deep into the bones of his neck. But Geoffrey did not cry out. He tried to think of his box garden, with its little green sprigs coming up through the dirt.

As the pain in his neck sent his fingernails into his knees, it occurred to him that he had never seen his own scarred body in a mirror. That peasant girl this morning—her look of revulsion, the way she had retched and run off . . .

What must Damaris think?

Damaris was busy amusing herself teaching Graycie to talk.

Geoffrey jumped up and pulled his shirt off the peg.

"I'm not done, boy," Silas said. "Sit down."

As Geoffrey buttoned his shirt, he heard a snicker. He looked at Damaris, but she was still cooing to Graycie. The snicker came again; Geoffrey whirled to see the face of the farm boy from this morning peeping in the window.

"Freak boy, freak boy!"

Geoffrey roared and charged the window. The boy's face disappeared. Damaris burst out laughing. Geoffrey looked at her then ran out the door.

The farm boy, in his haste, had fallen off the wagon wheel. Geoffrey swung at him. The boy ducked then tackled Geoffrey below the knees. They rolled away from the wagon in the dirt. The farm boy landed on top, astride Geoffrey's chest. He struck Geoffrey in the face, one fist after the other. Tiberias barked frantically.

"Papa!" Damaris was at the wagon door. "Come quick!"

Geoffrey tried to writhe away, but the farm boy outweighed him. A fist to Geoffrey's mouth split his lip. He punched at the boy's face, felt his knuckles connect, almost pulled free. The farm boy pinned him again, this time with his knees in Geoffrey's armpits, and rained punches onto Geoffrey's face.

"Papa!" Damaris screamed. She rushed down the steps, grabbed the farm boy's shirt, and tried to pull him off.

Geoffrey, blood in his eyes from a gash in each eyebrow, did not see Damaris, nor did he see Silas come up behind her and drag her, kicking and clawing, back to the wagon. There was a roaring in his ears as the farm boy slapped the sides of his head, but from somewhere far away, he heard the wagon door slam, thought he heard Damaris screaming. Or was she still laughing?

The boy finally stopped. "You don't know nothing 'bout fighting, do you?" He stood over Geoffrey for a moment then stomped him in the stomach. "Freak boy." He hocked into his throat, spat on Geoffrey's face, and walked off.

Geoffrey felt a moment of panic as he tried to inhale but could not. Finally, he sucked air into his lungs. He rolled onto his side. Blood, slick on his tongue, dribbled from the corner of his mouth. He thought he heard the muffled voice of Silas inside the wagon. He listened for Damaris to reply, but all he could hear, replaying in his head from a few minutes before, was her laughter—at him.

He did not know that what had amused her was the farm boy's startled reaction when Geoffrey charged the window. "Did you see that scamp's eyes pop out when Geoffrey roared at him?" she had said to Silas, still giggling, as Geoffrey ran out of the wagon.

Tiberias licked Geoffrey's hand, then raised his paw in the handshake Geoffrey had taught him. Geoffrey sat up. He took the proffered paw, hugged Tiberias onto his lap, and pressed his raw face into the dog's neck. He did not want Damaris to hear him cry.

At length, Geoffrey crawled to the wagon and retrieved, from its hook underneath, the gourd he used to water his plants. He struggled to his feet and walked to a well they had passed earlier that morning at the outskirts of the village. He stayed behind a tree until no one remained at the well then drew some water for his cut and swollen face.

The moon, nearly full, was cresting the eastern horizon when Geoffrey returned to the wagon. All was silent within, the window dark.

He sat down under the rear of the wagon and quietly slid a flat of plants from their makeshift shelf above the axle. With his fingertips, he pressed the soil down around the little sprouts—beans, about an inch high, from seeds Silas had bartered for—and gave each a few drops from the gourd.

He lay on his back under the wagon, his head pillowed on Tiberias, and listened to the crickets create their song, blending as it did with the steady snore of Silas.

The door scraped open and Damaris crept down the steps.

"Geoffrey?"

She crawled under the wagon and knelt beside him. He did not notice her shocked look when she saw his face.

"Oh, Geffy."

"Go away."

She scampered up to the wagon and returned with some liniment.

"Here," she said, and gingerly touched a fingertip with ointment to his abraded chin.

He threw her hand off; she reached out again.

"Leave me alone."

"Please, Geoffrey."

He rolled onto his side, back toward her.

The wagon creaked above them. "Damaris," Silas called. "Get back in here, you'll catch the ague."

"But, Papa, Geoffrey's hurt."

"Don't argue with me, girl."

Later that night, had Geoffrey awakened, he would have found Damaris curled against his back, her slender arm draped over his chest. But on hearing Silas stir at dawn's first light, the girl had fled, Geoffrey never knowing.

CHAPTER 6

The knifepoint *thocked* into the plank, missing the charcoaled circle completely.

"That's my girl," Silas said. "You've got a natural-born throwing arm."

Damaris kissed Silas on the forehead. "Thank you for the knife, Papa."

"Happy birthday, dearie."

Geoffrey hated it when he felt jealous of Damaris. Why should he care? After all, it was he who had shown her how to throw a knife long before Silas gave her one of her own.

"But don't throw quite so hard—let the momentum of the knife carry it—and finish so that your index finger points at your target." Silas pulled Damaris's knife free. "Now you, boy."

Tossing his own knife from his left hand to his right, Geoffrey stepped up to the line Silas had drawn in the dirt. Given him by Silas on his own twelfth birthday, the knife was still shiny three years later.

How foolish that I stabbed Bertraks in the leg that night and not the gut.

He hurled the knife, knew exactly where it would hit even as the blade tip left his fingers: the very center of the circle. Again.

Not a word from Silas as he pulled out Geoffrey's knife and tossed it back to him.

Then I would be doing this with my real father.

Damaris threw again; this time her knife landed just inside the circle.

27

"Beautiful *and* brilliant." Silas laughed. "But back to school with you both."

School for the past few years consisted of working ciphers on a slate and reading whatever books they could acquire. Damaris, to avoid his history lessons, often begged Silas to show her the use of his old silversmith tools. As they had no silver, she fashioned little items of tin. Silas had said she was a gifted artist.

Damaris got a book and sat in the shade of the wagon, where their marionette stage was set up for tonight's show. Several dozen barter and show wagons were arrayed nearby; it was the annual summer carnival in the village of Thewset.

Geoffrey tossed his knife to Silas. "You said you'd show me how to take it away, like they taught you in the army."

Silas jammed the knife into the plank and crossed to Geoffrey. "I wish you were as eager for book learning." He threw a punch at Geoffrey's midsection. Geoffrey's arm shot out and parried the punch, even as he pivoted and danced away. Surprised by the attack, he readied himself for another, fists raised, heart pounding.

Silas retrieved the knife. "Now do that again." He lunged at Geoffrey with the knife; Geoffrey deflected his arm as before. "See? Like fist fighting," Silas said. "But if you're cornered, you've also got to get control of my weapon hand." He demonstrated. "Now, disarm me."

Geoffrey tried to block Silas's knife thrust as before but missed and felt the knifepoint on his chin.

"What'd you do wrong?"

"Well . . ." Geoffrey replayed the skirmish in his head. "You feigned a move to the side—"

"And you fell for it," Silas said. "Your eyes were on the weapon, not my chest. I can't go anywhere without my midsection, can I?"

Since his thrashing three years ago at the fists of the farm boy, Geoffrey—who rarely asked Silas for anything—often engaged the man in talk of the Rebellion. He learned all he could from Silas about battle tactics, weapons use, and hand-to-hand fighting. It never occurred to him that Silas—

knowing Geoffrey would be a lifelong fugitive, like himself—had permitted that thrashing. It had proved a potent motivator, indeed. What it had cost Silas—to stand by as his boy was beaten to a pulp—Geoffrey never knew.

"Ho, there." A man wearing a tunic emblazoned with a crisscrossed pennant and scimitar walked up. Geoffrey's stomach lurched as he recognized the emblem of the Realm, which he had first seen the night his parents were murdered. He hid his knife under his shirt.

"Master Derrand, of his Overlord's estate." The man's fingers touched the hilt of the dagger at his belt. "Your name?"

"Silas Smitt."

"Produce your vendor's license."

"Ain't got one." Silas slipped into his country accent.

"Peddling pots and pans, are you not?"

"No."

"You passed through his Overlord's estate doing just that," Derrand said. "Last year."

"No," Geoffrey interrupted. "We—"

"Get, boy," Silas said.

Geoffrey shuffled up the wagon steps and sat across the table from Damaris, where she had been crafting a bracelet from tin. She hid the tools—a punch, file, small hammer, and some mandrels.

Derrand's voice was loud through the open window. "Your license, Silas Smitt, or you shall be arrested."

"Don't need no license. We stopped selling last spring."

"You will stand for inspection, then."

Geoffrey tried not to glare at the official as he trooped into the wagon like he owned it.

Silas remained in the doorway while the man nosed around.

Their teakettle was on the stove; a skillet, pot, and utensils hung on the wall. In the cupboard under the bunk was corn meal, tea, dried apples, lard, some biscuits. But when the man opened the cupboard above the bunk, a dozen tins of liniments, lotions, and ointments fell out.

"You're a traveling apothecary now?"

Geoffrey's face burned—was he going to have to show the man his scars?

"I've got a rash on my grunt," Silas said.

The official frowned.

"If'n you need proof, Mr. Derrand." Silas reached for his belt buckle.

"Forget it." The man waved him off. "Where are your wares?"

"Cost of the license got to be more than we was making on the goods," Silas said.

"What's your business, then?" Derrand smirked. "Thieving?"

The pressure of Damaris's bare foot on top of Geoffrey's under the table kept him in his seat. How did Silas remain so calm?

"We are puppet masters." Silas indicated the marionettes hanging from the ceiling near the birdcage.

"I shall collect the Palace Presidio tax, then."

"We already paid our Palace Presidio tax, for the whole year. Two and a half silver bob."

"Not to me, you didn't."

"We paid the official at Merston last week," Silas said. "Not ten miles from here."

"Do you have your proof voucher?"

When Silas explained that he had not been given one, Derrand named a sum, which amounted to nearly all they had earned since Merston.

Geoffrey gripped the edge of the table so hard his knuckles cracked. "Thieving's *his* business," he muttered.

The official swung his glare to Geoffrey.

"Don't listen to him," Silas said. "We're not 'leaving this business.' We got another show here tonight, and five more tomorrow." He counted out some coins.

With a stubby finger, Derrand prodded the dress of the marionette princess. "Perhaps I shall attend."

Geoffrey stood. "It's not that kind of show."

Silas quickly handed the coins to the official and hurried him out the door.

"I'll be needing a proof voucher," Silas said.

"You'll get the same as you got in Merston."

CHAPTER 7

"**S**o much for tonight's show." Damaris slapped the reins. "Giddup, Jenquilla."

She sat between Silas and Geoffrey on the wagon box, Graycie perched on her shoulder.

"You could have gotten yourself arrested, Geoffrey," Damaris said. "Or Papa."

"But I didn't, did I?"

"You didn't have to call him a thief," Damaris said.

"Dee," Geoffrey said. "He knew we'd already paid at Merston. And that none of those snakes give vouchers."

"Right you are, Cabbagehead," Silas said. "But Realm officials can be cruel if you rile 'em up."

"So we should sail to Markarian," Geoffrey said.

He pulled a flat from under the wagon seat and regarded some spindly plants. "We could get a farm and grow a whole field of beans."

"People like us can't buy a farm," Damaris said.

"Anyone can own land over there. It's not just families with certain names."

"Could Jenqy and Graycie and Tiberias go with us?" Damaris asked. "Otherwise, I'm not going."

"Just think how happy Tiberias would be with a couple of sheep to herd," Geoffrey said.

"Stop the wagon, Dee," Silas instructed.

31

Geoffrey saw the poster on the tree as Damaris reined the horse. He jumped off, looked up and down the road—no one in sight—and ripped the placard down. It said: "Rebels and Traitors." A list of names followed, including the name "Silas Marsden."

Geoffrey climbed aboard. "Another thing about Markarian." He shredded the placard.

"No more of these."

"We're not leaving Auldeland," Silas said. "Passage takes money. And now we got less than ever."

"Papa's right," Damaris said. "Why don't you get rid of your stupid map, Geoffrey?"

"Why did you steal my ship?"

"I did not steal your ship."

"I want it back."

"I told you, I don't have it." Damaris jabbed Geoffrey with her elbow.

"Talk about thieving," Geoffrey said.

"Liar." Damaris grabbed a couple fistfuls of his hair and shook him.

Silas recovered the reins and wedged himself between them. "Shut up, the both of you."

Damaris spoke nose-to-beak with Graycie, now perched on her finger. "What's in Geoffrey's head, Graycie? Papa says it's a cabbage." She giggled. "But it's not. It's a Brussels sprout."

Silas chuckled, which always started Graycie chirping and bobbing. Damaris laughed at the bird's antics. Silas was now laughing uncontrollably in a sort of fit, which happened occasionally. "A Brussels sprout," he choked out, tears streaming down his cheeks.

Geoffrey leaped off the wagon.

After a few miles of walking far behind the wagon, the air felt close; Geoffrey's scarf stuck to the back of his neck. Clouds collected in clots and the sun blanched, as though shadowed by the wings of a great bird.

Geoffrey turned his face skyward and caught the first cool drops. Ahead, he saw Damaris climb inside the wagon. He trotted up and resumed his seat on the box next to Silas.

The drops drummed into a downpour and the road became a quagmire. Silas urged the mare to a copse of trees. They stopped under dripping branches as the sky spat its last drops.

There was a crossroads ahead.

"Haggantown Road," Silas said. "Good girl, Jenqy." He leaned back. "Give her the nosebag, boy. We'll let her rest a bit."

But before Geoffrey could climb down, they heard a voice behind the trees ahead.

"Mercy . . . mercy . . ."

Silas ordered Geoffrey into the wagon. "Don't let Damaris come out 'til I tell you."

Geoffrey glanced down at the bunk. "She's asleep."

"Just get in there, like I told you."

"Mercy . . ."

Silas climbed down and started in the direction of the voice. Geoffrey followed a few paces behind.

Just past the trees, several feet off the road, was a man impaled on a stake. The post went up between his legs; his feet dangled a few inches above the ground.

"Mercy . . ." the man said.

Silas peered at the man's face. "Rufus Fergen?"

"Friend . . . mercy?"

"Rufus, it's Silas."

"Silas? Silas Marsden?"

"Yes, it's me." There was a catch in Silas's voice.

"Silas Marsden. The silversmith," Rufus said. "I thirst . . ."

"Water, boy, quick."

Geoffrey sprinted to the wagon and returned with his water gourd. Silas held it to Rufus's crusted lips. The man choked. He gritted his teeth then gasped out some words. "Hunting us down, Silas. One by one."

Rufus moved an arm as though to point, causing his body to shift on the post. He erupted with a guttural scream as he settled lower on the post, blackened toes now almost touching the ground. Nauseated,

Geoffrey watched a bulge on the victim's neck grow larger; the skin looked like it would split open any second.

The man's face contorted into bared teeth and gums. "Silas Marsden . . . mercy . . . Silas Marsden . . . friend . . ."

Geoffrey wanted to rush forward and lift the man's body off the stake. Something, anything, to ease his suffering.

Silas unsheathed his knife. "Forgive me, dear Rufus."

Geoffrey froze, eyes wide.

"Get in the wagon, boy."

Silas placed his knifepoint on the man's neck. "I'm sorry, Rufus."

Horse hooves sounded on the road. Silas hid the knife in his boot.

Geoffrey remembered the sleeping Damaris and ran for the wagon. He froze as three horse soldiers charged up, dismounted, and surrounded Silas.

Geoffrey felt for his knife at his belt. *Not there.* Not that it would have made a difference: two of the soldiers had crossbows in hand, and the third—a man of rank, judging by the embroidered pennant and scimitar on his tunic—drew his sword.

Geoffrey's water gourd lay on the ground. The captain stabbed it onto the tip of his sword. "Giving succor to a traitor. You know this man?"

"You wants 'em to live long, don't ya?" Silas said. "And suffer? So I gives him water, and he drinks." Silas laughed. "He drinks, the infernal fool, and now he won't die for another day." Silas spat at the base of the post. "Ain't that why you slits 'em in the grunt and sticks 'em on a round post 'stead of a pointy one?"

Rufus rasped, trying to speak. Geoffrey's heart caught in his throat. What if Rufus, in his delirium, gave Silas's real name—the name on the wanted poster?

Geoffrey scooped up a handful of mud and packed it into a ball.

A soldier searched Silas, found his knife, passed it to the captain. "Hastening this man's death is treason."

"He won't get no mercy killing from me," Silas said.

Rufus opened his mouth and started to speak. "Mercy . . . Silas Mar—" Splat! Geoffrey's mud ball hit Rufus in the throat, so hard the rest of the name came out as a whoosh.

"To all traitors," Geoffrey said.

Rufus whimpered.

Geoffrey, hating himself, grabbed up another mud ball and gripped it so tightly the tendons in his hand hurt.

A mud ball hit one of the soldiers on the shoulder. Geoffrey whirled to see Damaris packing a second mud ball.

"Sorry, sir," Geoffrey said. "She couldn't hit a bridge if she were standing on it."

Damaris wound up again, but Geoffrey caught her arm and wrenched the mud ball away.

Rufus spoke again. "Sila—"

Geoffrey hurled the mud ball into Rufus's face. "Please . . ." the man sobbed. A tear streaked the dirt on his cheek.

"Geoffrey," Damaris screamed. He clapped his hand over her mouth and kept it there, even as she bit into the fleshy part of his palm.

The other soldier came out of the wagon. "Look at this." He handed a mandrel and a delicate pair of pliers to the captain.

"You are a tradesman," the captain said. He studied the mandrel: a steel rod about the length of his hand, tapered on one end.

"I ain't nothing but a puppeteer," Silas said.

"It was tradesmen that fomented the Rebellion, not just farmers and peasants." The captain nodded to his two soldiers. "Arrest him."

The soldiers tied Silas's hands behind his back.

Damaris wrenched away from Geoffrey. "He's not a tradesman," she shouted, rushing up to the captain. "And these are not his tools."

"Whose are they, lass?" The captain seemed amused.

Damaris grabbed the mandrel and pliers out of his hand. "Mine." She slipped a bracelet off her wrist—several loops of shiny tin wire—and deftly cut and twisted the metal around the mandrel until she had a spiral earring with a hoop on the end.

"For your wife," Damaris said, and handed the trinket to the captain. "My uncle was a tinsmith, before he died."

The captain regarded the earring, stuck it in his pocket, and addressed the soldiers. "Put the prisoner on the bay; you two double up."

"Wait." Damaris fashioned a second earring and handed it to the captain. "In case your wife has two ears."

The captain guffawed. At that moment, Rufus gave a wheezing gasp; his chin slumped onto his chest.

The captain looked from the dead man to Silas.

"Release him."

After the soldiers rode away, Geoffrey helped Silas take Rufus's body down. They dug a grave among the trees, taking turns with their shovel.

Geoffrey sat on a rock and rested. Silas stopped digging; he was pale and his hand shook as he wiped his forehead.

"I'll finish," Geoffrey said.

Silas dropped the shovel. He walked up to Geoffrey and rubbed his knuckles so hard into Geoffrey's scalp that pain shot into his neck. Years later, Geoffrey would realize it was one of the only ways Silas—guarding his heart after having lost one beloved son—could express approval or affection for Geoffrey.

Damaris came out of the wagon as Silas was going in. "Isn't it treason to take him down and bury him, Papa?"

"Rufus and I were in every battle together," Silas said. "I'll not see him dishonored by gawkers and buzzards."

Geoffrey got to his feet, retrieved the shovel, and resumed digging.

"It was cruel, what you did." Damaris sat beside Tiberias and scratched his ears.

"Why do you always think the worst of me?" Geoffrey asked.

"Why did you hurt that man?"

"He knew Silas's real name—he'd already said it four times."

Silas exited the wagon with a small cloth bundle. "Damaris, how did that soldier find your tools?"

"I forgot to hide them with the others."

Geoffrey stopped digging and leaned on the shovel. Was Damaris going to get in trouble for once?

"I'm sorry, Papa."

"It was quick thinking, lass," Silas said. "Laying claim to that mandrel and pliers and showing your skill."

Geoffrey sighed. He helped Silas place Rufus's body in the grave.

Silas unfolded the cloth and placed the contents into the grave: pliers, a small hammer, assorted mandrels and files, several twists of solder, and a crucible.

"Papa," Damaris shrieked. "What are you doing?"

"Fill it in, boy."

Dirt pinged onto the tools.

"No," Damaris pleaded. "You said I had talent. You said I could be a silversmith like you."

"I should have gotten rid of 'em after we lost the war."

"But Papa, you said someday we would buy some silver and make a pitcher together, and a tray, and some lovely candlesticks . . ." The tools disappeared under the dirt. Damaris started to cry.

"Hurry it up, boy," Silas said. "When that patrol comes back and sees the grave, they'll be after us."

Damaris hurled herself into the hole and began digging like a dog for a bone. Geoffrey had never heard her weep like that.

He threw the shovel down and walked away.

CHAPTER 8

Whinto they stopped traveling late that night, they parked behind some bushes away from the road. Geoffrey and Tiberias settled into their shabby bearskin beneath the wagon.

The voice of Silas came through the floorboards. "It's supposed to be a Cat's Eye moon tonight—going to be cold."

Geoffrey thought Silas was addressing Damaris then remembered she was already curled up on the bunk, asleep.

"Ask Tiberias if he wants to sleep inside tonight," Silas called out.

An odd remark, considering the dog's thick coat. "He's fine," Geoffrey said, already shivering against the cold air.

The wagon door opened, and Silas dropped a blanket onto the ground—another mute attempt to thank Geoffrey, whose quick action with the mud balls that day had likely saved Silas from the same fate as Rufus.

The gibbous moon was floating a few hand-widths above the horizon. Geoffrey, propped on one elbow, started drawing a giant map in the dirt with a pointed stick. He first outlined the continent of Markarian, separated from Auldeland by a vast double ocean.

Not long after Silas was snoring, Damaris appeared under the wagon. "I knew you'd be making your map."

"Don't you mean my 'dumb old' map?"

"Geoffrey, a person can be anything in Markarian, right?" Damaris settled on her stomach opposite Geoffrey, chin propped on her hands. "Like a silversmith? Or at least a tinsmith, if they can't get any silver?"

Geoffrey nodded.

Damaris pointed to a linear array of small stones near the center of his map. "What's this?"

"That's the Rockline, between the Two Seas."

"Then I'm in Markarian, right?"

"Scoot back a little. Your elbows are in the sea."

Geoffrey retrieved a cloth bag from a peg above him and dumped out twigs, pebbles, grass, and leaves.

"Can I put the towns in Markarian?" Damaris asked.

"We have to do the forest first." Geoffrey gave her a handful of twigs to stick in the dirt. Then, he named off the coastal towns of Markarian and gave her a stone for each. The grass and leaves they placed over the land masses; the town of Caerdon on the coast of Auldeland was represented by a broken button.

From the pocket of her nightdress, Damaris produced a tiny hand-carved boat whose sail and mast was a bit of paper on a toothpick. She placed it in the harbor at Caerdon.

"My ship," Geoffrey said.

"Now, we sail to Markarian, the New Land." Damaris pushed the boat out to sea, toward the Rockline.

"Why'd you take it?"

Damaris didn't reply but continued moving the delicate ship along the ground.

"I just want to know," Geoffrey said.

"We never had fun anymore," Damaris said. "You wasted all your time building maps to Markarian."

"And you wasted all *your* time making junk out of tin." Geoffrey saw her lower lip quiver and remembered her buried tools, lost forever. He was trying to form an apology when Damaris snapped the little ship in half and threw it at him.

"You are a cruel, cruel boy!"

"You are a thief," Geoffrey said.

"I don't care what you say. Papa likes me better than you."

Geoffrey's face burned. "Even though you're a nobody."

"I'm not a nobody."

"You're nothing but the daughter of a servant girl."

"That's a lie. I'm from a noble family, same as you."

"Ask Silas. You were a naked mutt when I found you, just like your mother."

Damaris leaped across the map at Geoffrey; he rolled out from under the wagon, but she caught him while he was still on his back, jumped on top of him, and hammered her fists into his chest, her small knees grinding into his ribs.

"I hate you," she screamed. "Hate you, hate you!"

The tears of Damaris fell hot on Geoffrey's cheeks and dissolved his resistance. She collapsed onto him and her wet face was against his, her warm breath in his ear. Damaris slowly lifted her head and looked into Geoffrey's face. For a long moment not soon forgotten by either, they held one another with their eyes.

Then springing apart, Damaris scuttled into the wagon, and Geoffrey lurched off into the dark. A tree root tumbled him to the ground, and the night's curious stirrings vanished—for a time—on evanescent wings.

A few days later, Geoffrey found a new ship—crudely carved but with a stitched cloth sail—in one of his plant boxes. It was the best apology Damaris could give, and to Geoffrey— who had earlier made his own apologies to Damaris—it was more than enough.

After that, whenever Geoffrey built the map to Markarian, Damaris was there, despite Silas's claim that, being on the ground so much, she'd "catch the ague for sure." But Damaris didn't care, so loved she the special world that she and Geoffrey created and shared together.

CHAPTER 9

O ne day, four years later, Geoffrey was sixty yards away when he saw a soldier at their door stoop. He dashed for the wagon, his heart hammering in his ears.

The soldier raised his halberd. "What's your business here?"

"I live here." Geoffrey tried to catch his breath.

The soldier moved aside. Geoffrey took the steps in a leap.

Seated across from Silas at the table was a man Geoffrey recognized from three years prior: the tax collector for the local Overlord.

"Where have *you* been?" the man said.

Geoffrey bristled. He owed this man no explanation. He glanced at Damaris; her eyes warned him not to cause trouble.

"I already told ya, he's been looking for work," Silas said. "Where was ya looking, boy?"

"The quarry first, then the smithy," Geoffrey said.

The tax collector was a dishwater-faced man. "Did you get hired?"

"How is that your concern, if I may inquire?"

The official cleared his throat. "I register all local laborers on his lordship's tax roll."

Geoffrey fought the urge to punch the bobbing voice box on the skinny neck.

"Mr. Scudder here is just doin' his job," Silas said.

Geoffrey ignored him. "There's no work to be had in your county."

"I am sure that is not the case," Mr. Scudder said.

"Nor any of the counties adjoining, sir."

Geoffrey's tone produced another scowl. "The amount you owe, Mr. Smitt, is based on what you paid when you were in our county last year."

"We ain't been in your county in three years," Silas said. "And like I told ya, we ain't even done a show yet."

Geoffrey clenched his fists behind his back.

"I'm sorry, Mr. Scudder," Silas said. "But here's all we got." He put a coin on the table.

"Corporal," Scudder said. The steps creaked and the soldier appeared in the doorway.

"Debtor's prison for this one." He pointed at Silas.

"No," Damaris interjected.

"You may take his place, young lady," Mr. Scudder said. "Or you"—indicating Geoffrey—"until such time as the tax is paid."

The soldier pulled out wrist manacles. Silas retrieved a small jar from behind the cast-iron stove and dumped its contents—a handful of coins—onto the table.

"Papa," Damaris said. "That's all we have."

Scudder waved the corporal off and pocketed the money. As he left, he said, "Lying to an official of his lordship is also a punishable offense."

After the two men were gone, Silas addressed Geoffrey. "Why'd you show up?"

"I saw the soldier; I was worried."

"Couldn't you have hung back until that suckerfish was gone?"

"I told you we shouldn't come here, after what he did to us three years ago."

"We're not going to stay; we just need to earn a little money before we move on to Farharven."

"We shouldn't go there either, Silas. You always said it was too close to Caerdon."

"What does a cabbagehead know about anything?" Silas said.

Geoffrey's fists, still clenched, came up.

Damaris hurled a dishtowel at Geoffrey's face. "Last one to the dead tree is a rotten carcass-eater." She grabbed Silas's hand and pulled him out of the wagon, laughing.

Geoffrey threw off the towel and pursued her. Later he would be secretly grateful that—once again—she had intervened.

With Damaris egging them on, the three ran footraces and played tug-of-war with a harness rope. She even got them to play stone-toss and hop-square-hop, games they hadn't played since Geoffrey and Damaris were children.

They returned to the wagon for a meager supper of bread and cheese.

"Show me what you two did to the dragon," Damaris said.

Silas picked up their marionette dragon. "Light the candle, Geoffrey."

"Grrr, grrr," Silas growled as the dragon opened its mouth and flames shot out.

"Oh!" Damaris smiled. "How ever did you make it do that?"

The dragon barked out another flame. "Whale oil comes down through this tube and sprays over the candle when you squeeze the bulb in the tail," Silas said. "You like it?"

"It's so clever." Damaris inspected the mechanism. Geoffrey didn't tell her it had been his idea.

"Just in time for our new season," Silas said.

"People won't pay to see a puppet show anymore," Geoffrey said. "My cap was mostly empty last summer."

"*Marionette* show," Damaris said.

"We can add a night show, too," Silas said. "I built six torch holders."

"Papa, Geoffrey's right. It's not the same as when we were little. People would give us an extra coin or two, just for being—"

"Adorable?" Silas winked at Damaris.

She smiled. "But we're not children anymore."

"Who told you that?"

"Papa," Damaris giggled. "I'm sixteen and Geoffrey's nearly twenty." She refilled their mugs with steaming tea.

"We're going to have to do something different," Geoffrey said, "if we're ever going to get the money for Markarian."

"I told you to stop scheming about that. Look what you're doing to Damaris—she's practically starving herself."

"She wants to go to Markarian too, so she can be a silversmith."

"If I have to eat birdseed like Graycie," Damaris added.

"Graycie's going to starve too, if me or the boy can't find a couple weeks of work," Silas said.

"It's been two months since I sold a scarf," Damaris said.

"People don't buy scarves in summer, dearie," Silas said. "But keep knitting, for next winter."

Damaris fingered the locket on the chain at her throat. "I could sell this."

"Except it's worthless," Geoffrey said, and instantly regretted it. The locket—all that remained of her mother—had never left contact with the girl's body since the day he found her in the snow. He quickly changed the subject. "Some people go to Markarian as indentured servants."

"If you don't mind seven years without your freedom," Silas said.

"You call this freedom?" Geoffrey countered. "We can't own land. We can't appeal crooked tax collectors. If we get arrested, there's no trial." He motioned his mug of tea at Silas. "And you're still a hunted man because you once stood up against all that."

"Seven years is not forever," Damaris noted.

"We'd be separated, sure as hatchlings from eggs," Silas said.

"I don't want to be separated," Damaris said.

"Humph! You two would leave me stuck in Auldeland in a twitch of a toad's nose if ever you got the money for passage."

"That's not true, Papa."

Geoffrey drained his mug. "Silas, do you remember you once had me describe my childhood home to you—the house, the barns, the orchards, and croplands?"

Silas nodded.

"You said the estate—my parents called it Castleford—would be worth a fortune."

"You think that makes you a prince, don't you?" Damaris leaned back. "You think you're better than everybody."

"Dee, what I said . . . about your locket . . . I'm sorry."

Damaris saw the sincerity in Geoffrey's brown eyes and found she could not stay angry.

"Anyway, I believe it's time I reclaimed my inheritance," Geoffrey said.

Silas frowned.

"Or whatever part of it I can. That should be enough money to get us all to Markarian. Maybe even enough to buy a farm and some livestock. And some new metal working tools for Dee."

"You figure the men who killed your family will just hand Castleford over to you?" Silas's tone was mocking: "Good evening, my name is Sir Geoffrey and you should give all this back to me."

"No, but—"

"Yes, I'm a hunted man," Silas said. "But so will you be, Lord Cabbagehead, when they learn you're still alive. Have you forgotten the soldiers who stopped our wagon, looking for you the day after I found you? Or why we've never used your full name, or traveled in your father's province near Caerdon?"

"We're not far from Caerdon now," Geoffrey said.

"Only because Farharven hosts the first big fair of the summer."

"I'll start quietly, do a little research at the Library of Records in Caerdon," Geoffrey said. "Try to find out who owns the estate, how they acquired it. Maybe it has changed hands a few times. If I leave tonight, I can be at Caerdon by morning."

"Eat us out of horse and home, then go get yourself killed," Silas said. "How's this idea for raising money: I shall offer my services as a silversmith at some of the large manors near Caerdon. It was good money before the Rebellion."

"Papa, don't be foolish. You're still on the posters. And the new ones say 'Silas Marsden, *silversmith*.' Do you want to end up like your friend?"

"Geoffrey is the one who's going to end up like Rufus," Silas said. "Trying to reclaim his inheritance."

"You cannot stop me from reclaiming my inheritance."

"Nor can I be prohibited from returning to my trade."

Damaris leaped up, slamming both hands onto the table so hard the marionette dragon jumped. She clanged the metal plates into a stack, cleared off the utensils, and wiped the table.

Then she sat down and took a deep breath as if nothing had happened. "Papa, remember that idea I had for a new show?"

"Why didn't we do it?"

"You said Geoffrey wouldn't like it."

"I said no such thing."

"You said he wouldn't like his part."

"Would it make us some money?" Geoffrey asked.

"I think it could make us a lot."

"As long as it gets us to Markarian." Geoffrey crossed his arms over his chest. "But no puppets, right?"

"It's a drama," Damaris said. "And we'd have the whole season, if we got started right away."

"We'd have to spend some money on costumes and props," Silas added.

"Which we don't have," Geoffrey said. "Silas, when will you stop buying worthless skin potions? The last one—'melts scars and scrofula'— only melted the metal can it came in."

Damaris tapped the wall near the window. The sill popped off. She plunged her hand into the hidden space where Silas had kept the tinsmith tools and pulled out a little cloth sack of coins.

Geoffrey was even more surprised than Silas.

"Now do you want to hear about the new show?" Damaris asked.

CHAPTER 10

"Ai-eee!" Geoffrey's war cry split the morning as he lunged, sword in hand, at Silas. The older man sidestepped and parried the blow with a large battle-ax. Geoffrey wiped the sweat off his face and attacked again. He drove Silas along the bank of a stream to a huge tree, where Jenquilla was tethered, twitching flies with her tail.

"That'll do," Silas said, and collapsed onto one end of a log that spanned the stream.

Geoffrey sat on the other end. In the middle of the log, over the water, Damaris knelt in the sunshine. She held the marionette knight in one hand, the princess in the other, and voiced their conversation.

Geoffrey remembered Damaris as a little girl, blonde curls catching the sunlight, playing with cornhusk dolls and making him join her—and always giving him the doll that was missing its head or otherwise deformed.

"Can't you two make the fight look more realistic?" Damaris asked.

"Not without actually killing each other," Silas said.

"Guess it'll have to do. Have you been working on your lines, Papa?"

"I'm at the part where she don't get her head chopped off," Silas said.

"*Doesn't* get her head chopped off."

"I never talk that way around outsiders."

"But this is a dramatic performance, you have to speak correctly."

Geoffrey stood up and walked the log toward Damaris. He affected a stentorian voice. "And thus, the fair young maiden avoids a cruel beheading."

"That's it, Geoffrey," Damaris laughed. "Come on, Papa, let's hear you say it like that."

"She don't get a beheadin'," Silas said.

"Papa."

"I ain't to say don't?"

"And don't say ain't," Damaris said. "And the word is behead*ing*. Not behead*in*."

"I've had enough of this half-witted play—"

"Don't say play, Papa." Damaris giggled. "It's a *drama*."

Silas bellowed and pretended to lunge for her on the log. Damaris leaped into Geoffrey's arms. "Geffy, help!"

Geoffrey lost his balance and they both tumbled off the log into the stream. Damaris dunked Geoffrey's head. They chased and splashed each other, finally plopping down together in two feet of water.

Damaris turned her face to the sunshine, eyes closed, water droplets sparkling on her long lashes. Geoffrey, transfixed by the vision, was startled when her eyes flew open and found his.

"Rupert and Daniella!" she said.

The marionettes swirled fifteen yards downstream. As Geoffrey plunged toward them, something hurtled from an overhanging limb and somersaulted into the water. A young man scooped the marionettes out of the stream and skipped up the bank.

"How much you want for 'em?" he said. Straw-colored hair was plastered on his forehead above gray eyes and a freckled nose.

"Who in the name of botheration are you?" Silas said.

The intruder bobbed the head of the princess at the knight and mimicked Damaris's voice. "The question is, who in the name of all that's barmy, are *you*?" The similarity was uncanny. "Curly Locks plays make believe while Pretty Boy and Old Man have a fussy little duel."

Silas grabbed the boy's collar and cocked his fist.

"Papa, no."

The boy wriggled out of his shirt. He darted to the tree, vaulted onto Jenquilla's back, and leaped into the branches. He regarded them from a limb overhanging the water.

"Who's the trespasser?" he said. "I was sitting up here, singing the sun up, when up rolled your rig." He sang:

Sitting up a tree
Singing up the sun,
When up rolled you odd strangers three.

"What'd you do with the marionettes?" Silas demanded.

The boy pulled a flute from his waistband, played a few notes, then continued his song:

If you horse around
around a horse
around a horse you go of course.

Geoffrey looked at Jenquilla—the marionettes were draped over her neck, controllers on one side, little bodies dripping on the other.

"I hung 'em up to dry," the boy said. "I normally don't buy waterlogged marionettes, but I'll make an exception. How much?"

"Get down here, ya monkey," Silas said.

The boy screeched out a monkey sound, grabbed the branch above him, and looped around it like a trapeze artist.

Silas laughed. "He be a monkey, for sure."

Geoffrey looked at Damaris, who was peering up at the stranger from behind the log spanning the stream. She swiped the hair out of her face and smoothed her sopping frock. No matter how many trees Geoffrey might climb, or push-ups he might do, his scarred torso would never look like this young man's.

"Some watchdog you are, Tiberias," Geoffrey said.

"Your doggie likes bread and lard." The boy tossed a morsel from his perch. Tiberias snapped it up. The stranger leaped from the branch to the ground, rolling to break his fall. He cartwheeled to a stop in front of Silas.

"Singer Sandley, acrobat and songster. Call me Sandy."

When he made a low bow, Damaris ran for the wagon. Sandy, respecting her modesty, continued to look at the ground until he heard Damaris shut the wagon door. "So, how much for the marionettes?"

"They ain't for sale."

"Of course they are," Geoffrey said. "We don't need them anymore."

"Got any others?" the boy asked.

"We have a dragon that breathes fire."

"It ain't for sale either," Silas said.

"A marionette that breathes fire? Could I see it?"

Damaris reappeared in her best frock, wet hair wrapped in a scarf. "At least you didn't call them puppets, Sandy."

Sandy smiled at her.

"Geoffrey and I grew up doing marionette performances with Papa."

"And you still play with them." Sandy winked at her.

Damaris blushed. "I was working out our new drama."

"Are you at Farharven tomorrow?" Sandy asked.

Damaris nodded.

"Me too," Sandy said. "Opening day. What's your drama about?"

"He doesn't need to know any more of our business," Geoffrey said. He untied Jenquilla and walked her to the wagon traces. Forget selling him their marionettes; the sooner this scamp left, the better. He busied himself with the harness and pretended to ignore Sandy and Damaris.

"Where's your family?" Damaris asked.

"Don't need one."

"What's your act?"

Sandy leaped across the stream, did a handspring and a front flip, then leaped back across and bowed to Damaris.

"My lady, my queen," he said. "Singer Sandley, at your service, O fair queen."

Damaris giggled. "Do people pay to watch you flip around?"

Sandy produced the flute and played a lively tune as he danced. He finished with a kick-up-the-heels flourish. "It's more the music, I think."

"Our drama needs music," Damaris said. "Could you do it?"

"Tell me the story, we'll see."

"Time to get going, Dee," Geoffrey said. He swung up onto the wagon seat.

"Can Sandy come with us, Papa?" Damaris turned to the boy. "You want a ride?"

"Ride-walk-ride-walk." Sandy ticked off on his fingers. "Ride," he said, on the last finger.

"No," Geoffrey said.

"He's going the same direction we are, Geoffrey." She wanted to add "and unlike you, he sees me as more than a tomboy." But she didn't say it.

"We never give rides to strangers," Geoffrey called back.

"I'm not asking you," Damaris said. "Can we, Papa?"

Silas sighed. He hated to aggravate a Geoffrey-Damaris quarrel. In fact, he had long harbored a secret, irrational notion that someday, somehow, the two of them might come together as more than adopted siblings. And that was what made up his mind.

"Welcome aboard, Sandy."

CHAPTER II

Geoffrey climbed the makeshift ladder to a platform affixed to a tree, ten feet above the roof of their wagon.

"How about it?" Silas called from below.

"Still wobbly, but better," Geoffrey said. He reached up and tied a rope to the tree. The other end of the rope Silas secured to the base of a different tree thirty feet away, near the flatbed wagon they had borrowed to use as their stage.

"The line's too steep," Silas said. "She'll hit the tree."

"Not if she twists these handles together while she slides down—it'll slow her plenty," Geoffrey said. He looped a bit of rope—five inches that connected two wooden handles—over the line.

"Dee, you need to watch this." Geoffrey pushed off the platform. He shot down the line, slowing just before his feet touched the ground.

Damaris didn't look up from where she sat with Sandy on one of the benches arrayed in front of their stage. Sandy strummed a lute and sang:

Tale of young lovers
Scorched in flame
Tale of two
Who bear the name . . .

How many times did they have to go over the music together? Geoffrey grabbed Sandy's "drum"—a chamois stretched over a kettle—and pounded a rhythm on it.

"Geoffrey, stop." Damaris turned to him. "The drum doesn't play during this song, you know that."

"You need to practice sliding down the rope, Dee," Geoffrey said.

Damaris ignored him. "Now play the other song, Sandy, the one that goes at the end."

"You should let your brother show you how to slide down that rope, Damaris."

"He's not my brother."

"What is he, then?"

"Nothing," Damaris said. "We were both orphans, like you, until Papa—"

"—got stuck with 'em," Silas said. He was tacking a blanket up beside the flatbed wagon.

"Why do you need a blanket on both sides of the stage?" Sandy asked.

"So I can exit on one side, run behind the wagon and change costumes, then enter from the other. I play two different people."

"I could play the second person," Sandy said.

"Won't you be busy doing the music and drums?" Geoffrey said. "Besides, you're not traveling with us, so we have to be able to do this ourselves."

Damaris shot Geoffrey a look that singed his eyeballs. "Papa, the audience will see your legs when you run behind the wagon," she said. "They'll know you're the same person. Sandy—"

"That's what the crates are for," Geoffrey interrupted. "We'll stack them behind the wagon."

Silas slipped a bulky blindfold over Damaris's eyes. "I made a new strap for it," he said. "See if it's more comfortable."

"No," she said, pulling the blindfold off. She felt the inside of it. "It's the lining."

"Can't be helped," Silas said. "It's hammered tin—flame-proof. I made Geoffrey's shirt the same way."

"You already soaked it in lamp oil." Damaris sniffed the outside of the blindfold. "What if it smears the makeup Sandy gave me?"

"That would be a good thing, remember?" Silas said. "But we haven't even seen you in makeup yet."

"Do you have a mirror in the wagon?" Sandy grabbed Damaris's hand and pulled her up. "Come on, I'll help you put it on."

Geoffrey stepped in front of them. "Silas can help with that."

"What do you know about makeup, Papa?"

"You don't have a mother—but I once had a wife," Silas said.

Silas and Damaris disappeared inside the wagon.

Sandy cartwheeled back to the bench. "That rhythm you played, Geoffrey." He hammered the drum using Geoffrey's earlier pattern. "I like it. I think I'll use it for when the executioner comes out."

Geoffrey climbed back up the tower. It was hard not to like Sandy. He had taught Geoffrey and Silas how to leap off the platform and land without getting hurt, enabling them to build their tower higher than planned and "make the show wonderfully exciting," as Damaris had enthused.

Sandy had also remarked what a quick study Geoffrey was, praising his strength and agility. And Sandy was carelessly happy—maybe that was why Damaris liked him so much. But what did Sandy know about anything? There was not a single scar on that trim, well-muscled body. Nothing like the mass of keloids which encased Geoffrey—and mocked him every waking minute—for fleeing back to his bed instead of warning his parents that night.

Geoffrey gazed out at the harbor. His eyes followed a three-masted ship as it dropped below the western horizon. Probably sailing to Markarian.

Behind him stretched a pasture and forty wagons of various shapes and sizes, colorfully painted to advertise everything from magicians and sword swallowers to wild beasts and a troupe of midget jugglers. One wagon sold roasted turkey legs and sweetbreads, another hawked exotic treats "from across the Two Seas."

A jester on stilts—giraffing his way up the dirt fairway—saluted Geoffrey as he glided past their tower.

The wagon door opened, and Damaris flowed down the steps. Geoffrey's breath stopped in his throat. With Silas's application of makeup and a new grace in her walk, the child of the stormy night had become someone that Geoffrey had never seen before.

Sandy took Damaris by the hand, as a groom might greet his bride. "The fairest queen in all the land." He knelt before her on one knee.

Every muscle in Geoffrey's body bunched. He leaped off the platform, not seeing the man who was walking up to the wagon. He landed—rolling as Sandy had taught him—but crashed into the newcomer, tumbling them both into a sampling of cow pies.

Geoffrey sprang to his feet, slung the manure out of his eyes, and started toward Sandy and Damaris.

"Ooh, you stink, Geoffrey," she giggled, waving a hand in front of her nose. "Get away."

Geoffrey halted, unsure. Then he saw the stranger struggling to his feet and charged at him. "Get out of my way." The man plopped back down onto his ample bottom.

Geoffrey strode off. He had not noticed that the man's tunic was embroidered with the pennant and scimitar.

"Cabbagehead, get back here!" Silas hurried over to the man, helped him up, and tried to brush off the cow manure but only smeared it.

"Get your hands off me, pig." The man's evenly trimmed goatee divided fleshy lips from a double chin.

Sandy produced a bandana and held it out to the man, who wiped his pudgy hands on it.

He studied his manicured fingernails, now stained brown.

"Very sorry, sir," Silas said.

"Do you know who I am?" The purple veins on the man's nose seemed ready to burst.

Silas shook his head.

"I am Anry Edgewold. First officer of the Realm, tax collector for his Overlords Jalfry and Guernsey."

"Silas Smitt, at your service, sir. Don't mind that boy none."

"I will have him in irons."

Silas proffered several coins, fighting the tremor in his voice. "It were an accident; he didn't mean nothing."

Edgewold struck the money from Silas's hand. "His name?"

"Most folks calls him Cabbagehead," Silas said. "An ignorant boy, a clumsy boy. Not worth your time."

"That's for me and the magistrate in Caerdon to decide." The official stabbed a fat finger in Silas's face. "Not you."

Silas turned and motioned to Damaris. Edgewold's eyes tracked her as she disappeared into the wagon. She reappeared with her coin purse.

"Hoping this covers your clothes and your trouble, sir," Silas said. He plucked a bit of dirt off the official's shoulder as he placed the coin purse in the man's vest pocket. "Just a speck, really. A flea, sir, that ain't worth none of your valuable time."

The official patted his vest pocket. "Of course not."

Silas felt his heart rate returning to normal.

"The vendor's fee for this site has not been paid," Edgewold said.

"Perhaps the good gentleman will consider this sufficient . . ." Silas said.

"Perhaps I shall return with an arrest warrant for the boy who attacked me." Edgewold walked away.

Silas grabbed up the coins that Edgewold had knocked to the dirt, wiped them on his shirt, and raced after the man. "We always pay what is asked." Silas dropped the money into the fat hand. "And with a will, sir."

Edgewold pocketed the coins. "Not sufficient."

"It's all we have until tomorrow, after our first show," Silas said.

Sandy fished a coin pouch from his pants and handed it to the man, who added it to his pocket.

"Adequate for now," Edgewold said. "But your boy needs a thrashing that'll cripple him for weeks." He squared his vest over his paunch and strutted off.

CHAPTER 12

Geoffrey threw a fist-sized rock at the ship departing the harbor as though it were within range, instead of half a mile offshore. He grabbed up another stone from the rocky beach, then another, hurling hunks of flesh, as it were, from Sandy's body.

After a dozen of his missiles had splashed into the sea, a smaller rock plopped in, far short of his. Without turning around, he threw another. Again, a stone chased his into the water.

He glanced over his shoulder. A girl in her mid-teens crouched on the grassy dune behind him, ready to run. Geoffrey walked away from her, toward the water's edge, and sat down behind a boulder, out of her sight. He picked up a pebble and side-armed it out over the waves.

After a pause, a second pebble splished into the water beside his.

He stood and threw a rock out, as far as he could. A larger rock sailed after his and landed a full twenty-five feet farther.

That's when he heard the girl cry out. He whirled and saw a man grab the girl's arm and steer her away from the beach. She tried to pull free, lost her balance, fell. Her assailant yanked her up, half dragging her. She screamed.

Geoffrey raced up. "Let go of her." The man, about Geoffrey's age, was half a head taller and rock solid. His face was marked with several inflamed cysts and a dozen icepick scars.

"Beat it." Pockmark muscled the girl along.

Geoffrey blocked their path. The man hurled the girl away and in the same motion, swung at Geoffrey so fast that Geoffrey caught a hammer blow in the stomach that doubled him over.

Pockmark took off after the fleeing girl, but before he caught her, Geoffrey smashed into him with a flying tackle. Geoffrey rolled to his feet as the man leaped up and charged him. He dodged, and when the man swung about, hit him with a face and gut combo, then slammed the man's face onto his knee, as Silas had taught him. Blood gushed from Pockmark's nostrils as he fell to the sand. He got up slowly, cursing Geoffrey, and staggered off the beach.

Geoffrey walked to the water's edge. The girl came up and stood beside him. After a few minutes, she side-armed a stone in a neat double-skip across the tops of the incoming waves. She handed a flat stone to Geoffrey.

He looked at her. Her dark brown hair shone in the late afternoon sunlight. He returned the stone to her. She threw it in the direction of the departed assailant. "He's with one of the carnival wagons," she said. "Last summer he took 'no' for an answer."

The girl pulled out a small brown paper packet. "Want some sweet brittle?"

It was a treat Geoffrey had not had since a child, living with his parents. She folded it into his hand. The paper was sticky, with a fragrance of butterscotch. Resisting the urge to devour it at once, he pocketed it.

"You have a sweetheart," the girl said.

"I'm saving it for later."

"For her."

Who does she think she is? Geoffrey slapped the sweet brittle packet back into the girl's hand and strode to a new spot twenty yards down the shore, already regretting his hasty action.

Damaris would have loved such a treat.

The girl followed and faced him.

"I'm sorry." She smiled. "Granny says I talk too much. That I have no manners. She says it's because I have no parents, and she hasn't the time to discipline me properly." Her eyes studied his as she spoke. "You're an orphan too."

Geoffrey scowled. How did she know?

She again offered the packet of sweet brittle. He hesitated, thought of Damaris, then took it.

He sat down on the sand. The girl sat facing him, cross-legged.

"Wavy hair means you have a whimsical side. Like a child."

He looked past her, at the surf lapping the shore.

"Or it might mean you never really had a childhood. Like it got cut short."

"What are you, some kind of fortune-teller?"

"Sort of." The girl leaned forward and touched his hair. "May I?" She played his hair between her fingers from temple to shoulder. "Never cut your hair the month of two moons."

Geoffrey removed her hand.

"Actually, it's my grandmother. But I'm learning." She sighed. "Don't you want to know why you shouldn't cut your hair?"

He said nothing.

"You will never heal from what happened to you if you do."

Geoffrey changed the subject. "Why are you out here by yourself?"

"I'm always by myself. During the day, anyway. Granny's asleep; she works at night. So it gets lonely, and I come down here to see the birds fly and . . ." Her upward intonation invited him to finish her sentence.

"Watch the ships sail away."

"See? Fortune-telling is not that hard." She giggled. "You can call me Nissa, if you want to."

The name was pretty. It fit her somehow. Geoffrey started to get up.

"I can read palms," Nissa said. She grasped his wrist, tugged him back down, and studied his open hand. "Ooh, interesting."

"What?"

"This line means royal blood, or that you are wealthy." She fingered his frayed sleeve and blushed. "I'm still learning, like I said."

Geoffrey nodded.

"Where are you from?" Nissa asked.

"We travel."

"I wish I could travel. Me and Granny never go anywhere. This line means—oh my!"

"What?" Geoffrey withdrew his hand as if she had burned it.

"I need the crystal for this," Nissa said. "We live right over there." She nodded toward a line of buildings on the road near the shore.

Geoffrey did not notice the lengthening shadows, nor could he hear the shouts of Sandy, looking for him down at the harbor. He followed the girl up the bluff to an unpainted house on a lane of little houses and shops. The sign over the door said "Zeruba. See-ress & Soothsayer."

"Be quiet, don't wake Granny." Nissa reached for the door handle then stopped and looked at him for a few moments.

Had she changed her mind? He pushed his scarf a little higher.

"Uh . . ." Nissa blushed. "Granny gets mad if I work for free."

Geoffrey reached into his pocket, knowing he had no money. Embarrassed, he looked at the pink clouds streaking the western horizon where the sun had already dropped into the sea.

The summer air was cooling, promising a comfortable evening.

The show! Geoffrey took off running.

"Come back." Nissa wanted to run after him. "Please." Her voice trailed off. "Never mind about the money . . ."

CHAPTER 13

Geoffrey ran across the cow pasture toward the rows of carnival wagons. He could see Silas, silhouetted against the darkening sky, lighting the torches on both sides of their stage. He heard the drum rhythm begin, saw Sandy on the edge of the stage, the kettle between his knees.

Geoffrey climbed into the wagon from the front. Damaris whirled on him in the darkness.

"Where were you?"

She was trying to fasten a full-length cape over her shoulders. "Help me."

Geoffrey could barely see the tin clasp in the torchlight flickering through the window as he hooked it over her throat.

"How many?" she asked.

"The benches are full. And more are standing."

"Oh, Geoffrey, this is so exciting. Here's your costume, you'll have to put it on in the tree."

Geoffrey slipped out the front of the wagon and ran to a tree about ten feet from the one that braced their tower. He climbed—using the pegs they had placed that afternoon—and sat high on a leafy branch opposite the platform, hidden from the audience. Trying not to make a sound, he stripped off his shirt, dropped it to the ground, and donned a black mask and black flameproof shirt.

Below him, Silas—also in black—bounded onto the stage. The drum crescendoed and stopped abruptly. A hush came over the audience.

"Before your very eyes," Silas boomed. His was a commanding presence. "Before this very night is out. You, here present, shall see a woman struck blind . . . and a man nearly burned to death."

Geoffrey hoped their show could deliver the excitement Silas was promising. His palms were sweating. Maybe his heart would stop racing if he didn't think about the part he had to play.

With a whoosh, the flaming torches blazed up—Sandy's saltpeter pellets worked even better than promised. Acrid smoke billowed up to Geoffrey.

Then, a woman of entrancing loveliness glided onto the stage.

Geoffrey sensed the crowd's collective gasp. Damaris's violet eyes flashed in the torchlight. Golden curls spilled from beneath a silver crown and cascaded onto the bodice of her sequined dress. The gossamer cape Geoffrey had attached at her throat kissed gentle curves as it flowed to the floor.

Geoffrey watched Damaris look directly out at the spectators—as planned—making eye contact with as many people as she could.

"What do you see out there, my dear?" Silas said.

"A man on the third row." She pointed. "Holding a child."

"What else?"

"A woman with a bandana on her head."

"Maybe she's already blind," shouted a man in the back row. "You coulda planted them people."

"Thank you, my good fellow," Silas said. "Hold up some fingers, if you please. Any number, go ahead."

The heckler, a sailor with brown teeth, spat tobacco juice and held up three fingers.

"How many?" Silas asked.

"Three." Damaris's tone implied the answer was obvious.

Silas pointed to a woman near the front. "You ma'am?"

The woman held up one finger.

"One."

Silas swung his open hand toward Damaris's face, stopping an inch from her eyes. She recoiled, blinking.

"Nothing wrong with these beautiful eyes," Silas said.

Damaris stepped to the base of the tower and, like a trapeze artist, scampered up the ladder to the platform.

"And now, our story," Silas said. "The evil king wanted to marry our Princess. But her father and mother refused, so the king had them beheaded."

Silas climbed to the platform and stood beside Damaris. "Betrothed to another, our Princess, played by the fair Damaris, has chosen execution—rather than betray her true love."

Geoffrey shot an anxious glance down at the audience. Silas's proper elocution—requested by Damaris—betrayed his persona incognito. What if there was a spy from Caerdon on one of those benches?

Silas bound Damaris's wrists together then stretched her arms above her head and tied them to the tree that braced the platform. Silas used another piece of rope to tie her waist to the tree.

From Geoffrey's perch, ten feet away, it looked as if she was bound securely—hopefully the audience would think so too. But he could not make out the short rope with the handles; what if Damaris had forgotten it when she climbed?

"But, alas, in her hour of greatest need, where is her true love?" Silas tied the blindfold over Damaris's eyes then scuttled back down to the stage and faced the audience. "I, Silas, play the Executioner." He brandished a battle-ax and leather hood. "I go prepare."

Silas exited behind the curtain in front of the wagon. Geoffrey could barely see him as he ran behind the flatbed wagon that served as their stage.

When he reentered from the other side of the stage, Silas wore a black mask, identical to the one Geoffrey had just donned, and was naked from the waist up. Affecting a completely different voice—uncannily like his own, Geoffrey realized with shock—Silas said, "And I, Geoffrey, play the Hero."

Silas had the physique of a much younger man. As he buttoned a black shirt over his bare torso, he stood near the torches. No one in the audience would question the absence of scars on the Hero's body. He ducked behind the curtain and raced back to the other side; Geoffrey watched him tear off the Hero mask and throw on the Executioner's leather hood and robe before bounding back onto the stage and climbing to the platform.

Peering through the leaves at the platform across from him, Geoffrey could see the steady rise and fall of Damaris's bodice. Was she not even a little nervous behind that blindfold? He forced his eyes to study the chalked circle on the tree trunk above her trussed wrists. He wished he had practiced his knife throwing more.

Silas—eerily sinister in the hood and robe—reached the platform and faced the bound and blindfolded Princess.

"Prepare to die!" he roared. He took aim with a slow arc of the huge ax, touched the blade to Damaris's white throat, and drew back for the two-handed blow.

Geoffrey gave a blood-curdling yell and hurled his knife at the platform. His stomach dropped when his wrist brushed a twig—what if he hit her? The point of his blade slammed into the tree just above the Princess's bound hands. He grabbed the rope they had placed earlier and swung onto the platform. He drew his sword and attacked the Executioner, who fought back with the battle-ax.

Although Geoffrey and Silas had worked out each thrust and parry, they had not practiced with their masks on, nor in darkness illuminated only by torchlight from the stage below.

Sidestepping a swing of Silas's ax, Geoffrey's foot found only air. As he fell, he grabbed at the edge of the platform with his fingertips. He heard his sword clatter onto the wagon roof below him. Silas made a show of stomping on his fingertips; Geoffrey dropped onto the wagon roof, grabbed his sword, and leaped onto the ladder.

Silas again took aim at Damaris's neck with his ax and was halfway through a mighty swing when Geoffrey, regaining the platform, clanged the weapon out of Silas's hands. Geoffrey feigned a thrust to Silas's midsection and watched Silas hurtle off the platform, hit the ground, and roll out of sight behind the wagon.

Geoffrey nodded to the audience's applause then turned to Damaris. She hung limply from her tied wrists. Had the script called for the Princess to swoon? Untying her waist from the tree, he pinched her stomach. "I'm fine," she whispered.

Hoofbeats. Silas, again unrecognizable—this time in the full-face helmet of a soldier—was mounted on Jenquilla. He rode to the base of the tower and hurled a flaming spear at Geoffrey, which came faster than Geoffrey had expected. He managed to catch it as the blunted point struck him in the stomach. His shirt blazed up, hissing and crackling. The script now called for him to leap off the platform and attack the soldier, but . . .

Bertraks's torch. Geoffrey's body went rigid.

"Geoffrey," Damaris hissed. "Go, now!" He knew every spectator was watching him, but his feet would not move. His eyes watered from the smoke, blurring his vision of Silas below.

A scream exploded in his ears—Damaris—and vaporized his paralysis. He leaped off the platform onto Silas, pulled him off the horse, grappled with him in the dirt. Geoffrey got a stranglehold, shook Silas by the neck until he went limp. Geoffrey threw him aside then collapsed at the base of the tree that anchored the rope slide. His shirt was still on fire.

From behind the mask, he could see Damaris on the platform as she writhed to free her wrists. *Hurry!* Hands still apparently tied above her head, Damaris leaped off the platform.

Geoffrey heard the audience gasp, felt her body slam into him at the bottom of the rope slide. Her blindfold burst into flames. She yanked it off and threw her cape over Geoffrey, smothering the fire that engulfed him.

Geoffrey felt Damaris's heart pounding as she lay motionless on top of him, smoke rising from their bodies. Not a sound from the audience. After a few seconds, she rose; they helped each other to their feet. Sandy's song began as Geoffrey and Damaris came together in a tender embrace.

The audience erupted into applause.

"Papa, get up," Damaris whispered to Silas, motionless on the ground beside them. He did not stir. She shook him. "Geoffrey, something's wrong."

The clapping stopped as Geoffrey bent over Silas and shook him by the shoulders. "Silas?" No response. He lifted the limp body off the ground, laid him on the edge of the stage, and removed his helmet.

Damaris put her hand on Silas's chest. "He's not breathing. Somebody help!"

A balding man from the front row approached and felt Silas's wrist, then his throat. His voice was incredulous. "He's dead."

A murmur went up; several spectators edged away. Then . . .

Silas leaped to his feet and bowed with a flourish. A hesitant applause began and rippled through the crowd. Geoffrey saw his own relief mirrored on Damaris's face.

"Come into the light, my lady and gentleman," Silas said. He extended a hand to assist first Damaris, then Geoffrey onto the stage. They kept their backs to the audience.

"And so our Hero saved the fair young maiden from a ruthless beheading." Silas slowly turned Damaris to face the audience. "But was the executioner really cheated?"

Damaris's eyes, soot blackened and red rimmed, were fixed and staring.

Silas drew a sword and swung it at her face, coming within an inch of her eyes. Damaris did not flinch or draw back.

"Yes, our Hero saved the Princess from a quick and merciful death . . . only to condemn her to a life of cruel blindness." Silas grabbed a torch and thrust it at her face several times.

Again, she did not so much as blink.

There was scattered applause throughout the audience; some coins pinged onto the stage.

Silas acknowledged the donations with a gesture of his hand. "And our rescuing lover?"

Geoffrey let Silas turn him to face the audience, felt Silas's fingers at the back of his head untying the mask. He wondered if anyone in the audience could see how much he was trembling as the mask fell away.

"Handsome, yes," Silas said.

A woman in the second row nodded and flashed a snaggle-toothed grin.

"But he shall forever bear the painful reminder of his heroic folly." Silas unbuttoned Geoffrey's shirt where it was fastened at the back. "What could be worse, you ask, than *not seeing?*"

Silas paused and looked around at the audience, hushed in anticipation.

"Being seen," he shouted, as Geoffrey's shirt fell to the ground.

Geoffrey looked down. The massive, purple lumps of scar tissue—coursing in ridges and clumps from his chin to his waist—seemed eerily alive, writhing and undulating in the torchlight.

The shocked hush of the crowd exploded into a roar and built with whistles and shouts.

Coins rang onto the stage. An old woman shouted, "Show it all, boy!"

Geoffrey fought the urge to run, or at least snatch up his shirt and cover his nakedness. He forced himself, instead, to raise his arms and turn slowly in a circle. The roar gained new fury. He tried to blank his mind of everything except the sound of coins striking the stage. *And don't think of Damaris*—no doubt staring at him too.

A rotten tomato, flung from somewhere in the back, struck Geoffrey in the ear. Another rotten tomato hit him on the chin, splashing brown slime across his face. The clapping and cheering devolved into howls of laughter.

Geoffrey tried to focus on something, anything, beyond the crowd. A tall woman stood in the back. She was silent; her face held no derision. Her dark eyes locked onto his the instant before a rotten egg struck him in the eye. When he raised his arms to shield his face, a dried cow pie sailed onto the stage and slammed him below the waist. Pain shot into his abdomen; he doubled over and fell to the floor. The hoots and howls crescendoed to a deafening roar.

Geoffrey retched as he struggled to his hands and knees. He wiped the vomit from his mouth onto his shoulder, saw Sandy douse a torch then race to the next one. Crawling, Geoffrey reached the back of the stage as the last torch went out. He fumbled his way through the darkness to the base of the tree, found his shirt, and fled into the night.

Among the laughing faces, Geoffrey had glimpsed the hate-filled aspect of the man he had collided with earlier that day.

The thoughts of Anry Edgewold were indeed dark as he watched the performance. How obscene that a creature so ugly—and one who had disrespected him only hours before—should collect so much money. Edgewold had stared at Damaris in her princess gown as she took her bows. By what right did that misshapen man enjoy the every charm—as no doubt he did—of one so fair, while he, Edgewold, went home every night to a hag with fetid breath?

And so Edgewold had thrown a tomato. When it happened to catch Geoffrey on the ear, surprising the boy, someone in the crowd laughed. Encouraged, he threw another. Others joined in, flinging all manner of rotten fruit and anything else that came to hand.

But still the man was not satisfied, as we shall see.

CHAPTER 14

"Her hair's all gonna fall out if you don't stop brushing her." Silas came out of the wagon. "And how will I look tonight riding a bald horse?"

Damaris dragged the curry brush from Jenquilla's withers to her tail.

"We've got work to do." Silas climbed their tower and yanked Geoffrey's knife out of the tree, descended, and held the knife out to Damaris. "Needs sharpened."

She glanced at the knife but did not take it.

"The torches need more lamp oil, and your dress and cape need to be washed," Silas said.

Damaris picked the hair out of the curry brush.

"Dearie, you're quiet as a cricket who just got his back legs broke. By now, I should have heard: 'Oh, Papa, I just love the early morning. See how the sunlight through that tree makes a funny pattern on Jenqy's face?' Or, 'Mmm, Papa, smell the honeysuckle. Summer is my favorite time of year.'"

Damaris started braiding Jenquilla's mane.

"Then when autumn comes you say *that's* your favorite time of year."

Silas gently took the brush from her. "Sandy did himself fine with that drum and lute of his."

She felt her cheeks flush and moved away from Silas to the other side of the mare.

"He'll be along soon. We owe him his share of the take. Plus what he gave that official yesterday—saved Geoffrey a real lot of trouble."

Silas combed his fingers through the mane opposite where Damaris was working. "Mad at me for overplaying it last night?"

"That was a terrible surprise," Damaris said.

"Kind of surprised me too. I'm lying there real still when it hits me: do what I learned from that traveling Swami."

"Die?"

"Just make it look that way. Stop breathing and slow my heart way down. Same relaxing technique I taught you for when that torch comes at your face."

"You scared us half to death."

"I think it added to the drama, maybe even got us some extra coin."

"Most of that money was because of Geoffrey," Damaris said.

"Best we ever did, by a long sight. But we've got work to do. You can start by cutting out the cloth for your blindfold."

Damaris didn't reply.

"Need to make a new shirt for Geoffrey too," Silas noted. "The tin lining held up real well, though. Just like your blindfold."

"He was gone all night, Papa."

"Lots of nights he walks about, if he can't sleep. You know that."

"He's still gone."

"Probably off somewhere trying to talk a farmer out of a few vegetable seeds."

"Papa, let's do a different show. Change the story around."

"Has your mind gone to pottage, dearie? Every vendor on the fairway is coming tonight. Some of 'em are closing up early so they can get a seat."

"Did you see the look on Geoffrey's face when everybody started laughing at him?"

"Come inside," Silas said. "I've got something to show you."

Before following Silas into the wagon, Damaris glanced down the fairway. Where was Geoffrey? She wanted to talk with him, tell him not to care about those vile people from last night.

As a little girl, she had often seen Papa rub Geoffrey's body with various liniments, but she never saw a boy with scars. She saw her playmate, the one whom she climbed trees with, laughed with, sang with. She saw the boy in whose lap she sat as he read to her or conjured up make-believe stories for her. She saw the boy whose cap she loved to wear, the boy who carried her home one day after she got lost and tumbled down an embankment, wrenching her knee. Unaware of anything else as she pressed into his strong chest, she had felt safe—and special.

On the table in the wagon were six money pouches, plus a few loose coins. Damaris hadn't expected nearly that much.

"Ten more weeks like this, and we'll be on our way to Markarian," Silas said. "Maybe even get to sail before hurricane season."

"Papa, I don't care how much money we made last night. I don't want to do the show again."

"You want Geoffrey pursuing that fool idea of reclaiming his inheritance? Going to Caerdon, nosing about the government officials who had his family killed?"

"Papa, no, of course not."

"Geoffrey's the one who said he didn't mind doing the show. As long as it gets us to Markarian."

"That was before last night," Damaris said.

"And what about tonight's show? Elmond down at the 'Meats and Treats' wagon told me we are all the talk in Farharven. Said we'd have a huge crowd tonight."

"Papa, why did people throw things at Geoffrey? Why did they want to hurt him?"

"I don't know." Silas sighed. "Maybe some people, when they see someone worse off than themselves . . . feel contempt, I guess, instead of pity."

A shadow fell across the table.

"Pity?" Geoffrey said, standing in the open door of the wagon. His hair hung in filthy strands over his face, still streaked with last night's muck.

"Oh, Geoffrey," Damaris said. "I am so sorry." She went to him and took his hands. "I didn't know—"

"What a monster I really am?" He flung her hands away.

"Oh, no, Geoffrey, not a monster, never a monster." She brushed at tears in her eyes.

"You can tell 'Meats and Treats' Elmond not to worry," Geoffrey said. "We'll do the show tonight and every night until this fair closes. Then we'll go on to Shiresby and do it there, and on and on, like we planned. We need the money, don't we?"

Silas stood and indicated the bags on the table. "By rights, it's mostly yours, Geoffrey." He started to rub his knuckles on Geoffrey's scalp, but Geoffrey dodged, grabbed a few coins off the table, and strode out of the wagon.

"Geoffrey, wait." Damaris rushed after him.

Silas mumbled something about needing more supplies and hastened off up the fairway.

Damaris caught up with Geoffrey and grasped at his shoulders. He shrugged her off, tumbling her to the ground.

An approaching whistle.

Damaris looked up and saw Sandy.

"Morning, Geoffrey," Sandy said.

Geoffrey stopped, blocking Sandy's path. "You think you live here now?" He was a head taller than Sandy.

Damaris jumped up, brushed the dirt off her knees. "Now, Geoffrey, be nice to him. He left me some sweet brittle last night."

Geoffrey frowned. "He did, huh?"

"It wasn't me," Sandy said.

"Don't play dumb, Sandy. I found it this morning, on the wagon seat."

Sandy shrugged, smiled. Damaris's heart fluttered; she smiled back.

Geoffrey's hands clenched into fists. "Why'd you douse the torches?"

Sandy looked puzzled. "What?"

"Last night, at the end of the show."

"Well, the show was over, and I thought—"

"That was foolish of you. They were still throwing money."

"They were throwing everything *but* money," Sandy countered. "They were, uh . . ."

"They were what?" Geoffrey demanded.

Damaris's stomach tightened.

"Well, you know . . . they were laughing."

"You think that bothered me?"

"I thought it might. I mean, it would bother *me*. I just thought, well, you looked pretty upset, like maybe you might, uh . . ."

"Like maybe I might what, Sandy? Cry?"

Geoffrey lifted Sandy by the front of his shirt and flung him to the ground. "Get up!"

"Geoffrey—"

"I said get up."

Sandy got to his feet, caught Geoffrey's fist in the face, staggered backwards, and went down.

"Sandy?" Damaris knelt beside her friend then shouted up at Geoffrey. "What's wrong with you?"

Sandy wobbled to his feet and put a hand to his bleeding mouth. He shook his head to clear it, put his fists up to defend himself.

"Geoffrey, stop this!" Damaris grabbed at Geoffrey's arm as he swung again; Sandy caught a glancing blow, but it was enough to drop him to his knees.

"Get away from us!" Damaris was shaking all over. She shoved Geoffrey in the chest, but he was an ice wall, immovable. She pushed against him as he advanced on Sandy, her feet skidding backwards in the dirt. "You really *are* a monster!"

The resistance melted, and Geoffrey was gone.

Sandy held a bloody bandana to his mouth.

"Here, Sandy. Lie down, let me see that."

But Sandy was walking away.

"Don't leave, Sandy." A lump rose in her throat; she grabbed his arm.

Sandy detached her fingers. "I'm sorry."

"Wait. We owe you some money." Damaris darted into the wagon. She grabbed up one of the coin bags and rushed back out.

Sandy was nowhere in sight.

Damaris shuffled to their stage and flopped onto her stomach, her arm hanging off the edge. The raw ache in her chest merged into a deeper sense of loss that was always there, where her heart should have been. The coin bag dropped from her fingers; a tear trickled across the bridge of her nose.

"So you like sweet brittle."

CHAPTER 15

E dgewold.

The fat man was standing over her. Damaris scrambled to her feet beside the stage and swiped the tears from her face. "What do you want?"

"Your scar-boy is violent. He needs to be in prison."

"Get out of here," she yelled, hoping Silas was nearby.

"I'd say you're right, calling him a monster." The man stooped and picked up the coin sack, hefting it in his palm. "Quite a sum for a clumsy drummer who can't sing."

"Papa!"

"Good morning, sir." Silas hurried up. "Lovely day, ain't it?"

"He's got our money," Damaris said.

Edgewold unrolled a document, handed it to Silas.

Silas squinted and turned it upside down like he would read it if he could. "What is this?"

"A warrant for the arrest of one Geoffrey, carnival actor, for assaulting an official of the Realm," Edgewold said. "Duly signed and sealed by his Honorable Overlord Guernsey of Farharven."

A prison cart rolled up on creaking wheels, and a soldier climbed down. The driver remained on the seat, holding the reins.

"We settled that yesterday," Silas said.

"We settled nothing. Send the boy out."

75

"Papa, he knows Geoffrey's not here," Damaris said. "He's been spying on us."

The driver of the tumbrel was staring at her, picking at a huge boil on his neck. Chill bumps ran down her arms.

"There's money in your hand, Mr. Edgewold."

"Bribing an official is a punishable offense."

"Yes, sir. Consider that our earnings tax. Just paying it a mite early."

The man fake-smiled. "Earnings tax it is." He pocketed the coin bag. "You do not have enough money to make this go away."

He plucked the warrant from Silas's hand, delicately, as though the older man teemed with nits. He pointed to some writing at the bottom of the page.

"I am authorized to take the girl, in place of the criminal, to Starknell Tower, until such time as he shall return."

Damaris's mouth went dry. Starknell Tower was synonymous with rape, torture, and death. She clutched Silas's arm and pressed herself into him.

"Please, Mr. Edgewold," Silas said. "You seen our show last night. We took in a goodly amount. Mayhap you'll accept all of it. Not a bribe, mind you—but security, for the girl."

Edgewold snorted. The soldier grasped Damaris's arms, yanked her away from Silas.

"Papa!"

"There be fully five more bags like the one you hold, sir." Silas's voice was shaking.

Edgewold's chubby hand pulled at his goatee. "Surely I did not miscount as the pennies struck the stage."

"Not just penny coins was flung, sir." Silas dashed into the wagon.

The soldier's fingernails dug into Damaris's arm. He pushed her into the wooden cage and clicked the latch shut.

"Papa!"

Damaris felt the leering eyes of the driver on her. He milked some pus from the boil on his neck and smeared it on the slat nearest Damaris. Her blood turned to ice; she shook the cage door. "Papa!"

Silas raced up with the five coin bags, set them on the edge of the stage. "Search my wagon. If I be holding out even a half-penny, may I be stuck on the stake this very day."

Edgewold picked up each bag, opened it, and swirled a fat finger through the coins.

Damaris's pulse hammered in her throat; she fought the urge to vomit.

"Instead of prison, I am authorized to collect a fine, should the accused be of sufficient means," Edgewold said. "This is the first payment on that fine. I shall file a Writ of Owing at the First Magistrate's Court in Caerdon. Ten times this amount, payable by the Midsummer Moon. Failure to pay in full? Debtor's prison for all three of you."

He nodded to the soldier, who unlatched the cage door. Damaris burst out of the tumbrel, ran to Silas, and clung to him.

Edgewold climbed onto the cart and plopped down next to the driver. "Your phony accent intrigues me, old man. One day you may indeed find yourself impaled on that stake."

Inside their wagon, Damaris's hand trembled as she scooped more tea leaves from the canister. She couldn't get the rotten cabbage stink of the tumbrel—or maybe it was the pus—out of her nostrils no matter how strong she made the tea.

Silas scraped Geoffrey's knife back and forth on a whetstone. The sound made Damaris's fingernails hurt and her head ache.

"Papa, what he said . . . about your accent." She shivered and laced her hands around the hot cup.

"I think that fat little maggot was all bluster," Silas said.

"He was horrid. What did we ever do to him?"

"Hurt his pride, I guess, when Geoffrey knocked him down."

"But that was an accident. And you apologized, gave him money. Why wasn't that enough?"

"For jealousy, nothing is ever enough."

Damaris added water to the teakettle on the stove.

"Do you think Sandy will come back?"

"You'll see him soon," Silas said. "He travels to the same fairs we do, you know."

Silas placed the charred remains of the blindfold and shirt on the table, along with a roll of black fabric and some shears. "But right now we've got costumes to mend, torches to fill, a dress to wash—which you'd better do first, so it'll be dry by tonight."

"Papa, I told you, I don't want to do the show again."

"We do the show tonight, and we do it every night until that debt is paid. Or we all die in prison."

Silas handed her the mask that Geoffrey had worn. "This needs washed too."

Damaris held Geoffrey's mask up to her face and looked through the eyeholes . . . then dropped it and ran outside, not wanting Silas to see her cry.

CHAPTER 16

At the far edge of the pasture, near a stand of scrub trees, Geoffrey found a cattle pond. He splashed his face, but the water did nothing to stop his mind's relentless replay of the morning's events. Except in self-defense, he had never before tried to hurt anyone.

"See the world's only two-headed calf. Right here, alive, livin' and breathin'. And born under that same strange astrological sign: a pig, with seven feet."

Geoffrey latched onto the barker's voice as it drifted across the field, willing it to crowd out Damaris's pronouncement over him.

Monster . . .

He tried to imagine what such animals might look like. Could they be real? He found himself headed back to the fairway.

"Creatures so strange, so bizarre, so astounding, you won't believe your own eyes."

Geoffrey's steps slowed when he neared a magician's wagon. The illusionist was busy sawing a lady in half for the benefit of a handful of onlookers, promising even more spectacular feats if they would come back for the full show tonight.

A few yards down from the magician, a stubby man duck-legged it back and forth in front of a tent whose sides were painted with grotesquely deformed animals.

"Creatures so ugly their own mothers would kill them, if given the chance," the man said.

Geoffrey did not know how much money Nissa would charge to read his fortune. Maybe he should wait and see the animal-oddity show on his way back.

He went to an open-sided food wagon and asked for some sweet brittle. "We're sold out," gummed the woman. She seemed young to be without teeth. "How 'bout some molasses bobs? Four for a penny."

Geoffrey nodded. As she handed him the packet, he saw a man—probably a villager from Farharven—approach the bizarre animals exhibit.

"Yessir, seeing is believing." The barker stopped mid-waddle and held out his hand for the villager's money. "You won't be sorry, no indeed. One hundred percent guaranteed."

"Hey, Barney, don't waste your quid." Another villager limped up and joined the man named Barney. He pointed his cane in the direction of Silas's wagon. "Save it for the show down there on the end."

Barney hesitated.

"Big Eddy seen it last night. Says they set a couple of people on fire. He's still shook up."

"My good man," the barker said. "Do not miss the eighth wonder of the known world, right here in the tent behind me. Alive and breathing under water, the one and only gill-monkey."

"Still shook up, huh?" Barney pocketed his money. "Big Eddy McThuel?"

"Nature's freaks and rejects. Seen right here and right here only." The barker's voice was shrill now. "And, through a rare combination of peculiar and unnatural circumstances, we have the world's only sheep with six tails—growing out of her face. Alive, livin' and breathin'!"

"And bring something to throw," the older man said. The two ambled off.

"Something to throw?" Barney asked. "Why?"

"I don't know, I just heard that's what you do."

Geoffrey's throat went dry; he tried to swallow but couldn't. He ran his fingers across a bruise on his cheek.

"You." The barker pointed at him. "I heard about your so-called show. I wouldn't give a double donkey's pile for it."

Geoffrey looked at the man. With his flat nose and close-cropped yellow hair, he really did resemble a duck.

"And when it flops, you'll be working for me." He quacked out a laugh. "Step right up and see the one and only Reptile Boy, whose mother got too friendly one night with a crocodile."

Geoffrey fought the urge to fist-hammer the man's beak down his throat.

"Where you going, freak-boy?"

Geoffrey was on Nissa's street, a few blocks from her house, when the young man with the pockmarked face stepped in front of him. His left eye was swollen shut from Geoffrey's fist the day before. He gripped a wooden bowling pin by the neck, like a club.

Geoffrey tried to go around him, but two more young men stepped from an alley and blocked his path. The three toughs backed Geoffrey up against a building. His scalp began to sweat.

"You think that sweet little fortune-teller wants to see an ugly freak like you?" Pockmark jeered.

"Pinky here can read your future," one of the men said. His grin was a row of bronze-capped teeth. "Tell him, Pinky."

Pinky laughed. "You will soon have two black eyes, no teeth, and no money."

Geoffrey's hand moved toward his waist before he remembered that his knife was still stuck in the tree from last night.

"Whatever money you got is ours anyway. You didn't earn it." Pockmark yanked Geoffrey's scarf down. "You got it for being a freak."

"Here's another prediction," Pinky said. "A year from now, you'll still be a freak." The gang laughed.

Geoffrey tried to slow his breathing. Pinky was muscular, like some of the dockworkers he had seen at the harbor.

"Here," Geoffrey said, proffering his coins. "It's all I've got."

Pockmark smacked the coins away as Pinky and Metal-tooth pinned Geoffrey's arms against the building. Pockmark punched Geoffrey in the gut and then, with his club, delivered a savage blow to his chest. When the club slammed into Geoffrey a second time, something in his side felt like it broke. Pain ripped through his ribs; he sagged.

He felt them release his arms, tottered but did not fall. Pockmark slapped him across the face then again, backhanded. Geoffrey brought his hands up and tried to punch back, but the fists coming at him were beginning to blur. The gang took turns taunting him with slaps to the face and punches to the body. His knees turned to rubber; the rough siding dug into his back as he slid down the wall. *If I go down, I'm dead.* He tried to lock his knees.

"Now I got a prediction," Pockmark said. "While your old man is digging the hole to bury you, we'll be taking turns with your sister."

Geoffrey exploded off the wall, wrenched the club from Pockmark, and smashed it over his head. He spun, crashed his fist into Pinky's face. He dodged Metal-tooth's punch and used the man's momentum to pull him to the ground.

"You broke my nose," Pinky said.

Geoffrey bobbed away from Pinky's roundhouse punch then cracked him on the side of the head so hard the club broke. Pinky sprawled to the ground beside Pockmark. Metal-tooth got up and squared off with Geoffrey, who thrust the splintered club at him. The man turned around and snarled off.

Geoffrey stumbled the rest of the way to Nissa's house and waited for the letters spelling "Zeruba" to stop wobbling before he knocked. The door scraped open.

"Hello . . . oh, Geoffrey." The delight drained from Nissa's childish voice when she saw his face. She took his hand. "Come in."

How did she know his name? He pulled his hand from hers. Maybe she was at the show last night.

"I didn't see your show last night," Nissa said.

Was she a mind reader too?

"But someone told Granny about it."

"What did they say?"

Nissa seemed unable to reply.

Something about me being a monster, probably . . .

"It doesn't matter." Nissa put her arm around his waist. "Let's get you cleaned up."

The pain in Geoffrey's side was even worse than the time he fell out of a tree while showing off to Damaris as a youngster.

Inside the house, heavy curtains smothered out the sunlight. The air was a blend of stale cooking grease and incense.

Nissa seated Geoffrey at a small table. She began to clean the crusted blood from his face with a damp cloth. Her touch was gentle.

She must really need money, to be so nice to me.

Someone was snoring behind a door at the back of the room. Nissa motioned with her head. "Granny," she whispered.

Geoffrey set the packet of molasses bobs on the table. "They didn't have any sweet brittle. I'm sorry."

Even in the dim light, Geoffrey saw Nissa's neck flush. She fumbled to open the paper and smiled shyly at him as she popped one of the sweets in her mouth. She sat down across the table from him. "Shall I read your fortune?"

Geoffrey felt his pocket, realized he had lost his coins in the fight. "Uh . . . no."

"You already paid me." Nissa put another molasses bob into her mouth.

"It's not the same," Geoffrey said.

There was a break in the rhythmic snoring behind the door. Nissa touched a finger to Geoffrey's lips. "Shh . . ." The snoring resumed.

Nissa lit a candle. On the table between them, a luminescent crystal—about the size of a fist—cast a pale light on her face. The crystal was affixed to the top of a human skull. Geoffrey shuddered.

Nissa took his hands across the table, their arms encircling the skull and crystal, then closed her eyes and exhaled.

"You want to know when your life will finally begin." Her voice was low. "You are tired of never having the money you need."

Geoffrey nodded.

"That is all going to change, before many turns have passed."

He closed his eyes.

"You like plants, flowers, anything that grows . . ."

Only Damaris and Silas knew that. And his dead parents.

"I see a child. And your mother . . . there is much pain there."

The tender eyes of his mother seemed to search Geoffrey's as her cool palms held his cheeks.

"Your father too," Nissa said. "Much pain . . . and . . . guilt."

Don't think of the sounds mother made, burning up. Running to the woods, he could still hear her. And then—horribly—his father's surprisingly girlish screams. He yanked his hands out of Nissa's and jammed his fists against his ears.

"Geoffrey." She gently dislodged his fists. "Your father and mother have a message for you." One by one, Nissa uncurled and regained his fingers.

"They want you to know . . . they are not angry with you . . . they love you."

There was a constricting pain in Geoffrey's throat as he tried not to cry. Why had he stood there, watching the soldiers assemble in the moonlight, waiting as more arrived, and never warned his parents?

"Mama . . ." Geoffrey whispered. "I'm so sorry . . . Papa . . . please forgive me."

He coughed to get the lump out of his throat. The candle flickered and nearly went out.

"There is someone else . . ." Nissa's grip grew stronger. "A young woman. You have feelings for her . . ."

Geoffrey sighed.

"Buried in your heart is a secret wish." Nissa's voice was husky. "Something you hardly dare look at because it seems so far beyond anything that could ever be . . ."

A silent minute passed. Neither of them noticed that the snoring in the back room had ceased.

Nissa took a deep breath, exhaled, then released Geoffrey's hands. All was still save for the spitting candlewick.

"I'm not sure how you did that," Geoffrey finally said.

"It's nothing, really." Nissa shrugged. "Everyone wants to know the same things. Will my life change for the better? Will I get some money?"

Geoffrey nodded.

"A child whose parents died will often blame himself." Nissa blew out the candle. "And people especially want to know: will I ever find true love?"

"You knew I liked gardening, growing things."

"Just a guess from the soil under your nails."

Geoffrey felt his ears get red. "But what you said about a secret wish."

"I might have been talking about myself." Nissa blushed. "The truth is, Geoffrey, I really don't know much. I've never traveled more than a few miles outside of Farharven."

"Traveling's not that great."

"What would you rather do?"

"Farm."

"Not me. I'm almost sixteen and never had a beau. That's because Granny's afraid something might happen to me." She giggled, self-conscious. "I don't know why I'm telling you all this."

"Maybe you want me to know you're not really a fortune-teller."

"I guess," Nissa said. "But Granny's different. She really *can* predict a person's future. Of course, people tell her things. So she often knows all about a person before she meets them. And since no one knows their own future, she can tell a person whatever they want to hear."

"I'm sure every fortune-teller does that," Geoffrey said.

"Yes, but Granny has a gift. She sees things. Hears things."

"Like what?"

Nissa glanced at the backroom door and lowered her voice. "Demons, maybe. I don't know. She says there's an unseen world—a spirit world— just as real as this one. She gets frustrated with me, says I'm afraid to open up to it. Which I am, to tell you the truth." She sighed. "So . . . I'll never be any good at this."

The door at the back of the room creaked open. Startled by the striking visage of the old woman advancing on him, Geoffrey stood up so fast his chair clattered over. Zeruba's face was ancient but without wrinkles. Her eyes, owl-round, were without eyebrows.

The nimble old gorgon shoved Nissa aside and whispered in Geoffrey's face. "I know who ye are."

"Granny?"

"Ye leave and do not ever return."

"What's wrong, Granny?"

Geoffrey backed out the door. The sunlight was blinding.

"Or worse than dogs will I sic on ye." Zeruba slammed the door. There was a struggle on the other side as Nissa got the door open a crack before it shut again.

"Granny, please!"

"Hearken well, daughter," came Zeruba's voice through the door. "Ye have not seen this man."

"Geoffrey's gentle, Granny. He would never hurt me."

"Ye will say nothing, to no one."

"You don't understand!"

When he was half a block away, Geoffrey could still hear Nissa crying.

CHAPTER 17

"**A**nother hour of this and I won't have to fake being blind, Papa." Damaris tossed Geoffrey's tin-lined shirt, along with her needle and thread, onto the table. Moving her eyes made her head ache.

"Let's go out and tighten up the slide line," Silas said.

There was a noise outside. "Come out, old man, we got something to say."

Through the window, Damaris saw a dozen men armed with axes, clubs, and knives.

"Hitch up, Damaris," Silas whispered. "Quick and quiet." Silas ignored her questioning look. "And try to stay out of sight."

"We want the boy," hollered a squat, yellow-haired man.

Damaris climbed out of the wagon onto the driver's box and dropped cat-like to the ground.

Silas exited and stood on the little platform at the back of the wagon. Several men shouted at him.

"Your freak-boy attacked our kids."

"My young'un still ain't come to."

Jenquilla scuffed at the ground with a front hoof. "Easy, girl," Damaris whispered into the furry ear. She untied the mare from behind the stage and slipped the bridle on, hoping the animal would not sense her fear. "Just some nice visitors."

"Well, old man?"

"Well, what?" Silas drawled.

Damaris could picture him there on the other side of the scrim, lighting his pipe, like nothing was wrong. She wished she felt as calm as he sounded.

"Is he coming out or are we coming in after him?"

"Now, just you hold onto your feather dusters," Silas said.

Damaris cinched the breast strap on Jenquilla.

"C'mon!" The voice was angry.

"I'll go get him," Silas said.

Damaris heard the wagon door creak open then close again. "He ain't here. So you all can just go on about your business."

"No." Several voices.

"If you want to see him, come back tonight. Still got a few tickets left."

Damaris worked fast, hooking the harness traces to the carriage tree.

"We want him now."

"I'll give you each a free pass for tonight's show."

"We came for the boy, and we'll have the boy. Just a matter of time before he attacks someone else."

"My boy wouldn't touch no one, less'n it was self-defense." Now Silas sounded angry.

"He's a devil, I tell you, ain't fit to live. My kid's bad hurt."

"He wouldn't touch your ugly kid."

Damaris wished Geoffrey could hear Silas defend him.

"But we sure hurt your fake little peep show, huh, Ducky?"

Damaris's pulse quickened. That sounded like the kind of incautious remark Geoffrey would make. She hooked the shafts into their loops and secured the reins.

An ax chop sent the slide rope twanging into the tree. Two men clambered up the tower and rocked it. One of them looked down.

"Hey, here's the wench!"

A big bald man grabbed Damaris by the shoulders as the tower toppled. The man dodged the wrong way and went down under the falling platform.

Damaris twisted free. "Papa!"

But Silas was surrounded, his back against the wagon door. Damaris grabbed a piece of splintered wood and tossed it to him. He glanced at her, caught a punch instead of the stick, and fell against the door. Rough hands grabbed Damaris's arm and yanked her to the ground.

"Over here, you hairy no-neck apes!"

The hands left her as the mob turned and rushed at Geoffrey, twenty-five yards away in the cow pasture.

Damaris bent to help Silas up. "No, girl, get up there and drive."

Damaris scooted up to the wagon seat and grabbed the reins. "Giddup, Jenqy, yah!"

The wagon, shorn of its tower, took off after the mob, which was nearly upon Geoffrey. He stood like a statue.

"Run, Geoffrey!" Damaris shouted.

Silas came up beside Damaris.

"Why doesn't he run?" Damaris's heart was in her throat as the first man to reach Geoffrey swung his ax. Geoffrey dodged the blow then smacked away a knife thrust.

"Straight at Geoffrey then pull her left," shouted Silas.

The front wheels hit a rut and bounced Damaris forward. Silas caught her arm and pulled her back.

Geoffrey punched at one of the attackers, lost his balance, and went down. The ax-man swung at Geoffrey like he was splitting wood. Geoffrey rolled; the ax struck the ground an inch from his head as the mob scattered out of the path of the charging horse and wagon.

Geoffrey leaped to his feet a split second before Silas leaned from the wagon and yanked him aboard. Jenquilla stumbled, the wagon slowed. Four men scrambled aboard as the rest of the mob pursued on foot.

"Giddup, go!" Damaris shouted. Silas, still in lock-arm with Geoffrey, swung him around and swept one of the attackers off the top of the vehicle.

Damaris felt herself yanked off the seat and down into the wagon. The yellow-haired man vise-gripped her neck in both hands. She couldn't breathe. He forced her face toward the stovetop, now only inches away, the heat on her cheeks unbearable, her hair smelling of singe.

Her flailing fingers found the teapot handle, flung it backwards from its cradle. The man screamed as scalding water hit his face. Damaris half-kicked, half-rolled him out the door. He tumbled to a stop in the dust.

Damaris clutched her throat. It was as though she were still being strangled. Pain, spasms, her breath wheezing out. The wagon seemed to slow; the ruckus of the struggle overhead ebbed into oblivion.

"Dee . . . Dee, wake up."

The words reached Damaris from a distance. Someone lifted her, cradling her body in strong arms, and she was floating like a dandelion puff on the breeze. Then she was on the bunk, flowing along with the rolling wagon. The coolness of a damp rag on her forehead, someone stroking her hair.

Geoffrey? No, his big hands would not be so gentle . . .

Damaris opened her eyes. Geoffrey glanced away, cleared his throat, and picked up a cup of water.

"Dragon nectar, Dee?"

Geoffrey held the metal cup to her lips. She drank.

Over the rim, Damaris's eyes found Geoffrey's and held them until the last drop.

Always it seemed that his eyes were not merely looking, they were seeing—and understanding—her. And Geoffrey's eyes seemed always—unwisely, she thought—unguarded. If she focused a little deeper, inside the brown pools rather than on them, she saw strength and goodness, and something of sadness. And something timeless too—something that was also a part of her.

CHAPTER 18

Geoffrey tied his clothes into a bundle and donned his cap. He knelt beside the sleeping form of Damaris. Her hands, folded in at the wrists, were nestled together under her chin.

I bet that's how she slept inside her mother.

He was still beside her when moonlight began to filter through the window and bathe her face. Every few minutes her breath came out in a soft sigh. Maybe she would wake up and try to stop him.

Geoffrey slipped out of the wagon, stood on the step, and inhaled the cool night air.

Tiberias slept beside their dying fire. Were the dog younger, he would be a good companion for the days to come. Geoffrey lifted his fingers through the dog's fur like a comb, wishing he could wake the mutt and pour his heart into those tufted ears, like he had as a child.

"Goodbye, old boy."

Geoffrey stepped onto the road, feeling a curious mix of fear and excitement for the adventure ahead.

"Geoffrey."

He turned. Damaris, in a white nightdress, her hair loose, stood beside the wagon. The breeze played a tress of hair across her face. She brushed it back.

"It's because of me," she said.

"No."

"I told you I was sorry, Geoffrey."

"That's not it."

"Papa?" She shivered, hugging herself.

"What about him?"

"When he accused you of picking a fight with those boys. Blamed you for losing our tower and props and things."

"You didn't believe me either, Dee."

"Well, you picked a fight with Sandy."

"I told you I was sorry," Geoffrey said. "And if I ever see Sandy again, I'll try to make it right with him."

Behind her shone the moon on the water of the abandoned stone quarry, where they had camped after fleeing Farharven. The water was so still that the reflected moon seemed steadier than the true one floating overhead.

"The Writ of Owing is not your fault either," Damaris said. "Papa knows you didn't knock down that man on purpose."

"None of that matters."

Damaris took a few steps toward him. "It matters to me."

"Damaris. We have no money. In three days, we'll have no food."

"We'll do another show," she said. "Not that one—ever again—but something."

"I don't care what people think of me."

"People are horrid."

"Don't you get it? I'm a danger to us," Geoffrey said. "That mob—our fellow vendors—will be at every fair. Yesterday we got away. Next time we might not be so lucky."

Damaris shook her head.

"And if we don't pay the Writ by midsummer, we'll all be in Starknell." She sighed.

"We're going to need a lot of money, Dee."

"Like an inheritance?"

Geoffrey didn't reply.

"Caerdon is too far away, Geoffrey."

"A night's walk. I am sorry, Damaris. I wish things were different, with all my heart."

Geoffrey forced himself to turn away. *Go now, or you won't be able to.* He took the first steps.

Damaris followed, ran in front of him. Geoffrey stopped, saw the tears streaming silently down her cheeks, and felt his resolve break.

His insides trembled as Damaris removed her chain and locket, reached up, and fastened it on him. The touch of her fingers on the nape of his neck, the warm fragrance of her scalp . . .

Geoffrey ran down the dark road, his vision blurred with tears. He had gone a good two miles before he realized he was being followed.

Tiberias.

CHAPTER 19

Nissa was bored; she had given only one reading all morning. She was also hungry. As she sat on the step, she debated whether to risk her grandmother's wrath and sneak back into the house for some salt pork and bread.

But Granny forbade her to be inside whenever Hamewith was there. "You can't be hurt by what you don't know," she said.

Hamewith emerged and sat down beside her on the step. He was a plain young fellow with a harmless face—a man who could easily blend into a crowd. Nissa liked him, if only for the fact that he didn't treat her like the naïve child Granny thought she was.

"That didn't take long. Didn't Granny tell you anything this time?"

"Not much," Hamewith said. "You got anything for me?"

Nissa laughed, flattered to be asked. "You mean, do I know if there's a tax revolt afoot or some assassination plot? No, I don't."

Hamewith sighed. "I just hate going back to Lord Nostromal empty-handed."

"Tell me about his castle again." Nissa had heard about the lavish lifestyle enjoyed by the Chancellor of the House of Overlords and his grand entourage.

"Maybe I ought to take you there sometime," Hamewith said.

"Don't tease me."

Hamewith picked up a twig, scratched some mud off his boot. "You must have heard *some* gossip."

"The only people I ever meet are the lovelorn and the lost, you know that."

"I bet you have all kinds of beaus coming to call," Hamewith said. "What about the carnival?"

Nissa bit at a hangnail until it bled. Hamewith studied her. "You met someone?"

She shrugged.

"I bet he was nice."

"What difference does it make?"

"Why do you say that?" Hamewith's voice was gentle.

"I'll never see him again."

"I'm sorry to hear that, Nissa."

It felt good to talk to someone about it. Hamewith cared more than Granny, it seemed.

"What happened, if you don't mind me asking?"

"Granny sent him away."

"Surely not."

Nissa, still picking at her fingernail, did not notice the new intensity in Hamewith's voice.

"I'm not lying," she said.

"Uh huh." The man feigned a yawn.

"'I know who ye are.'" Nissa imitated Zeruba's piercing snarl. "Then she told him never to come back. And Geoffrey wouldn't harm a housefly. I just wish I could talk to him, apologize for Granny."

"Hmm . . ." Hamewith stroked his chin. "If only you had some way to get a message to him."

"You travel around. Maybe you could tell him for me."

Hamewith shook his head.

"I mean, if you run into him."

"That's unlikely."

"But it's possible, right?"

"I don't know what he looks like, or anything about him."

"He was at the carnival, an actor," Nissa said. "But some of the men ran him off."

"Why?"

"They said he attacked their kids. But I think they were just jealous of how much money his show made. They said he's ugly too."

"Ugly?"

"All scarred up or something," Nissa said. "But it must be part of their act somehow because he's not ugly at all." She sighed, remembering the gentle depth in Geoffrey's eyes.

"Is there anything else you can tell me that might help me recognize this—Geoffrey, was it?"

CHAPTER 20

Geoffrey arrived in the city an hour after sunup and found the Palace Presidio. Centuries old, it was magnificently set on a bluff above the river and best known as the meeting place of the House of Overlords. But it also held the Library of Records and, hopefully, the information Geoffrey sought.

Geoffrey left Tiberias resting in the sunshine. The vestibule, as he entered, smelled of old wood and unwashed bodies. He inquired of a woman who was scrubbing the flagstone floor and was directed toward the furthest of three cavernous hallways.

At the end of the hallway was a door, guarded by a massive desk. Behind the desk stood a clerk with outsized gray sideburns. The clerk looked up. "Where's your process?"

"Process?"

"No one gets in without it."

Geoffrey, trying to guess what was meant by "process," patted his pockets. "Must've dropped it."

He turned to go. Another man arrived and handed the clerk a paper. The clerk gave it a glance, stuck it in a cubbyhole with like papers, and admitted the man through the door behind his desk.

Geoffrey returned momentarily with Tiberias, who plopped onto the stone floor. "Found it."

"You can't bring a dog in here," said the clerk.

"Not my dog."

"Get! Shoo!"

Tiberias ignored the clerk.

When the clerk picked up a scroll rod and whacked Tiberias on the back, Geoffrey plucked a paper from the cubbyhole. He stopped the clerk's second swing.

"Let me try," Geoffrey said. "Come on, dog."

Tiberias followed Geoffrey back outside, who thanked the animal with a bread ball from his pocket. "I didn't know he was gonna hit you, boy. I'm so sorry. Wait here."

Geoffrey returned to the clerk, handed over the pilfered paper, and entered the Library of Records.

The room was a cramped jumble of scrolls, parchments, and record books, scattered and stacked on shelves and tables. Geoffrey perused the materials for several fruitless hours. At last he located a land ownership book for the environs of Caerdon. But the page of entries for the estate known as Castleford was missing—torn out.

While Geoffrey conducted his research, several officials came and went. One man—evidently a curator—offered assistance, but Geoffrey declined. His precaution was insufficient, for after Geoffrey departed, the man made a careful examination of the volumes and pages that had occupied Geoffrey's attention.

Finally, in a ledger that listed members of the House of Overlords going back several hundred years, Geoffrey found his father's name and date of death. The line following "Wellam Davenant" read "Haviwade Bertraks."

Fury burned inside Geoffrey's chest like fiery coals in a blazing stove.

PART TWO

CHAPTER 21

On the outskirts of Caerdon, in the ornate parlor of a large country manor—known to Nissa as Dunnesmore, the castle of Lord Nostromal—a young woman turned pirouettes on the inlaid floor.

A servant girl, lugging a silver tray of tea and biscuits, limped into the room.

Lady Lorica twirled over to her. "What do you think?"

Mousy looked around—the great lady was indeed addressing her, a mere servant of only seventeen birthdays, and one with a misshapen leg, at that. *Is she seeking my opinion of her dancing? Her gown? The weather, maybe?*

"I asked you a question—what do you think?"

"It's very nice, miss," Mousy said. That should cover everything but the gown, a gaudy sack more suited to a clown than the consort of the Lord Chancellor.

Lord Nostromal strode into the parlor. The other servant girls in the household—notwithstanding his fifty-odd years—thought the big man handsome, but Mousy was afraid of him. She hurried to finish placing the napkins.

Lady Lorica gave a cry of delight and spun into Nostromal's arms. His stern face softened into a charismatic smile.

"You have been away so long," Lorica said.

"A week and a half."

"A year and a half, to me."

Nostromal linked arms with Lorica and walked her to the large window overlooking the front lawn. On the sill were a dozen potted orchids.

Mousy poured the tea and watched sidelong as Nostromal moved along the row of orchids, adjusting a stake on one plant, blowing a speck of dust off another.

"You act as if it's these silly flowers you have missed," Lorica said.

He selected a small pair of shears from a tool basket and snipped off a blossom.

Lorica knelt to the floor and retrieved it. "What was wrong with this one?"

"An imperfection where one of the petals joins the stem."

"That's silly," Lorica said. "But I'll take your word for it."

There was a knock. A man wearing the pennant and scimitar on his tunic and a bushy-browed scowl on his face stood in the open doorway.

"My apologies, your grace. But I have information that may require your urgent attention."

Nostromal waved the man in. "You remember Captain Axelrad, my dear." He seemed relieved at the interruption.

"A young man has been seeking information about the family and lands of Wellam Lord Davenant," Axelrad said.

"How do you know this?"

"Our spy in the Library of Records."

"You are certain of whom he inquires?"

"The late Baron Castleford, yes."

"Arrest the man, captain. Starknell Dungeon."

Axelrad nodded. "The See-ress Zeruba may also know something."

"According to whom?"

"Hamewith."

"Regarding this same young man?"

"Yes," Axelrad said.

"Bring Zeruba to me at once," Nostromal ordered.

"Very good, sire."

Mousy stepped aside as Axelrad, a stocky mass of muscle, pinched five biscuits on his way out.

"It appears I must return to affairs of state, my dear." Nostromal drew Lorica close. "Allow me to call on you tomorrow afternoon at Darrowick?"

"Of course." Lorica turned her face up for a kiss. Mousy looked away.

"It's not as if you have Scourge." Chagrin tinged Lorica's voice.

"What have you heard?" Nostromal's reply was sharp.

Mousy made for the doorway, willing her misshapen foot not to clump.

"Nothing but mad rumors," Lorica said.

"Rumors?"

"One story has it that you sold your soul to the devil so you wouldn't die of Scourge." She laughed. "How ridiculous people are."

"What if I did have Scourge?"

"I would think you the most repulsive man ever. Any woman would." Lorica giggled then pirouetted from Nostromal, reaching the doorway before Mousy. "But you'd be dead, so it wouldn't matter what I thought, would it?"

And Lady Lorica was gone.

Mousy had finally gained the main hallway when she heard her carefully laid tea tray crash against the wall.

CHAPTER 22

"He didn't even look at me," Lady Lorica said. "And why should he, when you dress me in this peasant costume—"

She ripped a sleeve off her dress and hurled it at Derina, her lady-in-waiting. "It isn't even a dress, it's a rucksack."

Derina retrieved the sleeve from the floor of Lorica's bedchamber and sat on the divan.

Now fifty, she had served the girl's family at Darrowick Manor since before Lorica was born. And because the lord and lady of Darrowick had wanted a son, Derina became as much father and mother to Lorica as nursemaid and governess. And Lorica became the child that Derina would never have.

"You tell Marenda to go sew body bags for the prison from now on. And for the asylum." Lorica ripped the other sleeve off. "Why did you let me go to Dunnesmore? Nostromal should have called on me *here*, if he cared at all."

"I did try to tell you, milady, but—"

"No, you didn't. You wanted to see your scrawny doctor friend."

Lorica collapsed on the floor in front of Derina and flopped her head onto Derina's lap.

"Nostromal thinks I'm ugly."

"I'm sure that's not true, pet."

"He's never even kissed me."

Derina stroked Lorica's hair. The young woman—even had she been ugly—was a most desirable catch among the nobility. With her father dead and her mother so senile she barely recognized her own daughter, Lorica was the sole heir to a vast estate.

"Maybe you should forget about Lord Nostromal." Derina hated to say it. She had dearly hoped Lorica would be visiting Nostromal's estate often, so she could, indeed, see more of Dr. Qwenten. "There are others, men closer to your own age."

Lorica snorted. "I wouldn't give a bag of dirt for the lot of them."

"But if Lord Nostromal does not care about you—"

"No, Derina, he does care."

"What makes you think so?"

"He confides in me."

"How so?" Derina asked.

"He's working on a bill for the House of Overlords—part of some grand plan he has to improve the country." Lorica stood and walked to the dressing mirror. "He told me all about it."

"That doesn't mean he loves you."

"Maybe not yet." Lorica primped her hair in the mirror then turned sideways and ran her hands down her form. "But he will."

Derina's brow furrowed. "Lorica, dear, Dr. Qwenten is worried about you regarding Lord Nostromal."

"What does he know?"

"He works for Lord Nostromal—some kind of research."

"So?" Lorica fished a necklace from her jewelry box and modeled it in the mirror.

"He gave me no details—doctors have to keep secrets, you know— but he advises against this, milady. And I think we should listen to him."

"How many times have I told you to stop this constant fretting over me? And stop bossing me—it's tiresome."

Derina hesitated. How to convince Lorica to heed Lucius Qwenten's warning? Maybe remind her that the doctor had once saved Lorica's life . . .

The image of ten-year-old Lorica—unconscious in a pool of blood, wrists slit on a broken hand mirror—still haunted Derina. Nights were the worst. It had taken but a minute for Derina to grasp why the child wanted to murder herself. It would take a thousand lifetimes for Derina to forgive herself.

The Duke of Anxbury, staying at Darrowick Manor for a month, fell ill (feigned, as Derina learned too late) on the last day of his visit. That was the day Derina met Dr. Qwenten, who prescribed bed rest for the Duke, and a walk in the garden for himself with Derina. Derina, who doggedly remained at Lorica's side when certain male guests were visiting, made an exception that day—the Duke was bedridden, after all—and spent the most magical hour of her life with the young doctor.

The second time Derina saw Dr. Qwenten was a month later, when he saved little Lorica's life. Lorica's parents, away at the time, assumed it was her clumsiness that broke the hand mirror, and if they noticed the sutures on her wrists, they did not remark on it. In fact, Lorica's mother saw to it that the mirror (a rare heirloom with a silver serpent handle) was reglazed and replaced atop her daughter's bureau. Derina, of course, promptly secreted the hand mirror elsewhere. Neither she nor Lorica ever needed to see the silver serpent mirror—tool of Lorica's suicide attempt and reminder of Derina's failure to protect the child from the Duke of Anxbury that day.

It was Derina who nursed Lorica back to health and watched her grow into a beautiful young woman. It was also Derina who defended her lady's reputation when Lorica unwisely bestowed her favors on unworthy gentlemen. For Derina understood Lorica's unconscious belief that she was no longer worthy or special . . .

"Lorica." Derina's temples were throbbing. "Do you remember when you were a little girl, and Dr. Qwenten—"

"Tomorrow we visit Madame Charteges," Lorica interrupted. "She shall make me a dress like no other."

CHAPTER 23

Asolitary human moan came to Geoffrey's ears every few
minutes, but it was the stench in his nostrils that finally cause
him to open his eyes.

He was on his back on a stone floor. Except for a few shafts of light
from a barred window high on the wall, the cell was dark. His fingertips
found a painful lump on his scalp; his cap was gone.

Geoffrey stood up into the hot air, raw with four centuries of human
filth. The moaning ceased . . . silence reigned except for the buzzing of
flies and the skittering of rodent claws.

Geoffrey ripped strips from a crusty blanket and knotted a loop
through an iron ring in the wall above his head. He pulled himself up on
the ring and stuck his foot into the blanket loop, then into the iron ring,
one foot atop the other, leaning into the cornered wall.

The barred window was now just inches above Geoffrey's upstretched
fingertips. He leaped for the bars, missed, and fell hard to the floor. He
felt for broken bones, glad for Sandy's instruction on how to fall. Four
jumps and as many bruises later, his hands grasped the sill, and he pulled
himself up to a perch on the window ledge.

Geoffrey yanked on the bars and found that the mortar in which they
were set was crumbling. If he could work a couple of the bars loose—

"He's gone!"

Geoffrey froze. A guard's face appeared at the hatch in the cell door.
Keys jangled, the door swung open, and a pair of guards burst in.

"Up there." One of the men pointed to Geoffrey on the ledge. The guard's shouts into the corridor brought the warden, a whip, and a crossbow. Geoffrey came down under pain of death, although that might have been preferable to what came next.

"Twenty strokes for trying to escape," the warden said on his way out. "Ten more for punching the arresting officer yesterday."

The two guards bound Geoffrey's arms to the iron ring above his head, turned him to face the wall, then stripped off his shirt.

"Well, look at this." The guard with the whip reminded Geoffrey of a bear—hairy, and with a slouch in his thick shoulders.

The other guard poked his finger at the scar tissue encasing Geoffrey's trunk. "What are you, a hunchback or something?"

Geoffrey did not reply. The man bounced Geoffrey's forehead off the wall. "I asked you a question." He had a sparse red beard and watery eyes. Geoffrey wondered how anyone could smell worse than the stench he was already breathing.

The Bear swung the whip and struck the top of Geoffrey's shoulders.

"Hey," the red-bearded guard howled. The tip of the whip had flicked him on the arm.

The pain of that first blow was worse than Geoffrey had expected. He swallowed a scream, clenched his jaw muscles, and tried to remember that time long ago when Damaris had stood on his tender shoulders to return a baby bird to its nest.

Don't let her know it hurts.

The man lashed him again, and again, each blow harder. Geoffrey dug his nails into his clenched palms. The whip now struck Geoffrey's lower back—exquisitely tender since his burn injuries. He ground his teeth until they squeaked.

It's just Damaris's feet, her little feet . . .

"Give it." Redbeard grabbed the whip handle. "I'll make him yell." He attacked Geoffrey's bleeding back with a ferocity that nearly elicited the cries they craved.

"I reckon that's about thirty," Bear said. "We ain't supposed to kill him."

But the other man continued to swing the whip.

Had he still been on the window ledge, Geoffrey might have seen Silas and Tiberias below, on the road outside the prison. Tiberias had loped back to their wagon after Geoffrey's arrest and led Silas straight to Starknell.

"Ya dumb beast of a dog. He ain't gonna be *here*." Or so Silas hoped. He coaxed Tiberias to walk with him to the Library of Records, where he learned nothing, then—with sinking heart—followed Tiberias back to Starknell.

He loitered near the prison's main entrance, shivering in the chill evening shadows. The massive oak gate groaned open, and a guard brought a man out. The prisoner, shuffling in ankle shackles, bore a wooden post on his shoulder. Silas sprinted up and looked into his face.

Not Geoffrey.

"Outa the way," the guard said.

The gate swung shut. Silas knocked on the peep hatch. No answer. He kept knocking. His knuckles aching, he changed hands. The portal opened.

"My boy may have been brung here by mistake," Silas said. "I want to see the warden."

"So does his mother." The hatch slammed.

Silas knocked again, but to no avail.

"You may as well rap on the gates of Doom." A man stood behind Silas, gripping the neck of a chicken.

Silas ignored the man, hammered the hatch with both fists.

The chicken merchant cackled. "Them that goes in there don't never come out. Exceptin' like that." He jerked his head in the direction of the condemned man. "Or this." He dangled the dead chicken in Silas's face.

Silas struck the bird to the ground. "You think I care?" He shook the man by his grimy smock. "That boy's been nothing but trouble." Silas thrust him away, and the man skittered off, leaving his poultry on the ground. Silas kicked the dead bird into brief flights after him.

Something in Tiberias's mouth caught his eye. In the waning light, it looked like a rag. Silas dropped to his knees in front of the dog.

Geoffrey's cap.

Silas changed his sob into a cough when he felt a spear point in his back.

"On your feet, old man, move along." The sentry prodded Silas with his spear.

Tiberias growled.

"And take your mutt with you."

"I need to see the warden," Silas said.

"Move on or you will." The sentry was about Silas's age.

"I need to find out if my boy was brung here by mistake."

"Nobody's brung here by mistake."

"Maybe he was released."

"Nobody's released." The sentry seemed tired. "Except to the abyss."

"Has anyone died here in the last three days?"

"Two by the rack, one by the thousand cuts, and one old crone of consumption." The sentry spat. "And a Rebel taken out and impaled."

"Bearded fellow, right?"

The sentry nodded.

"How old were they? The ones dead of the rack and cuts?"

"Here's some free advice, mister. You wanna find something out about a prisoner in Starknell, hire a solicitor. Assuming you got a lot of coin. Now pick up your chicken and get outta here."

"I'll lay odds he's been tortured." Panting, Redbeard threw the whip down. "That's why he don't holler."

Geoffrey hung by his wrists from the iron ring, barely conscious.

"Maybe he survived the brazen bull," Bear said.

"No one survives the brazen bull, you mutton head."

"Maybe they pulled him out before he was all the way roasted."

Still arguing, they cut Geoffrey down, locked irons around his ankles, and chained him to the wall.

As the key grated in the lock, Geoffrey's fingers found a bit of rock. When they were out of earshot, he would begin filing at the chain that bound him to the wall. But first, Geoffrey stretched out on his stomach, straining against the ankle irons to reach his shirt, wadded against the opposite wall. Inch by agonizing inch, he pulled it over his raw back and fastened it up to his chin.

Redbeard had said something about sending the other guards in to see the "crocodile man."

CHAPTER 24

"Well?" Nostromal said.

Dr. Lucius Qwenten's hand trembled as he decanted the yellow fluid. "The new serum, I fear, will disappoint."

"Why?"

"Only two of Disicorum's patients recovered," Qwenten said.

With his fist, Nostromal hammered a dusty scroll on the lab bench. "Do you forget what this cost me?"

"I have completed his second formula, as you requested."

"Get on with it, then."

"I dislike losing another monkey," Qwenten said.

"Who do you think pays for your monkeys?"

True, unfortunately. What physician-alchemist could do research without a patron? Not one of Qwenten's colleagues had such a beautifully equipped laboratory at their disposal—albeit in the cellar of Nostromal's castle.

"After this," Qwenten said, "I will devote all my efforts to the materials we recovered from the Gypteziam tomb."

"No. That tomb had already been plundered."

"I speak, Lord Nostromal, of the things the early grave robbers did not take: the tiny jars, the dried plants, the mortar and pestle with its residue of powdered mosses and molds—all the tools of the ancient medicinal arts. And all of which our expedition brought back by the crate full. I need yet a little more time."

"Time?" Nostromal thundered. "On your claim a few months ago that you were nearing success, I have initiated plans that will shortly lead to matrimony."

"Nearing success," after two decades, had meant another few years to Qwenten. But his patron was so relentless that Qwenten's progress reports were often designed to appease rather than enlighten.

Nostromal rolled up his sleeve. His inner forearm was crisscrossed with dozens of short linear scars. There were also some small round sores, which resembled minor burns.

Qwenten slid the lid from a crockery vessel. With tongs, he fished out a thumb-sized black leech and placed it, dripping, on Nostromal's forearm. The creature rapidly embedded its needle-like teeth and began pulsating.

"Three thousand years ago, a cure for Scourge came out of the land of Gypteziam," Qwenten said.

"You've been over this nonsense before."

"You've never listened."

"The Sun King of the Fourth Reign captured a tribe of nomads," Nostromal recited in a bored voice. "Then half his army was wiped out by Scourge, so he freed the nomads."

"But," Qwenten said, "not one of the *nomads* perished of Scourge. The Sun King believed it was divine intervention."

"He foolishly forfeited ten thousand potential slaves."

Qwenten placed two more leeches on Nostromal's arm.

"The point is—how could the Sun King allow the god of the nomads to remain stronger than himself?" He produced a cage containing three rats, each the size of a large squirrel. "He couldn't. So I believe he charged every sorcerer, alchemist, and physician in his empire with finding a cure for Scourge."

With his tongs, Qwenten picked the engorged leeches off Nostromal's forearm and dropped them into a ceramic bowl. He knew he was fortunate not to have contracted the disease himself over the years. His new leech method for drawing Nostromal's blood was much safer. And Nostromal favored it because the leech bites did not scar like the knife.

"So effective was the treatment they devised that Scourge was all but gone for the next nine hundred years," Qwenten said. "Great rulers can, on occasion, make use of great resources for the good of humanity."

That might get Nostromal's attention.

"When Scourge finally returned—as it always does—the formula had long since been forgotten. But do you not think that the Sun King, to be fully prepared for the afterlife, would be buried with his Scourge medicine?

"And those are precisely the materials our recent expedition recovered from his tomb."

"Then why are you not working with those materials?" Nostromal demanded.

"You ordered me to focus on the Disicorum manuscript."

Although Nostromal was apparently well regarded as a statesman, Qwenten never understood why the man should assume he was also an expert in medicinal research, whereas Qwenten had devoted his life to it.

Qwenten dumped the bowl of leeches into the rat cage. The rats fought and shrieked as they devoured the writhing blood morsels— Qwenten's innovative way of transferring the infection to the rats. He opened another cage, pulled out a small monkey, and dropped it in with the rats.

For a moment, nothing happened. The next instant the rats swarmed the monkey and bit it viciously, over and over. The terrified little animal slammed around inside the cage, screaming, unable to escape.

Qwenten turned away. But Nostromal lost interest only when the monkey, curled up on her side, had been reduced to pleading whimpers.

Purple spots appeared on the monkey's muzzle; her breathing slowed to a labored wheezing, and her neck swelled to a lumpy, grotesque shape.

Dr. Qwenten donned chain mail gloves that extended to his armpits, reached into the cage, and extracted the semi-comatose monkey. He placed the animal on its back, secured her with leather straps, and poured the vial of yellow serum into the creature's mouth.

Removing his gloves, Qwenten picked up a notebook and quill pen. He flipped an hourglass and gazed at the tumbling grains as they grew into a tiny pyramid.

The monkey's breathing became labored. Then, with a gurgling gasp, she died.

Nostromal muttered a curse.

As Qwenten made the entry in his notebook, the cellar door opened.

"Lord Nostromal," Axelrad said. "You requested to be informed upon the arrival of a certain person."

"I shall join you presently."

"Very good, sire." Axelrad left the laboratory.

Nostromal addressed Qwenten. "When can I expect the Gypteziam serum?"

"I confess I have been working nights on it."

"And?"

"I have narrowed the possibilities to thirty-seven different formulae. The most promising is a mixture of several mold strains, which grow very well in this damp cellar of yours. By growing these molds on ordinary bread—"

"If it works, how long will it take to rid me of this?" Nostromal interrupted.

"An early infection would likely be cured by one or two doses, but you, carrying the disease for decades—"

"Answer the question! How long to cure me?"

"Medical science has no experience with a human who carries Scourge, but cannot be killed by it," Qwenten said. "You may have to take many doses over many months."

The door slammed as Nostromal left the room.

Limuel—Qwenten's fifteen-year-old assistant—emerged from under a lab bench, where he sometimes hid during Nostromal's visits.

Qwenten did not watch as the young man picked up the rat cage and submerged it in the salamander pool. When Limuel pulled it out of the water, the rats were dead. He then dropped them into the firepit at the end of the room, along with the dead monkey.

"Use the bellows, Limuel," Qwenten said.

Dr. Qwenten had decided that, whether he found the cure for Scourge or not, he would leave Nostromal's employ in another three months and request Derina's hand in marriage—two things he should have done years ago.

CHAPTER 25

Nissa was drawing stick figures in the dust near the stoop when Hamewith showed up and told her that she was indeed going to visit the castle of Lord Nostromal, Chancellor of the House of Overlords.

"Your grandmother's invited too," Hamewith said.

Nissa, flushed with excitement, ran inside.

"What have you done?" Granny's stricken look pierced Nissa's heart.

The door burst open. A soldier herded them outside into a waiting tumbrel. Hamewith was gone.

That afternoon, in an ugly chamber his servants called the Rattlesnake Room, Nissa and Zeruba stood before Nostromal. Axelrad and two soldiers were stationed near the door.

Nissa wanted to cry out that it was all a mistake, she was an admirer, had always heard wonderful things about the Lord Nostromal and his great castle. But her words couldn't get past the choking sensation in her throat.

"My dear Zeruba." Nostromal's voice was somewhat high-pitched for such a big man. "You had information about someone we both had thought dead. Yet you failed to inform me."

Nissa wished she were wearing a shawl over her thin shirt. She hadn't expected the great man to seem creepy.

"I had thought to make further inquiries before troubling you, my lord." There was an unfamiliar quaver in her grandmother's voice. "I did not know who he was."

Nostromal gave a harsh laugh. "Which is why you said to him, 'I know who ye are . . .'"

Nissa stopped breathing. How could she have recited Granny's exact words to Hamewith?

"His name be Geoffrey, of the house of Davenant, heir to those lands and titles," Zeruba said.

"What of his companions—an old man and a girl?"

"I have no knowledge of these," Zeruba answered.

"Whom else have you told about this man's existence?" Nostromal waited for Zeruba's reply with the patience of a vulture whose prey cannot flee.

"No one, my lord."

"Have I not, upon personal recommendation, provided entrée for you to some dozen castles, Zeruba? And have not the Overlords and ladies therein paid handsomely for your services?"

"I am grateful, sire."

"I do enjoy your news of the intrigues among our aristocracy," Nostromal said. "And you once sent word of a treasonous whispering which proved useful to me. But why did you not tell me of this Geoffrey?"

"I am undone, your grace."

Nissa had never before heard the fierce old woman apologize. Her stomach trembled.

"And I know naught else—except to caution you, my lord."

"I can assure you, he is no threat to me," Nostromal boasted. "Where is his army? His horsemen, lancers, bowmen?"

Nostromal hunched over Zeruba like a wolf with a field mouse. "Tomorrow, Zeruba, you shall be released and escorted to Castle Loridine—Lady Tyrus always enjoys your readings. And I shall expect a full report—her husband has of late been heard to speak ill of me."

"Thank you, your grace."

"But I am left to wonder. What other information do you withhold from me? And how to be certain that you will henceforth tell me all?"

"I have told all, my lord. I swear so."

Nostromal addressed Axelrad. "Captain, see that this girl is returned to her grandmother in the morning. Alive."

"Please, sire, she has done nothing!" Zeruba cried.

Axelrad shoved Nissa into one of the soldiers. A hand clamped the back of her neck as a fusty mouth crushed her lips.

"I beg of you," Zeruba said. "She is innocent of men!"

Nissa screamed and tried to twist away as a boot kicked her ankles out from under her. Her back hit the ground; the air whooshed out of her lungs.

"How long, Captain Axelrad, does it take a young woman to die on the culla di Giuda?"

"About three days, Lord Nostromal. Less, if weights are tied to the feet."

"Should you fail me again, Zeruba, your eyes shall be stitched open for the entire spectacle," Nostromal said.

Each soldier grabbed a leg and dragged Nissa to the door. She shrieked in terror. Her shirt rolled up past her shoulder blades, the stone floor scraping skin off her back.

"Granny!" She tried to kick herself free, grabbed at the doorframe with her fingers as they yanked her into the hallway.

Zeruba hobbled out after them, pleading.

Axelrad slammed the door against Nissa's cries and returned to Nostromal.

"Summon Haviwade Bertraks, the present Baron Lord Castleford, at once," Nostromal said.

"As you wish." Axelrad bowed his head. "If I may, sire—what is to be done with the prisoner Geoffrey Davenant?"

"Execute him." Nostromal strode to the door.

"Very good, sire. They say he is too ugly to live."

"Ugly?" Nostromal turned back. "Tell me about this."

"Deformed, somehow," Axelrad said. "He was a freak in a traveling sideshow."

"I should like to see him."

CHAPTER 26

D r. Qwenten checked the row of flat dishes. "Limuel? When did number thirty-one turn?"

"You were up in the kitchen," Limuel said.

"You kept the temperature constant?"

"Yes, sir."

"And added nothing else?"

"No, sir."

A happy cradlesong—forgotten since his childhood—popped into Qwenten's head, and he hummed.

"Is everything all right, doctor?" Limuel said.

"Limuel, what happens when cultured Scourge blood is added to a plate of agar?"

"It changes color."

"And what happens when we add a test serum?"

"Nothing, usually." Limuel was not ambitious, but neither was he stupid. "Except this time it turned back to brown."

"Yes, it really did." Qwenten pulled his stool close and stared at the dish of brown gel, as though it might vanish if he took his eyes off it. "Read it to me."

Limuel read from the open notebook on the bench. "Serum thirty-one: equal parts tomb bread molds A and D. And the entire F series from small pots number 11 and 17."

"Run to the kitchen and bring the two largest baking pans they've got, and a dozen small trays. Hurry."

CHAPTER 27

Lord Bertraks had consumed nearly her whole tray of pastries, Mousy saw with alarm. Was he a glutton? Or just nervous? People were often uneasy in the presence of Lord Nostromal of Dunnesmore.

The man's bulk overspread the side chair in Nostromal's parlor. Had he always been this large? Padding himself for protection, perhaps. From what? It annoyed Mousy that she could not stop analyzing people, especially the foul ones who frequently came in and out of the master's presence.

"Surely, Lord Nostromal, you did not bring me to Dunnesmore to hector me again for your Amendment of Justice." Bertraks's mouth was full of pastry. "Although a sufficient quantity of these little delights might almost persuade." He forced a laugh and popped another tart into his mouth, crumbs dribbling through the stubble on his double chin.

Nostromal, at his windowsill of orchids, trimmed some blemished leaves then pressed dirt around a bulb in one of the larger pots.

Axelrad lounged on a silk settee across the room, picking his blocky teeth with his dagger.

"I have heretofore voted with you on every issue since I first sat in the House of Overlords." Bertraks sounded defensive. "But I hold with those who argued last session that your bill gives too much power to the Lord Chancellor."

"Were I not the current Lord Chancellor, you would no doubt vote for these added powers."

Bertraks started to agree, checked himself. He waved his empty wineglass at Mousy. She filled it, wishing she could close her nostrils like a river otter against the unwashed folds of flesh.

"Who do you think gave you your seat in the Assembly and the power you wield as Lord of the Castleford estate?" Nostromal stabbed a stake into one of the flowerpots. "And speaking of the late Lord Wellam Davenant, a young man named Geoffrey Davenant has been brought to my attention."

Bertraks choked in mid-swig and coughed until his eyes watered. "That boy could not have lived."

"How do you know?"

"No one survives the 'neck of fire.'"

"Maybe you forgot the pitch. Or the torch."

Mousy watched the man's face turn almost as purple as the birthmark on his forehead. The ensuing silence burgeoned like a boil that must be lanced. Could an otter close its ears too?

Bertraks banged his glass onto the side table. "I myself set him on fire."

Because I walk with a limp and am too shy to spit at a leafhopper, they think I'm also retarded, and confess murder in front of me.

Nostromal poured water onto one of his plants. "Did you not account for his body?"

"There was no need. No child could have survived the blizzard that night." Bertraks wiped his palms on his paunch. "This Geoffrey must be someone else—an imposter, trying to claim my title and estate."

Nostromal stared at Bertraks, and the silence built again to uncomfortable levels. The chamber door flung open. Lady Lorica stormed in, followed by Derina.

"My lady, please, I beg you, reconsider," Derina said.

"Leave me at once," Lorica hissed at her.

Derina took a few steps back but remained in the room.

"Lady Lorica, what is this?" Nostromal said.

Mousy numbered the goggle-eyed Bertraks among those who had heard of Lady Lorica but never seen her. The woman's beauty was now heightened by the color in her cheeks and the fire in her eyes. Nevertheless, Bertraks seemed relieved for a chance to edge out.

"Might I have a word, my lord?" Lorica said and then whirled on Derina. "Leave this chamber or leave my service."

Derina bowed herself out of the room. Bertraks was already gone, followed by Axelrad.

Mousy, limping, was the last one out.

"There is a reason for this rudeness?" Nostromal said.

"Is it rudeness that you arranged to see me today but did not come?" Lorica said. "That you ignore my messages? That you allow rumors to spread concerning your intentions toward me?"

"My dear—"

"Even my servants now mock me—the entire household was prepared for your arrival."

"Please accept my apology."

"And today I learn that you are still seeing that little strumpet, 'Lady' Sahana."

"Mean-spirited gossip," Nostromal said.

"Is it true?"

"Of course not."

"Liar." Lorica snatched up one of Nostromal's orchid pots and hurled it to the floor. "You care more for these than you do me." She raked the entire row off the ledge, crockery crashing in a tangle of shoots, petals, and mud.

Nostromal knelt to touch a bleeding stem, rubbed the sap between his fingers. He sprang at Lorica, grabbed her shoulders, and shook her.

"Ha!" Lorica said. "So you *are* a man and not a stone."

She launched her lips at his, but the pain as he crushed her mouth shocked her.

He's devouring me, teeth and tongue, like a ravenous wolf. Should not have waited so long, I tried to tell him . . . must breathe . . .

Lorica pulled away, sucked in a breath. "I love you, Nostromal." She found his mouth again with her bruised lips. But this time she kissed a face of stone.

"I love you," she tried again. She pulled back to look at him but was dizzy now and faint. She sagged against his chest, caught at his stiff arms to keep from dropping to the floor. "I don't feel . . . myself."

She stumbled to a couch, sat down, pressed her fists into her forehead. "I . . . I don't know what's wrong with me."

"You have contracted Scourge," Nostromal said.

"Do not jest, my love," Lorica said.

"In a very short time, you will be dead."

"Perhaps the luncheon did not agree." She looked at him. He was studying his fingernails. She forced a laugh. "You yourself would be dead, or dreadfully sick."

"I survived it as a young man, the only way I could."

"I don't understand."

"I appealed to the Author of sickness and death."

"You . . . you can't sell your soul," Lorica said. "Is that what you mean?"

He adjusted the cuticles on his thumbs.

"Nostromal, look at me."

What she saw in his eyes pierced her to the core.

"Somehow," Nostromal said, "he heard my plea."

Nostromal's face blurred and Lorica fell sideways, sprawling onto her back on the couch. She reached up for his hand. Not there.

"He keeps me alive but will not rid me of the disease."

"But why do this . . . to me . . ."

"You did it to yourself." Scorn in Nostromal's voice.

Lorica began to cry, her breaths tearing at the lining of her throat.

"But the cure is imminent—after which I shall no longer need him."

She felt hot patches on her cheeks, raised her hands, and saw purple splotches on her skin.

"Then I shall be whole again," Nostromal said.

Her fingertips found tender lumps on her neck.

"And I shall have a son . . . such as you could have borne me."

I was to be a brood mare?

Lorica's eyes, painful to move, followed Nostromal as he turned his back and walked to the door. She tried to scream; steel claws ripped at the flesh inside her throat, but no sound came out. The room spun. She closed her eyes against a surge of nausea.

"Get the doctor," she heard Nostromal say. "Your lady has taken ill."

"What's wrong with her?" Derina's voice. "I want to see her."

"I said get the doctor."

The door closed. Lorica was alone. Why did it take forever to suck air into her lungs and even longer to force it back out? If she could just get her fingernails under the lumps crowding her windpipe, maybe she could breathe . . .

Footsteps.

"Nostromal?"

She heard a whisper, sensed a face above hers. "I'm here."

"I would have . . . always . . . loved you." Lorica strangled each word out in a rasping whisper. "Only you."

She raised her head off the pillow and opened her eyes onto an ugly face. Bertraks.

Derina ran into the parlor, Dr. Qwenten right behind her. Lady Lorica lay face-up on the couch, eyes and mouth open in a frozen scream.

Derina shrieked.

A bubble of mucus bloomed from one of Lorica's nostrils. Her throat was scratched bloody, her new dress torn at the neck.

Derina dropped to her knees and stroked her lady's face, crying.

Qwenten pulled Derina away. "You mustn't touch her."

"Let go!" Derina fought him. Finally subsiding, she wept on Qwenten's shoulder.

Qwenten was still holding the sobbing Derina when Nostromal entered, grabbed a coverlet from a couch, and threw it over Lorica. "No one is to see her. She would not wish it."

"You." Qwenten clenched his teeth.

"Food poisoning," Nostromal said. "From her luncheon at Darrowick."

"Not food poisoning." Qwenten forced quiet into his voice.

"Dr. Qwenten, you are to cremate Lady Lorica's body against this illness being infectious, as per the usual custom," Nostromal said. "I shall convey the sad news to her mother." There was a crack in his voice.

The first time Qwenten had seen tears in Nostromal's eyes was when the man begged him to work full-time for a Scourge cure: "I am no longer a man, doctor, but a leper." Back then, Qwenten was still naïve of Nostromal's ability to imitate human emotion as a means of manipulation. Nostromal, he knew, would allow a few members of the household staff, and select outside acquaintances, to see his "grief"—thus preserving a certain benevolent image.

Nostromal wiped his eyes and moved to the doorway, where Axelrad waited.

"Captain, please see that the doctor carries out my instructions regarding the late Lady Lorica."

Axelrad nodded. "Lord Bertraks awaits you in the solarium. I took the liberty of ordering that his glass be kept full with your finest."

Nostromal slid out.

Qwenten felt Axelrad's stare and glanced up as the man widened his stance and folded his arms across his chest.

"Yes, Lord Nostril, I'll vote for your Amendment of Justice," Bertraks slurred.

Mousy saw courage flowing into Bertraks with each swallow. He belched and stuck his glass out for a refill.

"That's what you do, girlie, tell 'em what they want to hear."

Mousy nearly dropped the wine bottle when she saw, over Bertraks's shoulder, the towering form of her master silhouetted in the solarium doorway.

"But when his stinking bill comes up, old Bertraks will just vote against it."

She forced her eyes away from Nostromal and tried to focus on the bottle in her hand.

"Here's something else, girlie: 'I would have always loved you,'" Bertraks said in a mocking falsetto. "'And only you.'" He laughed. "Lorica promising to be faithful? That is rich, girlie, let me tell you. Ask any of the blokes down at Blunco's Tavern if they don't think that's rich." He laughed again, drained his glass.

Mousy's hand shook so violently that she brought the other hand up to steady it as she poured. Earlier she had heard a murder confessed. Was she now going to witness one?

"Relax, monkey-face," Bertraks said. "You got the good stuff by mistake, but never you mind. The old weasel won't miss it."

To Mousy's relief, Nostromal withdrew, Bertraks remaining none the wiser.

CHAPTER 28

Nostromal stepped into Qwenten's laboratory. "My steward informed me that you wish to leave my employ."

Instead of standing as he normally did upon Nostromal's arrival, Qwenten remained on his stool and continued to write.

"Have I not provided everything that was necessary, all these years, for your research?" Nostromal demanded.

Qwenten nodded. *Especially the blood samples.* One cannot test new medicaments without a regular source of the disease element. Not to mention last year's astounding excursion to the tombs of Gypteziam.

"And have I not shielded you from the struggle to live as your impoverished colleagues do, delivering the babies of peasants who cannot pay and draining the boils of nobles who will not?"

"I have copied out the main information for you, including the preliminary results of the Gypteziam experiments." Qwenten indicated the paper on his writing desk. "I should like permission to take my notebooks with me." He tied a strap around a half-dozen shabby folios and put them in his satchel.

"You break our agreement, and I will see you brought before the magistrate and imprisoned."

"I myself may have something to say to the magistrate."

"And what might that be?"

Qwenten felt his insides tremble. "Regarding the death of the Lady Lorica." A long shot against an Overlord, let alone the Lord Chancellor himself.

Nostromal sighed, like a parent addressing a trying child. "Doctor, I have given you twenty years to find the cure and invested many pounds of silver. But you have failed me. That woman's demise is a matter for your conscience, not mine."

Qwenten mouthed silent epithets as he donned his cloak, picked up his satchel and a canvas bag, and started toward the door.

"If you leave before completing our project, your friend Derina will be arrested," Nostromal said.

"On what charge?"

"Murder."

Qwenten's viscera went cold. He stopped, turned.

"Rumor has it that Derina poisoned her own mistress," Nostromal said.

Qwenten spoke through clenched teeth. "Lady Lorica died of Scourge."

"Lord Darrowick, Lorica's father, also died under peculiar circumstances."

"Lord Darrowick died of bleeding ulcers," Qwenten said. "I myself attended him."

"I have two physicians in my occasional employ who, if Lord Darrowick's body is exhumed, will testify that he was poisoned," Nostromal said. "With the death of Lady Lorica under similar circumstances, suspicion will naturally fall upon your Derina. She was present, as any number of people can attest, at both deaths."

Qwenten dropped his belongings, felt his neck flush red. He threw off his cloak, ready to attack the man and strangle the life out of him. He brought his hands up. White and small—even the veins were just tiny blue squiggles—and hated himself. He loathed especially the weakness that had led him into an agreement with this creature in the first place.

"You will continue to give our work here your best effort," Nostromal said.

Qwenten sank onto his stool.

"You will also stand when I enter and address me properly."

But Qwenten remained seated. He dug his fists into his eyes and did not see Nostromal pull his dagger, cut his own forearm, smear the blade in blood.

"Doctor."

When Qwenten looked up, Nostromal feinted at him with the bloody dagger. Qwenten jerked back, fell off his stool.

"Who knows, you yourself might need the cure someday," Nostromal said. "Or perhaps Derina will contract Scourge."

He thrust his bleeding forearm in Qwenten's face.

"Clean this up."

CHAPTER 29

Silas found a solicitor in a row of dumpy buildings near the Palace Presidio in Caerdon and learned the cost of gleaning information about Geoffrey.

Now, as he hurried down the main street, Tiberias beside him, a lute came sailing out of a tavern and boinged onto the street, followed by a tumbling young man who almost managed to regain his balance and avoid the mud.

Silas helped the teenager to his feet.

"Hey-yo, Mr. Silas!" Singer Sandley said. "Thank you, sir."

Sandy's knee was bleeding. Silas felt Sandy's arms—no broken bones. He picked up the ruined lute.

"I'd rather have busted my arm." Sandy caressed the broken instrument. "Guess they don't want an acrobat-musician again tonight." He sighed. "Least not one they have to pay much."

"Yeah? We'll see about that." Silas started to march into the tavern.

"Mr. Silas, wait." Sandy opened his fist and displayed a coin. "It'll do. But thanks, sir." He laughed, delighted to have a friend willing to stick up for him. "Anyway, the crowd loved me last night."

Silas resumed his journey, Sandy beside him.

"Where's Damaris? And Geoffrey?"

"They're not here."

"If you don't mind me asking—"

"Damaris is with friends."

"What about Geoffrey?"

"Geoffrey's in some trouble."

"Anything I can do?"

A visit from Sandy might cheer Damaris up. *But to divulge where they were staying, even to Sandy . . .*

They arrived at the livery stable where Silas had boarded Jenquilla and the wagon. Silas found the owner repairing a fence in the corral. "How much will you give me for my horse and wagon?"

The man named a price. "Less what you owe me."

"The wagon is solid poplar, built strong," Silas said. "And there ain't a worthier horse than Jenquilla. Powerful but gentle."

"Wagon's old. So's the horse."

Silas didn't have time to locate a more generous buyer. *What if they brought Geoffrey out of Starknell while he was gone?*

He entered the wagon one last time. With Sandy's help, Silas sacked up dishes, utensils, pans and teakettle, tobacco and coffee. He said goodbye to Jenquilla, in the corral, with the last of the sugar.

Within six blocks and an hour—peddling door to door—Silas and Sandy had disposed of the household goods. At a market stall, they bought bread and apples and ate standing at an overturned barrel.

"Is there anything else I can do, Mr. Silas?"

"You can take these off my hands." Silas brought the marionettes out of his rucksack.

"The dragon breathes real fire." He showed Sandy the oil tube in the dragon's mouth.

Sandy examined dragon, knight, and princess, admiring the craftsmanship. "You could get a lot of money for these." He set them on the barrel top. "But I've got only the four silver bob to my name, and I'm going to need that to get my lute fixed."

"They're yours, son," Silas said. "And if you try to pay me or thank me, I'll destroy 'em."

"I gotta give you *something*." Sandy produced a small clasp knife, several marbles, and a bright yellow handkerchief.

Silas snapped a back leg off the dragon and threw it on the ground.

"Oh, no, please." Sandy dropped to the ground and retrieved the leg. "Truly, Mr. Silas, I don't know how I can ever thank—"

Silas grasped the dragon's wings this time.

"No, wait. I mean . . . I'll give them a good home. Really good." Sandy affected a theatrical voice. "Once upon a time, there was a fierce, fire-breathing dragon. He was more mad than fierce because he had only five legs 'stead of six. And a boy who wanted to tame that dragon and marry a princess someday . . ."

"If you start now, Sandy, you can still make it in time for the last two days at the Shiresby carnival."

"That's where I was going before my neck got snapped." Sandy tapped the broken lute, hanging by its strings around his shoulders. "After I earn a little money, I'll go see Damaris, take her a present. If that's all right with you, sir."

"She'd like that." Silas extended his hand to Sandy and decided to chance it. "We're staying with Dr. Avery and his wife, in Cliffhaven."

"See you soon." Sandy skipped a few paces away then stopped. "Thank you for the marionettes." He laughed. "Thank you, thank you, thank you."

Silas shook his fist and laughed in spite of himself. Sandy saluted then whistled his way down the crowded street, soon disappearing among people and animals, carts and wagons.

The money from the sale of their wagon and Jenquilla Silas delivered to his solicitor, who promised to send a message to him as soon as he knew something.

Silas kept his vigil outside Starknell the rest of that day and all night. At noon the next day—with no word from the solicitor—he wrote a note on a strip of cloth and tied it around Tiberias's neck. "Take this back to Damaris so she doesn't worry. Go on, now, git."

Tiberias arrived but the note did not, snagged on the first bramble the dog had marked after Silas started him on the road to Cliffhaven.

CHAPTER 30

Mrs. Jolecia Avery tried to comfort Damaris, telling her that when Dr. Avery—two villages away—returned, they would decide together what to do. Mrs. Avery also reasoned that Silas might need more time.

"But don't you see?" Damaris said. "Tiberias would not have returned alone unless something had also happened to Papa."

Sometime after midnight, the older woman—exhausted by Damaris's distress—fell asleep. Damaris donned some old clothes, coiled her hair under a cap, and left the cottage with Tiberias as her guide and one of Dr. Avery's walking sticks for protection.

As she walked beside Tiberias, Damaris thought of the inquiries her peasant-boy persona might foster—she didn't want to arouse suspicion. Geoffrey and Silas, if alive, could be in prison. If Tiberias did lead her to the prison, she would approach the place as a relative bringing food to loved ones.

The basket of food she carried—which included meat—was her downfall. She heard the howls of the wild dog pack just after Tiberias caught their scent. She ran, but the lead dog was upon her in seconds, fangs ripping into her calf.

She swung her stick, went down. Tiberias bit her attacker on the muzzle. Damaris wrenched her leg free, rolled, and scrambled up a sapling. She heard the rest of the dogs—a dozen or more—hit Tiberias as one.

Then the dogs were below her, leaping at her feet as she stood on a branch, the spindly tree swaying. The branch shuddered as a dog hit it near her foot. She stretched up for a higher branch and nearly lost her balance. She felt dizzy, fought it, and vaguely wondered how much of her blood was going to drip into the mouths of the beasts.

CHAPTER 31

"L ast name?"

"Smitt," Silas said. "Like I told you yesterday."

"Uh-huh . . ."

The knot in Silas's stomach became a ball of lead. Did Mr. Basenbowd, his solicitor, know his true surname? He edged toward the door of the airless office. Probably a soldier waiting on the other side.

Mr. Basenbowd crossed to the door, jerked it open. "Shall we get some air, Mr., ah, Smitt?"

Silas struggled against the urge to run and instead followed Mr. Basenbowd out to the wharf along the river, a stone's throw from his shabby office. They came to an older section of the abandoned dock.

Silas squatted, picked up a gull feather, and surveyed the area. Soldiers could be hiding in the abandoned building behind them, but it was far enough away that he would have a head start. Unless they were armed with crossbows.

"I wish I had the kind of news you were hoping for," the solicitor said.

From a season many years gone, the Scourge-ravaged face of Silas's little son—eyes closed in death—filled his vision.

"Your boy was arrested two days ago and taken to Starknell. That evening, he was given twenty strokes for trying to escape."

To displace the image of a whip striking Geoffrey's tender back, Silas focused his eyes on a flatboat drifting downriver near the far bank.

"Was Geoffrey charged with a crime?"

"That information is vague," Mr. Basenbowd said. "Geoffrey apparently entered the Library of Records without proper authorization and may have insulted the government clerk there. One of my sources averred that he pretended to be a nobleman, seeking to acquire property that was not his. None of my informants knew that he is the surviving heir of the late Wellam, Lord Davenant, of Castleford."

"A man should have the right to know the name of his accuser and the charges brought," Silas said, startled to hear himself speaking his thoughts out loud. Such verbal incaution was deadly for a former resistor with a price on his head.

Mr. Basenbowd looked at Silas. "A pity the Rebellion failed, eh?"

Silas studied the gull feather. *Does he think I will now incriminate myself?* He smoothed the vane down the shaft, then backwards. A rustle behind him, he swung around: only a pelican, landing on a post.

"As to the identity of his accuser," Mr. Basenbowd continued, "again, there is no definite information. It is possible that the usurper of the Davenant estate wanted to avoid any legal battles with long-lost heirs. A man named Haviwade Bertraks."

Silas returned his gaze to the flatboat on the wide muddy river.

"Geoffrey was to be executed, but the sentence got postponed. I could not determine the reason."

"Where is he now?" Silas asked.

"Yesterday morning he was removed from Starknell, presumably for the sentence to be carried out."

Silas's gut turned over. Yesterday morning he had sold the horse and wagon—and for a few hours was absent from his post outside the prison.

"Geoffrey's cell has been empty since that time, according to one of his guards."

"How do you know he was talking about Geoffrey?"

"He described Geoffrey's scars as you described them to me."

Silas crumpled the feather and let it sift through his fingers. "What did you mean, 'presumably'?"

"I can find no evidence of his execution yesterday, either by torture or the blade."

"So Geoffrey may be alive?"

"Most unlikely." Mr. Basenbowd sighed. "I think that whoever wanted him dead also wanted no notice taken. I'm sorry."

Silas felt like his insides had been scooped out. The flatboat disappeared into a mist.

"He was probably buried in the Pit," Mr. Basenbowd said.

Silas, numb, walked away.

Mr. Basenbowd caught up with him and placed a bag of coins in his hand. "It's all there, minus what it cost me to get into Starknell and back out."

Silas handed the money back.

"No," the solicitor said. "I am one of those who believe that former Rebels should be thanked, not executed."

The scent of alfalfa fields, the tap-tap of a woodpecker, the sunshine—simple things that usually made him appreciate each day he remained alive—were lost on Silas as he walked the road to the Pit.

The Pit, a giant smoldering sinkhole outside the city, stank of garbage and sulfurous gases. Silas peered through the smoke, picked up a stick, then climbed over the rim and inched his way down. His feet slipped, and he slid down the loose stones toward the abyss. He planted his stick and skidded to a stop just before going over the edge.

Silas poked around in the rubble on the ledge, found a femur bone—too small to be Geoffrey's—and a charred skull fragment. Coughing against the foul fumes, he finally crawled out of the Pit and flopped onto his back near the rim, gasping for air.

White clouds journeyed across the sky above him in unhurried tumbles. A red-tailed hawk screamed *kee-eeeee-arr* and floated up until it was a tiny speck against the blue. A breeze carried the scent of a coming summer shower.

By what means, Silas brooded, could these things continue languorously on, as though nothing had happened?

Silas was still lying there—as close to Geoffrey as he knew how to be—after midnight, when it began to rain.

CHAPTER 32

How many hours had passed when the rain began, Damaris could not tell. One by one the dogs slunk away. Shivering, she slid down the tree, crawled into the road, and found the remains of Tiberias. His hind legs were gone; his lower jaw dangled by a bloody strand. She cradled the broken body and cried.

The rain ended and a bird began its pre-dawn chirp, answered by another. Voices, coming along the road. Damaris wobbled to her feet, thinking to drag Tiberias out of the way. Dizziness, then blackness, overtook her. She collapsed facedown on top of the dog's remains.

"Look." A boy of fourteen ran up, a halter rope in one hand. Another boy—a year older—joined the first and crouched beside Damaris.

"Better leave him alone," the younger boy said. "We don't want to be accused of no murder."

"Ain't dead," the older boy said. He turned Damaris over.

"He's purty."

"It's a she," the older boy said. "Don't you know nothing?"

"That's a lotta blood."

"It's from the dog, stupid."

"Come on," the younger boy said. "Pappy will thrash us if we don't find them goats directly."

"I wasn't the one let 'em out," the older boy said. He grabbed Damaris under the arms and started to drag her off the road.

"Trampas, what you gonna do?"

"You really don't know nothing, do you?"

The younger boy considered this. "Hey, I found her first."

"Run along, baby brother."

Baby Brother's first punch caught Trampas on the side of the head.

———————————————

A gray light was forming in the eastern sky as Silas neared Cliffhaven. He heard a commotion on the road ahead. Two boys grappled in the mud, punching each other. On the road lay a body, face upwards, and a mangled dog. Silas's heart unraveled. *Damaris.* He ran and knelt beside her.

The boys stood up. "Hey, old man," one said. "Get away from her. She's ours."

Damaris was still breathing.

"But we might sell you a turn."

The warrior's cry erupted from Silas as he charged the larger boy. But the other boy tripped him. He went down hard, struggled to get up through a hail of kicks and punches.

"Damaris," he shouted. "Damaris!"

Damaris roused, grabbed up a makeshift weapon, and hammered the bigger boy's head. Silas sprang free, slammed the boy's neck with a whiplash punch, kicked the other one in the throat. He slashed the air with his knife. "Who's gelded first?"

The boys grumbled to their feet and loped off.

Damaris still gripped her weapon: the jawbone of a dog . . . the jawbone of Tiberias. "Oh, Papa."

She cried all the way home.

CHAPTER 33

Geoffrey, in leg irons and a blindfold, was marched up a half-dozen stone steps. Door hinges creaked, and he was propelled across a threshold.

The smell of floor polish and tallow candles brought to mind Geoffrey's home as a child. His chains clinked as he shuffled down a corridor into a room. A door *thunked* shut behind him, and someone removed the blindfold.

He stood blinking in a large chamber, a soldier on either side of him. The stone-mantel fireplace, the wrought-iron chandelier ablaze with candles, the smell of leather furniture: except for the immensity of the room, he might have been standing in his father's study when he was a boy.

A man sat at the massive desk, flanked by a uniformed officer, who said, "The prisoner you requested, Lord Nostromal."

Lord Nostromal rose, strode toward him. He was taller than Geoffrey. "You will state your name."

Geoffrey's mouth was dry, but he managed to corral some moisture and spat it at Nostromal, who dodged; the mucus glob hit the uniformed officer. Geoffrey was shoved to his knees. A sword blade measured the back of his neck.

"Not yet, Captain Axelrad."

The guards yanked Geoffrey to his feet, the flayed skin on his back screaming.

"Geoffrey Davenant, son of the late Wellam Lord Davenant, of Castleford," Nostromal said. "That is who you are, is it not?"

Geoffrey pulled himself up to his full height but did not reply.

Nostromal drew his sword, placed the point at Geoffrey's midsection. Geoffrey's pulse hammered behind his eyes. Better to die like this than rot in a prison cell.

With the tip of his sword, Nostromal lifted Geoffrey's filthy shirt and exposed the thick scar tissue. "You were an innocent child when you were marked like that." He let the shirt drop and sheathed his sword. "I would like to see that justice is done for you."

"Strange justice," Geoffrey said. "To be arrested, imprisoned, flogged."

"You were arrested on false intelligence that you were an imposter. As to the flogging, I had nothing to do with that." Nostromal nodded to Axelrad, who left the room. "During your time at the Library of Records, did you happen to learn the name of the present owner of the Castleford estate?"

Geoffrey, following Nostromal's eyes, turned around. Captain Axelrad had re-entered the chamber with two soldiers and a corpulent middle-aged man.

Geoffrey had imagined this moment so many times that the instant he saw the purple birthmark—now running into a balding scalp—he sprang, grabbed the fat neck, and slammed the man to the ground. But before he could strangle the animal who had murdered his parents and set him ablaze as a boy, the guards yanked him away.

Bertraks, coughing, got himself to a sitting position on the floor. "What is the meaning of this?"

"You two seem to have met," Nostromal said.

"I have never laid eyes on this foul creature in my life," Bertraks said, and heaved himself to his feet.

"Haviwade Bertraks, allow me to introduce to you the rightful heir, lost these many years, of those lands and titles which you now hold. This is Geoffrey Davenant, son of Wellam Lord Davenant, Baron Castleford."

"That's impossible."

"This man is to be released and restored," Nostromal said.

"Lord Nostromal," Bertraks said. "I most strenuously object."

"On what grounds?"

"He's an imposter. Anyone can see that."

"Let the man show his scars." Nostromal nodded to the soldiers who still held Geoffrey's arms. They released their grip.

Geoffrey hesitated then pulled the top of his shirt down to reveal the ropy webs of scar tissue that connected his jaw to his collarbone.

"If he is the Davenant heir, he is a member of a treasonous family," Bertraks said. "Furthermore, he is alive only because he escaped their house the night they were executed."

"Executed, Bertraks?" Nostromal said. "In a home?"

Bertraks shifted his weight from one foot to the other.

"That would be murder, of course," Nostromal said. "And how could you know that, unless you were there?"

"But—"

"Where were you the night your parents died?" Nostromal asked Geoffrey.

Geoffrey's tongue stuck to the roof of his mouth. He had never before spoken of that night, not to Silas, not even to Damaris.

"With them," he finally said. "At home."

"And what happened to you?"

Geoffrey's throat felt like it had closed up.

"Go on," Nostromal said, his voice gentle, encouraging.

"I was . . . burned."

"Set ablaze, to be more precise?"

Geoffrey nodded.

"By whom?"

"This is the man." Geoffrey pointed to Bertraks.

Nostromal motioned to Axelrad, who gave an order. The soldiers flanking Bertraks trussed his hands behind his back.

"Haviwade Bertraks, you shall be taken to the Tower at Starknell, from thence to stand trial for the crime of murder."

"This is outrageous!"

"Did you not brag to me yesterday—Captain Axelrad was witness—that you set this man ablaze? You murdered his parents, the Lord and Lady Davenant, because you wanted their estate."

"He's an imposter, I tell you!"

"It is you who are the imposter," Nostromal said.

Bertraks yelled obscenities as the soldiers dragged him out, followed by Axelrad, who had drawn his sword.

"Release this man," Nostromal said to Geoffrey's guards. The guards unlocked Geoffrey's leg irons.

Nostromal assumed a formal tone. "As Chancellor of the House of Overlords, in accordance with our laws and by virtue of your hereditary rights, I hereby declare that you, Geoffrey—"

Bertraks's voice could be heard from the corridor—helpless yelps of pain and fear.

"That you, Geoffrey Davenant, son of Wellam Lord Davenant, Baron Castleford, are, on this day, to assume all lands and titles heretofore held by the usurper Bertraks, as well as the seat in the House of Overlords, appertaining thereto."

Geoffrey's fists opened slowly.

"I shall have the Clerk of the House draw up the proper papers," Nostromal said. "The House of Overlords itself, when it meets next week, will officially ratify your restoration. But that is a mere formality, I assure you, Geoffrey, Lord Davenant, Baron Castleford."

Axelrad re-entered the chamber, one of his boots spotting the floor crimson. "The prisoner Bertraks tried to escape."

"And?"

"He did not survive."

"Lord Geoffrey, you shall dine with me tonight."

Geoffrey did not reply. *Bertraks . . . dead?* Axelrad's voice intruded. "His lordship is addressing you."

"Captain Axelrad, see to it that Geoffrey, Lord Davenant, is properly attired and present here this evening, in my dining room."

"No," Geoffrey said.

Nostromal frowned.

"I mean, not wishing to sound ungrateful, but there is something I must attend to."

"Of course," Nostromal said. "You no doubt have relatives to inform of your circumstances."

Geoffrey hoped it was not disrespectful to ignore the Chancellor's remark. He became aware of his matted hair, dirty face, and the prison smell that clung to his ruined clothing. He started for the door.

"I shall provide an escort for you," Nostromal said.

"That is not necessary, sir, uh, I mean, your grace."

"Let me at least see that you have a clean tunic for your journey."

"I am very grateful." Geoffrey wondered if he should bow or say something on his way out.

After the door closed behind Geoffrey, Nostromal addressed Axelrad. "What do we know of his companions?"

"An old man and a girl," Axelrad said. "Traveling sideshow trash, according to Hamewith."

"Let me know when they are located." Nostromal returned to his desk. "But don't arrest them yet."

"Your grace, might I inquire . . ."

"What?"

"It is good, of course, that Bertraks will no longer be voting against your bill," Axelrad said. "But are you not taking a risk, installing this Geoffrey in his stead?"

"As a small boy, he witnessed the murder of his parents," Nostromal said. "Such a wound never heals. You have also seen the scars on his body."

Axelrad nodded.

"Ugliness further confuses the soul. Such a one can often be maneuvered to useful purposes."

"But to give him a seat in the House of Overlords?"

"That seat is the vote I need to pass the Amendment of Justice. Without it, my plans are defeated."

"You also gave him the Castleford estate, my lord," Axelrad said.

"We'll see how long he keeps it," Nostromal said.

"One more thing, if I may, as it relates to your plans," Axelrad said. "What of the loss of access to the fortune of the Lady Lorica?"

"That woman was not a lady."

CHAPTER 34

By the time he realized he was being followed, Geoffrey had exited the main road from Caerdon and was within a few miles of the abandoned stone quarry where he had left Silas and Damaris.

He sprinted ahead a hundred yards and scooted up a tree. Soon a wiry young man, wearing the garb of a commoner but moving with the gait of a hunter, passed beneath him. Geoffrey waited. When the man doubled back, Geoffrey leaped on him, wrested his knife away, and put it to his throat.

"Who sent you?"

"Captain Axelrad."

"What's your name?"

"Hamewith."

Geoffrey marched the man about forty yards off the road to a denser part of the woods.

"Remove your tunic."

He used Hamewith's leather belt to bind his hands behind a tree. With the spy's knife, he cut off a tunic sleeve and bound the man's neck to the tree. The other sleeve he draped around his own neck. For the first time since losing his scarf at the prison, he felt fully dressed.

"Are you going to kill me?"

"If you shout for help before dawn tomorrow, yes."

When Geoffrey reached their campsite on the banks of the stone quarry, he found nothing but Jenquilla's hoofprints and the remains of their cooking fire.

The next carnival of the summer was at Shiresby. *Why did I think they would wait for me?* Here was the familiar ache in his chest that often struck him when day's light turned to night.

He sat at the water's edge. He was a child again, Silas making him walk—but he couldn't keep up, and the wagon soon disappeared from sight.

Geoffrey removed the borrowed tunic and eased his body into the quarry. After the initial shock of cold water on raw flesh, the pain of his damaged back subsided somewhat.

When Geoffrey arrived back at Nostromal's castle that evening, Rigdin—the butler who had provided him the clean tunic—received him. "I was wondering if I might borrow a horse."

"I shall inquire," Rigdin said.

"No need to bother anyone," Geoffrey said. "I'll bring it back in a day or two."

"I shall inquire, Lord Geoffrey."

"Is that necessary? When I was a boy, our butler could arrange such things by himself."

"I am not at liberty to acquiesce to such a request." Rigdin fumed off, returned, and ushered Geoffrey into a large room with glass walls on three sides.

Nostromal stood at a table transplanting tiny green shoots from large wooden trays.

"Lord Geoffrey." Nostromal wiped his hands. "How pleasant to see you again."

The fragrance of roses.

"What brings you back to Dunnesmore so soon?"

Potted roses lined the glass walls and sat on tables. *Mama had a rose garden.*

"How may I be of service?"

Her arms were always brown in the summer.

Rigdin, behind him, cleared his throat.

Geoffrey squeezed his eyes shut. His boyhood hands were pinning a rose in his mother's dark tresses, the flower's scent blending with hers.

He felt a sharp pain on his shoulder. "Lord Geoffrey." The butler tapped him again. Geoffrey opened his eyes. He should probably start out saying something nice, but . . . "Why did you have me followed?" he blurted.

"My dear fellow," Nostromal said. "A gentleman would never interpose in another gentleman's affairs unless he hoped to render a service. I perceived that you were not well—perhaps related to your unfortunate stay at Starknell—and I wanted to have a man standing near should you be in need."

"I am fine," Geoffrey said, although the agony of his back was worsening by the minute.

The last time he had felt this dizzy he ended up facedown in the dirt.

"Even now you appear, shall we say, less than sound."

"I'll be all right." Geoffrey leaned against a table of potted rosebushes.

"I do owe you an apology on another matter," Nostromal said. "Earlier today I had no choice but to expose, as it were, your injuries, to make the case for your restoration. I trust you understand."

Geoffrey nodded.

"It is never pleasant to be vulnerable to judgment or ridicule. I myself once had an illness that, for a time, made me something of an outcast."

Geoffrey leaned over to smell a variegated white blossom. Sweet, not unlike clover.

"That particular specimen is my own creation: a graft of Rosa alba and Rosa gallica. I would be happy to give you a start for your gardens at Castleford."

Castleford. He was now the owner of his parents' estate. But he needed to find Damaris and Silas.

"Sir, I wonder if I might borrow a horse."

"You have not yet located your companions?"

"No."

"My stable is at your disposal, Lord Geoffrey, of course," Nostromal said. "May I inquire as to the reason for your urgency?"

"They have little food and less money."

"Night is upon us, young man. "Would it not be better to wait until tomorrow?"

"I should like to leave at once."

"If you begin your journey with the light of morning, you could reach Shiresby by tomorrow noon."

"I should like to get there sooner," Geoffrey said.

Nostromal whispered something to Rigdin, who departed the room. Much later, Geoffrey would realize that—naïve of Nostromal's cunning—he had unwittingly confirmed Shiresby as his destination.

"Should you wish, I could send you with a coach and driver, to bring them back in comfort and style."

"Just a horse is fine, if you please."

"Lord Geoffrey, you must take refreshment before you depart," Nostromal said. "I insist."

A protest faltered on Geoffrey's lips. But he was sandstorm thirsty . . . maybe some water, at least, would make the dizziness go away.

CHAPTER 35

"From peasant to prisoner to peer," Nostromal said. "You have had an eventful few days." He raised his glass. "To Geoffrey, Lord Davenant, Baron Castleford."

Geoffrey drained his wineglass. By the bottom of his second glass, the grip of pain was loosening. He settled into the cushioned chair, careful not to lean back. The servant girl poured him another. He watched the rosy liquid splash up from the bottom of the crystal and swirl to the top.

At the other end of the massive dining table, Nostromal smiled. "Best of all, a longstanding wrong has, on this day, been made right."

"My gratitude, sir," Geoffrey said. "For the reversal in my circumstances."

Geoffrey hadn't been able to eat the weevil-ridden prison biscuits. He now attacked every plate of food the servers set before him, not considering whether there might be special table manners for dining with the Lord Chancellor of the Realm.

"Tell me," Nostromal said, "what will you do now? That is, after you are reunited with your companions."

"We shall go to Markarian."

"Markarian? Whatever for?"

"I should like to earn my living there."

"Young man," Nostromal said, "you have just acquired, in a single day, more wealth than you could earn in a lifetime of work, anywhere in the known world. Do you not realize that you are the owner of Castleford?"

His father and mother were the owners of Castleford. They were murdered.

"Castleford, as kept by your family, was a magnificent estate. With the removal of Bertraks—and under your stewardship—it will be so again, I have no doubt."

"I'd like to sell it as soon as possible," Geoffrey said. "Use the money to book passage to the New Land. Maybe buy a small farm when we get there."

"You want to be a . . . *farmer*." Uttered like it was a coarse word.

Geoffrey nodded. He'd best say no more if the idea of being a farmer so disgusted the man.

He still needed to borrow a horse.

"Do you have any idea how many acres of tillable land are part of the Castleford estate?" Nostromal said. "And why Markarian? I have never understood why anyone would wish to leave the civilized world for such a foul place."

"Freedom," Geoffrey said.

"You seem an intelligent young man, Geoffrey. How long do you think it will be before a man with an army—either from across the sea or from within Markarian—puts that rogue people into the chains they belong?"

The server brought in a yellow cake smothered with fruit sauce. Geoffrey found it delicious, as everything else had been, but sudden stomach cramps made him unable to eat another bite.

"There is something else you need to consider," Nostromal said. "Do you not realize that as a member of the House of Overlords, you have the opportunity to make a difference?"

"I don't think it's for me," Geoffrey said.

"Nonsense. It is to this you were born."

Geoffrey shook his head.

"The House of Overlords convenes next week for its biannual session," Nostromal said. "Can I count on you to be there, Lord Geoffrey? I shall need the support of all my friends in that chamber."

Surprised that Lord Nostromal should call him a friend, Geoffrey tried to choose his next words carefully. "I'm not interested in being part of a body that devises a vague system of rules, taxes, and laws and then empowers petty and cruel men to enforce it."

"You are a most original thinker, my young friend," Nostromal said. "I like that."

Geoffrey—unused to compliments of any kind—was flattered but not convinced. "One wonders how many other murderers—like Bertraks—sit in that chamber."

Nostromal chuckled. "You would bring a unique perspective. We need your wisdom; the country needs it. I encourage you to think it over."

Geoffrey looked away from Nostromal to the dancing fires in his goblet and tried to comprehend how so many candles had squeezed themselves into such a small space. He dashed his hand across his eyes and restored the candles to the chandelier above him.

"Whether you decide to serve kin and country as a statesman or sell Castleford and leave Auldeland, please remember that I am at your service and shall help you all I can."

"There is one thing you can do." Geoffrey told Nostromal about the Writ of Owing, levied against them at Farharven.

"In the morning, Lord Geoffrey, I shall dispatch an order to the clerk at Smerton Hall in Caerdon to determine the amount. I shall then pay it myself, on behalf of you and your companions."

The room wobbled. Geoffrey tried to focus on a painting behind Nostromal, but the mahogany paneling moved over it and created a dark void where the colored canvas had been.

Then came the distant voice of Silas, proud that Cabbagehead "got us quit of the back taxes."

"You are very generous, sir," Geoffrey said. "I shall pay you back as soon as I sell the estate."

Nostromal's voice was now coming through a dense fog, asking Geoffrey for the names under which the tax writ would be filed, where his companions were last seen, their exact ages and physical descriptions. But first, wanting Silas's full name.

"Smitt," Geoffrey mumbled. "Silas Smitt."

"Not an alias or stage name, his *given* name."

The name "Marsden" was on Geoffrey's tongue when he heard a crash and felt liquid splash onto his lap. He stood, saw his water glass rolling toward the edge of the table, lunged to catch it, missed, heard the crystal splinter into shards on the floor. Or was it laughter he heard?

"Well." A female voice. "At last we have a guest who stands when a lady enters the room."

Geoffrey looked in the direction of the voice and saw a statuesque woman in a red velvet evening gown. A diamond pendant sparkled from the hollow of her throat. He glanced away, but she was still there when he looked back, her dark eyes drawing his.

"Lord Geoffrey, may I present my daughter, the Lady Sapphira," Nostromal said.

"You may close your mouth and be seated, young man," the woman said. She laughed again, the high-pitched hooting a jarring contrast to her deep voice.

Geoffrey obeyed. He was dizzy, and the room was hotter than a stone oven.

"Lord Geoffrey," Nostromal said, "you will reside with us until the family of the interloper Bertraks can be removed from Castleford."

Geoffrey felt his head nod and vaguely wondered about the people he was displacing from Castleford.

Nostromal rose from the table. "After dessert, my dear, would you be so good as to show our guest to his quarters?"

"Of course," Sapphira said.

Nostromal melted through the doorway as Sapphira glided over to Geoffrey and slid into a chair beside him. The servant girl materialized with a cake plate and glass of wine for Sapphira.

"Bring more water, Mousy," Sapphira said.

Geoffrey's throat burned; his mouth was full of fur. He tried to recall Dr. Avery's warning from many years ago about not getting too hot.

"You must relax, Geoffrey," Sapphira said. "I have seen you before, you know."

"I don't think so."

"'Handsome, yes . . .'" Sapphira mimicked Silas's stentorian tone. "'But he shall forever bear the painful reminder of his heroic folly.'"

Geoffrey's hand groped his makeshift scarf.

"Why should a few scars keep us from getting to know one another better?" Sapphira rose, took his hands, and pulled him to his feet. Her forefinger stroked the fabric at his neck. "Every survivor carries a mark of some sort. A testimony to his courage."

She took his face in her hands, pressed into him. He jerked away, and the room flipped upside down.

The last thing Geoffrey heard as he hit the floor was the high hooting laugh.

Mousy arrived in the dining room with water to replace what Geoffrey had spilled. Seeing Sapphira standing over Geoffrey's body on the floor, Mousy wondered for a moment if the lady might have killed him.

Sapphira grabbed the pitcher of water from Mousy and dumped it onto Geoffrey's upturned face. He didn't respond.

"Mousy," Sapphira said, "you and Dwenko get this cheap drunk to his room." She stepped over Geoffrey's body and sat down to eat her cake.

"He's burning up with fever, milady," Mousy said. "Should I get the doctor?"

"No. Get me something I can eat—not this chamber pot sludge." Sapphira flung the cake plate at Mousy, missing her head by an inch.

CHAPTER 36

Damaris opened her eyes the next morning and saw Silas sitting beside her bed. She tried to sit up but was too weak. "Where are we?"

"Dr. Avery's house."

Jolecia Avery appeared with a cup of tea. "I thought the girl would never wake up. This is my fault. I am so sorry. Can you ever forgive me? Here, drink this, dearie."

Damaris pushed the teacup away. "Where's Geoffrey?"

Silas could not reply.

"Papa?" She took Silas's hand and uncurled his fingers from Geoffrey's cap.

"He's not dead, Papa," she said. "I would know, here." She clutched the cap to her breast, closed her eyes, and was soon sleeping again.

Dr. Avery came in, examined Damaris's torn leg. "We are going to have to amputate."

Silas had seen soldiers with injured limbs during the war. The appendage first turned a dusky purple—like Damaris's foot—then, in the absence of a surgeon, blackened as the victim died of a wracking fever.

Dr. Avery washed Damaris's leg with hot water then laid out his tools: bone saw, clamps for the arteries, scalpel for the muscles, needle and thread to suture skin flaps over the exposed bone end.

"Pray that she remain unconscious." The doctor placed his blade on the skin just below Damaris's knee.

154

Silas looked at Damaris's pale face, a helpless ache in his chest. His eyes caught the motion blur of Dr. Avery's arm.

Damaris screamed, sat bolt upright.

"Hold her down, Silas."

Damaris shrieked, "What are you doing?"

"It's your leg," Silas said. "I'm sorry—"

"He's not going to cut my leg off!" Damaris's eyes looked terrified.

Silas put his hands on her shoulders, gently tried to push her back onto the bed.

"Papa, no!"

"It's going to be all right, Dee."

"Get your hands off me!"

"Jolecia," the doctor called. "Come in here, please."

"Papa, no, you have to protect me! Please! Don't let them do this to me."

Silas's heart came apart. He looked at Dr. Avery.

"She'll die," the doctor said.

"I won't die. I won't. Tell him, Papa."

Silas had a fleeting sense that Damaris was right. He clung to it. He looked at Dr. Avery and shook his head.

The doctor sighed, collected his instruments.

"Jolecia, we will bathe her leg every three hours in hot water and sphagnum salts. Silas, you will rub her leg at the same interval, to stimulate whatever circulation remains."

Damaris grabbed Silas's hand, interlaced her fingers with his. An hour later she was asleep, still gripping his hand.

And for only the second time since his wife and son had died of Scourge decades earlier, Silas prayed.

CHAPTER 37

"You must squeeze harder, Mousy," Dr. Qwenten said.

"I don't want to hurt him."

"You won't, he's still unconscious. But you have to get all the pus out of each pocket."

Mousy pressed her thumbs against a red lump on Geoffrey's back, forcing out thick yellow fluid. The foul odor coated her tongue. How did doctors ever get used to this?

"That's better," Qwenten said. "Now, the wet linen compress. Leave it on about twenty minutes. When you peel it off, some of the scabs and crusts should stick to the cloth. If not, let it dry a bit longer."

"Yes, sir."

"You remember how to do the dressing?"

"First," Mousy said, "I put some of the yarrow and wormwood mixture on the worst places, then a thin layer of chickweed and lard ointment over all, and wrap with the linen strips."

"But not too tight." The physician walked to the door. "I'll send someone to relieve you for the night."

"Oh, no, sir. That won't be necessary. If you please, sir."

The door closed behind him, and Mousy was again alone with Lord Geoffrey.

She had been sick to her stomach when she first saw the man's back: a mass of abscessed lacerations, scabs, and pus. But under the instruction of Dr. Qwenten, she quickly grasped the tasks he assigned her.

Mousy remembered the doctor's kindness to her as a little girl in this household, when he had made various braces for her misshapen leg. Although none of his contraptions ever worked—and some chafed sores on her leg—she had wanted to be a doctor herself ever since. Something in the touch of Dr. Qwenten's hands, as he worked on her leg, always made her feel less ashamed somehow.

After doing the wet-to-dry compresses and the dressing, she turned Geoffrey on his side. She smoothed the chestnut curls away from his forehead. His long eyelashes fluttered when she bathed his fevered face with cool water, but he did not wake up. She found herself wondering about the thick scars on his neck and torso.

I bet they made fun of him when he was little.

No doubt he had been a lonely child. She herself stopped playing with other children at the age of four after being laughed at when she tried to run. She pictured Geoffrey as a boy, desperately trying to stop his ears from the jeers of others. Such a man would understand someone like her . . . and she, him.

In all her lonely years, Mousy had never dared imagine herself in love . . .

CHAPTER 38

D
r. Lucius Qwenten, in his chain mail gloves, extracted a monkey from the rat cage. The animal was covered with bite marks and offered no resistance.

Nostromal rolled his sleeve down over his bandaged forearm and fastened it with a jeweled cuff pin. "Why is that sideshow man still not awake?"

"Lord Geoffrey's back is severely infected," Qwenten said. "If the fever breaks soon, he may pull through."

"How long after that until he can be up?"

"Scar tissue heals very slowly. Full recovery may take—"

"Just be sure he is ready to attend the House of Overlords session in three days."

Qwenten had his doubts about that. He strapped the monkey, neck swollen and wheezing, onto the lab bench. "Limuel, Gypteziam serum number thirty-one."

The boy removed the cork stopper from a vial and handed it to Qwenten, who forced the monkey's mouth open and poured in the liquid.

Limuel flipped the hourglass over.

After several long minutes, the monkey's breathing normalized and the neck swelling diminished. His tiny eyes came open. He blinked at one wrist strap then the other, as if asking why he should be tied down.

Qwenten unfastened the straps. The little animal rolled to a sitting position and fished a biscuit from a pocket of the doctor's smock. The monkey held the biscuit in both hands and gnawed it, like a tiny child eating an apple.

Qwenten placed the monkey in a clean cage, removed his gloves, and busied himself with his notebook. He silenced the celebratory grin on Limuel's face with a shake of his head. The master would not be sentimental about this success.

"How much of this serum have you made for me?" Nostromal demanded.

"None, so far."

"Why not?"

"The preparation of that vial took two days," Qwenten said. "And we need to observe the monkey for a period of time, to determine the permanence of the effect, or any unwanted effects."

"I'll be back day after tomorrow." Nostromal was already at the door.

"One vial will not cure you," Qwenten said. "As I have tried to explain."

"How fast can you make it?"

"If I set up a larger hot box to grow the mold and construct more distilling apparatus, I can make a vial and a half, perhaps two, per day."

Nostromal grunted his dissatisfaction.

"I must caution you," Qwenten said. "Take more than one dose each day and the toxins suddenly released may kill you."

"I doubt that." Nostromal left the cellar.

Qwenten hurried through the door after him. "I should like to visit Darrowick this afternoon."

He had tried to go to Derina the day after Lady Lorica's death, but Nostromal ordered him to treat Lord Geoffrey in addition to his work on the serum—and had alerted the castle guards to prevent the doctor departing.

Qwenten scurried to keep up with Nostromal. "Limuel knows what to do in my absence. I will be back by nightfall."

"If you leave these grounds for any reason, you shall find it necessary to seek your friend Derina in the torture pit at Starknell."

CHAPTER 39

"D r. Qwenten?"

The door to the cellar opened, and Mousy hobbled in.

"What is it, Mousy?"

"Geoffrey—I mean Baron Castleford—is awake."

"I shall be up shortly," the physician said. "In the meantime, he should not be left alone."

"He's not alone. The Lady Sapphira is with him."

"Why her?"

"She ordered me to summon her the instant Baron Castleford woke up."

"Please return to him at once, my dear." If there was anyone living in Castle Dunnesmore whom Qwenten loathed more than Nostromal, it was the man's twenty-six-year-old daughter. Sapphira's mother had died of Scourge when Sapphira was a child. That same epidemic had infected Nostromal and—among thousands of others—killed Silas's wife and little boy.

Mousy made her way back upstairs as fast as her limp would allow and slipped into Geoffrey's room.

Sapphira was sitting in the bedside chair, her back to Mousy. "I have been so worried about you, Geoffrey," she said.

"Lady Sapphira?" Geoffrey's voice was weak.

"I am here," Sapphira said. "I have never left your side."

Mousy could not believe her ears. Lord Geoffrey must have a lot of money to attract such interest from this creature.

"I remember you bathed my face. I wanted to thank you but couldn't speak." Geoffrey tried to sit up, fell back, closed his eyes.

Mousy cleared her throat and moved to the other side of the bed. She was met by Sapphira's glower and felt herself flush from neck to hairline.

"Thank you for singing to me, Sapphira," Geoffrey said, eyes still closed. "It was dark. Your song . . . found me."

Sapphira's eyes stabbed Mousy to silence.

"Your voice sounds different today," Geoffrey said.

Dr. Qwenten came into the room, grasped his patient's wrist. "Pulse is stronger. You are a tough young fellow, Lord Geoffrey."

"Thank you, doctor. It's just Geoffrey, if you don't mind. I should like to pay you when I can."

"Stick your tongue out."

"Do you know where Silas and Damaris are?"

"Who?" Dr. Qwenten said.

"His companions," Sapphira said. "Geoffrey, darling, when you fell ill, my father dispatched couriers to locate and bring them here."

"They're here?" Geoffrey tried again to sit up and made it this time.

"They have not yet been found, but do not worry, they shall be." She turned to Mousy. "Let us leave the doctor to his patient."

Mousy limped out ahead of Sapphira, who grasped her above the elbow, steered her into a room across the hall, and shut the door. The tall woman tightened her grip. Pain shot down Mousy's arm into her fingers.

"What are you going to tell your precious Lord Geoffrey?"

Mousy opened her mouth, but no words came out. A rabbit in the talons of a hawk.

The first blow was a backhand slap. Mousy's face burned as tears sprang to her eyes.

"That's right," Sapphira said. "Nothing. Because you are never to see him again."

A blow to the side of Mousy's head dropped her to her knees, ears ringing.

"And what will you tell Dr. Qwenten?"

Mousy tasted blood in her mouth.

"The little songbird can't speak?"

Mousy was trying to form the word "nothing" when the toe of Sapphira's riding boot smashed into her ribs. Her little body crumpled to the ground.

When Mousy heard Dr. Qwenten exit Geoffrey's room, she picked herself off the floor and waited, listening.

All quiet.

She crept out into the hall. Fighting her fear of Lady Sapphira, she entered Geoffrey's room. She was startled to see him crawling toward the door.

"Oh, sir, you must not be out of bed." Ignoring the pain in her ribs, she helped Geoffrey back to bed, where he lay panting, sweat glistening on his forehead.

"You are very kind, miss."

"Are you hungry, Geoffrey, uh, Lord Geoffrey?"

"You know my name, but I do not know yours," Geoffrey said.

"Musette."

Mousy had neither spoken nor heard her real name since her mother died. Why had she told this man?

"But everyone calls me Mousy," she quickly added.

Gentle brown eyes regarded her. "Musette is a lovely name. It becomes you."

Mousy's heart hopped into her throat.

"And yes." Geoffrey's eyes twinkled into a smile. "I think I could eat the entire larder and just be getting started."

"I will return shortly, sir."

"Musette, could you also please find me some clothes?"

When Mousy returned, Geoffrey was asleep. She placed the clothes at the foot of his bed and set the food on the night table. Lingering, she adjusted his pillow and with her fingers combed the wavy chestnut hair off his forehead.

What if Sapphira came back? The thought nauseated Mousy with fear. She hurried to the door and peered out, then turned back for a last look at Geoffrey. His face was calm, with some color in his cheeks.

Mousy watched his chest rise and fall, found herself taking a step toward him, then another. She would sit beside him for just another minute or so. She wanted to wake him, look into his eyes, tell him it was she who had sung to him. Most of all, she wanted to hear Geoffrey speak her name again. Her heart replayed his kind voice:

"Musette . . ."

Geoffrey . . .

She leaned in and kissed him on the forehead. A sudden shift in the light caused her to look up, and she saw that the shadow springing toward her was Sapphira.

CHAPTER 40

"How hard can it be? They are sideshow performers."

Axelrad seethed under Nostromal's scorn. A soldier by training, he always sized a man up by how easy he'd be to kill. Bare hands? Or would a weapon be required? Remaining composed, Axelrad replied, "We are checking every village within a hundred miles that has ever had a carnival, my lord."

"Geoffrey regained consciousness this afternoon," Nostromal said. "I need that half-wit in the House of Overlords, not chasing around the countryside looking for his fellow freaks."

"His stepfather, Silas, was here in Caerdon a few days ago."

"How do you know?"

"He gave some puppets to a traveling minstrel who calls himself Singer Sandley. We found Sandley in Shiresby, doing a show. He claimed not to know Silas's whereabouts."

"And?"

"Sandley was part of their show at Farharven," Axelrad said. "We think he knows where the girl is, at least. But he declined to tell us, not even under torture."

"Torture him some more," Nostromal said.

"He died this morning in the skull press."

"Idiot. You still have nothing."

Axelrad held up a burlap sack. "I have the puppets, sire."

"Get out of my sight."

"Yes, my lord."

Smoldering, Axelrad left the room. Something about Nostromal made him ponder whether it might take several men to kill him. Not that he would ever be foolish enough to try . . .

CHAPTER 41

"**G**eoffrey!"

He startled awake. Mousy's quick calculation that Lady Sapphira would do no violence to her in front of Geoffrey was borne out, and the woman's hands came off her throat.

"Uh, I mean, Baron Castleford," Mousy said. "The Lady Sapphira is here."

Geoffrey blinked. "Hello."

"Mousy was just leaving, Geoffrey." Sapphira sat. "I'll stay with you awhile."

At the door, Mousy glanced back at Geoffrey.

He smiled at her.

It was enough.

But as Mousy shut the door, she saw that Sapphira was already halfway out of her chair.

Mousy ducked into an alcove as the door flung open. She heard Sapphira stalk down the corridor. Slipping her shoes off, Mousy headed in the opposite direction, but not fast enough. She glanced behind her as she reached the stairs.

Sapphira, running, was gaining on her.

Mousy had always been painstakingly slow on stairs.

It would be an accident, of course. And who would dispute the Lady Sapphira?

The crippled girl stumbled and fell down the stairs. How sad . . .

Mousy sat on the top step, launched herself with her hands as she had done as a child, and washboarded down the steps. Same thing on the next flight, then a lurching run toward Dr. Qwenten's cellar door. Locked. Mousy hammered on it. Sapphira rounded the corner.

"Dr. Qwenten, hurry!"

The door opened. Mousy dove inside.

"Out of my way," Sapphira said to Qwenten.

Qwenten brandished the beaker in his hand.

"One step more and you will be hideous during the two months it takes to heal, and ugly for the rest of your life."

"You wouldn't dare. Daddy will have your head off."

"He needs my head. More than he needs you." Qwenten slammed the door in Sapphira's face.

Mousy, breathing hard, was frantically trying to drag a small table under the cellar window.

"What are you doing?" Limuel said.

"Running away."

"You can't go by yourself," Qwenten said.

"I can't stay here, doctor. When that woman takes a hate to someone in this household, they are finished."

Limuel nodded in agreement.

"I never wanted to be a servant the rest of my life anyway," Mousy said.

"Why not?" Limuel said.

"I'm going to be a doctor."

So assured was Mousy's tone that Limuel scurried off and returned with some clothes he had outgrown, plus a tattered carpetbag. Qwenten wrote a letter recommending Mousy as an apprentice to a colleague of his to the north. "When you get to Marmet Crossing, ask for Dr. Rudolph Tarrold."

Sometime after midnight, they opened the cellar window and boosted her out.

"Blessings to you, Mousy," Qwenten said.

"It's Musette now, sir, if you please."

"Musette." Qwenten smiled as the girl disappeared into the night. "Good for you."

CHAPTER 42

Blades clanged as Nostromal, in facemask and chest armor, sparred with a man in similar gear.

Axelrad ushered Geoffrey into Nostromal's presence and cleared his throat.

"That will be all, Riker," Nostromal said.

The pugilist collected Nostromal's weapon and equipment. "Same time tomorrow, sire?"

"Yes," Nostromal said. The man exited.

Geoffrey remained near the doorway. "I wanted to thank you, Lord Nostromal, before I left."

"And you wish to borrow a horse."

"I no longer require it."

"You have word of your companions?"

"No. But Rigdin has informed me that any livery stable in Caerdon will loan horses to a baron on credit."

"Surely Dr. Qwenten would not yet want you to travel."

"I am grateful for his services as well." Geoffrey turned to leave.

"Lord Nostromal," Axelrad said. "I have news that may interest Geoffrey regarding his kin."

"You did not inform me, captain." Nostromal sounded annoyed.

"My apologies, sire," Axelrad said. "A party of my men captured a highwayman. He confessed to the murder of an old man and a girl."

"How do you know they were Geoffrey's companions?" Nostromal said, recognizing Axelrad's ruse and playing his part.

"The victims were apparently traveling performers, last reported at Farharven." Axelrad turned to Geoffrey. "You were recently in Farharven?"

"So were many others," Geoffrey said.

"The killer said the girl was about seventeen, blonde hair."

"That could have been anybody."

"Said she was pretty to look at. Called the old man Papa."

Everyone calls their old man Papa, Geoffrey told himself.

Axelrad reached into a burlap sack, pulled out some marionettes, handed them to Geoffrey. "The robber had these in his possession when we caught up with him."

A princess, a knight, and a dragon. Geoffrey's stomach twisted into his chest.

Of course, any puppeteer worth his salt would have a knight and princess, possibly a dragon.

"Ever seen 'em before?"

With his finger, Geoffrey probed the dragon's little fabric mouth. The oil tube.

CHAPTER 43

"Castleford, my lord."

The voice was far away.

"Master Geoffrey, we have arrived."

Geoffrey did not respond.

Rudy was persistent. "Are you going to get out, sir?"

Geoffrey sighed. Why had Nostromal thought he would want to borrow a servant?

"If you please, sir," Rudy said. "I've got to unload the carriage so I can send it back to Dunnesmore."

Geoffrey forced himself to open his eyes.

In the way a man who has just lost both legs might regard a found penny, Geoffrey gazed at his childhood home through the carriage window.

Sagging shutters, peeling paint, vines creeping over the stone walls like a disease.

Geoffrey moved toward a garden near the main house where his mother had grown herbs for the kitchen. He climbed over the stone wall, dropped to all fours in front of a headless cherub, and mindlessly groped in the overgrown lavender plants for the statue's head.

He fitted the head with its pudgy cheeks onto the ancient sculpture. The spiced sweetness of crushed lavender stems filled his nostrils, and he was once again helping his mother weed this garden, the sun-warmed soil on his fingertips. He pulled one weed, then another.

Geoffrey was still pulling weeds two hours later when Rudy approached. "I have stowed the food and drink in the larder. And sent the carriage back to Dunnesmore. What would you have me do next, sir?"

The servant cleared his throat and repeated his question twice more. However, the lack of an answer suited Rudy, who had been instructed that his main job was to spy on his new master's doings and report regularly to Captain Axelrad. He disappeared into the house for a long drink and a longer nap.

The stars were glimmering through the gloom when Geoffrey ran out of weeds to pull. He curled up on his side under the cherub.

The night his baby sister had died, Geoffrey's mother held him so tightly that he almost couldn't breathe. He had felt sorry for his father, who seemed to have no mother to hold him.

The next morning found Geoffrey shuffling to Castleford's dilapidated barn in search of some garden tools.

The barn door scraped against rotting floorboards as Geoffrey shoved it open. He took a few steps into the barn and stood for a moment to let his eyes adjust to the murk. Silence, then a flutter of wings as a swallow flitted past him out the door.

A sword point jabbed Geoffrey in the back.

"This place does not belong to you." A man who looked like the swordsman's brother pinned Geoffrey's arms behind his back.

"Set foot here again and we'll kill you."

Geoffrey nodded. The man released him.

Geoffrey started toward the door then dove at the swordsman's feet and knocked him down. The other man yanked Geoffrey up into a headlock. He was unable to move against the leveraged arms.

The first man put his sword at Geoffrey's throat.

"Augie, Kirken, Bayon!" Geoffrey shouted. The headlock loosened for an instant, and Geoffrey twisted away. He punched his would-be executioner in the side of the neck, but the headlocker was on him again.

Hoofbeats outside. "In here!" Geoffrey yelled. The assailants released him and ran out the back of the building.

Geoffrey stepped out of the barn, blinking in the sunlight. Sapphira dismounted. Her roan was leading a black gelding.

"What was that about?" she asked.

Geoffrey pointed to the two men as they disappeared over a pasture fence.

"Are you hurt?" Sapphira asked.

He flexed his neck. "No."

"Who are they?"

Geoffrey shrugged. He went back into the barn and found a trowel, some rusty shears, and a spade with a broken handle.

When he came out, Sapphira was still holding the reins of the horses. She brushed some straw off Geoffrey's shoulder. "I am so very sorry about the loss of your companions."

Geoffrey said nothing.

"I thought a gallop in the fresh air might be good for you. Jakers here is a fine mount, one of Daddy's favorites."

"Maybe some other time." Geoffrey headed for the herb garden.

"I brought you some new clothes."

Geoffrey continued walking, Sapphira following with the horses. When he reached the ruined stone wall of the herb garden, Geoffrey knelt and began to restack the fallen stones.

"Daddy said someone in your position shouldn't dress like a servant."

Geoffrey, sizing the scattered stones, tried to ignore Sapphira's voice.

"At least try them on."

The servant's clothes that Musette had smuggled to Geoffrey were, in fact, uncomfortably small. Maybe the woman would go away if he acquiesced.

Inside the house, he donned new leggings, a fitted shirt, and waistcoat. The fit was perfect, the fabric finer than anything he had worn since his boyhood at Castleford. But ruffled sleeves? He tore them off.

As he headed back outside, he heard a scream. Sapphira's horse skittered away from a pear tree, leaving her gripping a branch, dangling in the air.

Geoffrey sprinted to the tree and arrived underneath just as Sapphira released the branch. He caught her in his arms; she fainted.

Geoffrey carried her inside to a couch in the parlor then found some brandy in the larder that Rudy had sequestered behind a flour sack.

Sapphira sat up, took a long drink, and patted the cushion beside her. "Please sit with me for a moment."

Geoffrey balanced himself on the edge of the couch.

"I should have known better than to expect Sugar to stay put, standing on his saddle. But the pears looked delicious."

"They aren't ripe yet," Geoffrey said.

"I'm curious," Sapphira said. "Who are Augie, Kirken, and . . . Bayon, was it?"

Geoffrey's ears reddened. "Some friends from my childhood." Imaginary playmates, actually, who had died the night his childhood ended. But Sapphira didn't need to know that.

"How clever of you to make it seem like many men were arriving."

"The hoofbeats helped."

"You didn't even thank me," Sapphira said.

"Are you well enough to head home now?"

"If you don't mind accompanying me."

Outside, Geoffrey helped Sapphira onto her horse and mounted the black gelding she had brought for him. It was a short ride to Dunnesmore. When they arrived, Geoffrey declined her offer to have the liveryman drive him home.

"Whoever attacked you may try again." Sapphira caught his shirt as he turned away. "Why don't you stay here for a few days at least?"

"I belong at Castleford," Geoffrey said.

Belong at Castleford.

Those words had a strange sound to Geoffrey. Since being orphaned, he had belonged with Silas and Damaris, wherever that might be, and had hoped that one day they might together reach the shores of Markarian.

He had had his hands in the soil of Castleford. He had also defended his life on that soil. Furthermore, his rightful name had been restored to him. Geoffrey, Lord Davenant, of Castleford. Perhaps he did belong there.

CHAPTER 44

Geoffrey guessed there was no proper way to spit out the chewy chunk.

At the other end of the dining table, Nostromal forked the lumps into his mouth with gusto. "Snails, Geoffrey. Imported from the waters of eastern Frinacea."

Geoffrey swallowed the slimy glob and resisted a wave of nausea.

"If I may presume." Nostromal lifted his glass. "To the memory of the man who raised you and the girl you grew up with."

Geoffrey stared at his plate. Had he really needed to accept Nostromal's dinner invitation? Yes, the man had saved him from execution, restored his estate, paid their back taxes, and provided Dr. Qwenten's services.

"I regret that I had not the pleasure of knowing him—Silas, was it?—as I did your father," Nostromal said.

Geoffrey looked up.

"Wellam Lord Davenant was a good man," Nostromal said. "His death, and that of your mother, were terrible tragedies."

A thousand questions rushed to Geoffrey's mind. "I have always wondered—why?"

"Mobs are an ugly thing," Nostromal said.

Like that mob at Farharven.

"Your father had published a tract which some claimed incited the Rebellion. So Bertraks, and others, proclaimed your father a traitor.

"It was a wicked exaggeration, of course, and a pretext. Bertraks was a little man with a big appetite. He coveted Castleford and a seat in the House of Overlords."

Bertraks was dead—another thing for which Geoffrey was indebted to Nostromal.

"I have fought such injustice my entire life," Nostromal said. "And the bill I now have before the House of Overlords—the Amendment of Justice—is a huge step toward a better country for us all."

"Who else was involved besides Bertraks?"

"The affair was never investigated. Then, as now, there was no central power to deal with such matters. My bill would allow me—as Chancellor of the House of Overlords—to establish an interior armed force to deal with events like that which befell your family."

"But that would not have prevented it," Geoffrey said.

"Justice for such perpetrators will be swift. It will serve notice to others who would do the same."

The butler entered. "With apologies, my lord, but Dr. Qwenten requests audience."

"Later, Rigdin."

"He insists."

Dr. Qwenten stepped into the room carrying a ceramic bowl. Geoffrey caught a glimpse of writhing black leeches and reflexively covered his plate.

"The second batch must be checked for efficacy," Qwenten said.

"You tested it this morning." There was an edge in Nostromal's voice.

"That was the first batch. I have changed the broth formula to encourage faster growth."

Nostromal rolled his sleeve up. "Geoffrey, you remember the doctor."

"I am in your debt, Dr. Qwenten," Geoffrey said.

Qwenten placed a glistening leech on Nostromal's forearm.

"This is but one of many projects I am engaged in for the betterment of our country," Nostromal said. "Is it twenty years we have been working together for the advancement of medical science, Dr. Qwenten?"

"Twenty years, four months, three weeks, and a day."

Spoken like a prisoner citing time served, Geoffrey thought. He watched the leech embed itself as Qwenten placed several more.

Nostromal chuckled. "For some reason, Dr. Qwenten seems to have a shortage of volunteers who are willing to donate blood."

Geoffrey stared as the leeches pulsed and swelled. "Your dedication . . . is commendable."

"Dedication can only accomplish so much," Nostromal said. "Geoffrey, we are at a time in history wherein we have the chance to remake Auldeland into something grand, something wonderful. A golden empire, as it were, not seen since the days of Dartanyen."

Qwenten tonged the leeches back into his bowl, the last one making a squeaking sound as he dislodged it from Nostromal's skin.

"But without your presence in the House of Overlords day after tomorrow, a grand opportunity for our country shall be lost, perhaps forever."

The snails Geoffrey had just eaten seemed to writhe in his stomach.

"A crisis, like a foreign invasion or a resurgence of Scourge, might allow me—us—to assume the power needed," Nostromal said. "But there is no guarantee."

Dr. Qwenten dressed Nostromal's arm and left the room.

Nostromal fastened his cuff pin. "I have never quite gotten used to the feel of those creatures on my flesh."

"Just as I would never get used to being a politician," Geoffrey said.

"May I suggest you attend this one time? If, after that, you still believe serving your country is not your path, so be it. I shall then assist you in finding a buyer for Castleford, and you can sail for Markarian—or do anything else you wish."

"Thank you for the meal and for all you've done for me." Geoffrey stood. "But, begging your pardon—"

"Your father was a man of principle who worked tirelessly for those who have no voice. Do you not think that he would wish you, his son, to assume your rightful place and carry on his work?"

Nostromal rose and walked the length of the table. He looked straight at Geoffrey. The man's short beard was immaculate, as if each hair had been trimmed individually.

"I am not asking this for me," Nostromal said, his voice husky, "but for your father's sake."

Geoffrey's throat tightened; he turned away.

"Should you change your mind, let me know. If you wish, I can provide you a copy of my bill beforehand."

Geoffrey shambled home and spent the night in his mother's rose garden, unable to sleep. Memories of his early childhood had faded with the years. But what kind of son would fail his father at such a time? If only he could talk to Silas and Damaris . . .

CHAPTER 45

"Geoffrey."

The ground was cold against his back, his hair damp with dew. Geoffrey blinked awake. Faint sunrise colors painted the sky above him, darkness fading into dawn.

"Geoffrey."

Geoffrey rose, grabbed his spade, approached the garden shed.

A figure stepped from the door but stayed in the shadow of the building.

Something stirred in Geoffrey's chest.

"Hello, Cabbagehead."

"Silas!" Geoffrey ran to Silas, and they embraced one another.

"Damaris is all right?"

"She is," Silas said.

"I thought you both were dead."

"We thought *you* were dead," Silas said. "At least I did. Damaris insisted you were alive. Said she would know it if you weren't."

"Why didn't she come with you?"

"She hurt her leg."

"But she's all right?"

"Yes." Silas pulled something from his pocket. "She wanted me to bring you this."

His cap.

Geoffrey became aware of his fine shirt and leggings. "Let's go see her. I'll get some better clothes on." He headed for the house.

Silas, however, stayed rooted in the shadow of the shed.

"It's safe," Geoffrey said. "Come on."

Silas followed him to the well. Geoffrey pulled up a bucket and scrubbed the soil off his hands.

"Who told you Damaris and I were dead?" Silas said.

"Captain Axelrad."

Geoffrey described his arrest at the Library of Records, his imprisonment, and his restoration to Castleford by the Lord Chancellor.

"The Lord Chancellor—Nostromal of Dunnesmore?"

"Yes. At first they thought I was an imposter. But when Lord Nostromal learned who I was—"

"Lord Nostromal . . . you trust him?"

Geoffrey nodded.

"Why?"

"The man didn't have to reinstate me, but he did. When I got sick after being in prison, his personal physician attended me. And his daughter nursed me back to health."

Silas shook his head.

"He has provided me with food, tools, supplies—everything I need to get started here. And he paid off our back tax debt—the Writ of Owing from that blackguard Edgewold."

"The Lord Chancellor of the Realm paid off the debt of a peasant."

"Former peasant," Geoffrey said.

"Oh. *Former* peasant."

The old pain of being mocked by Silas stabbed at Geoffrey. "I will pay him back as soon as I can, of course."

They crossed the overgrown lawn to the mansion.

"The House of Overlords has its annual session tomorrow morning," Geoffrey said. "As Baron Castleford, I'm expected to attend."

"Will you?"

"I have decided not to."

"You want the title but not the work," Silas said.

"I don't care about the title, Silas. And I have no knowledge or experience for that type of work."

When they reached the front porch, Geoffrey said, "What would you think about living here? Repair the house, bring the land back into production. It's what we've always wanted—a place of our own."

"In a free country," Silas said.

They walked into the house; Geoffrey called for Rudy.

Silas ducked behind the open front door when Rudy tottered into the entrance hall.

"Where are the clothes I was wearing yesterday?" Geoffrey asked.

"I burned 'em."

"Why?"

"Lady Sapphira," Rudy said. "After you carried her inside and laid her down on the couch. It was while you was fetching her some spirits, she says to me, 'Rudy, take them servant's clothes out and burn 'em.' So that's what I done. I seen some other clothes upstairs, might fit you. Shall I fetch 'em?"

"Yes," Geoffrey said. "Then I want you to sweep this house from top to bottom. Dust off the furniture, tidy up the kitchen, and bring in some wood for the cookstove."

"You ain't gonna live outside no more?"

"I'm bringing my family here tonight."

———

After Rudy brought the clothes into the parlor, Geoffrey dismissed him and began changing. The clothes did not fit.

Silas emerged from behind the door. "Hurry up, Geoffrey."

Silas felt exposed at Castleford; the sooner he left, the better. Dr. Avery had warned him that inquiries had been made at the Penny Pony Inn regarding a former Rebel—a silversmith—of Silas's description, including the fact that he had performed at the carnival in Farharven.

Word of other inquiries—spawned, no doubt, by Axelrad's search for them—had also reached Dr. Avery's ears.

At the sound of a noise outside, Silas ran to the entrance hall and watched through a window as an ebony carriage with matching Percherons rolled up the lane and stopped outside. With the assistance of two footmen, a tall woman alighted. She ascended the steps to the front door.

Silas slipped behind the floor-to-ceiling curtains in the entrance hall.

"Ah, Geoffrey." Silas heard the woman's deep voice as she swept in. "Father sends china for your dining pleasure, wine for your wine cellar, candlesticks for your table, and delicacies for your palate."

The footmen entered bearing boxes.

"And me, to see that everything is properly arranged."

"Thank you, Lady Sapphira."

"No need to call me 'Lady', my dear."

Silas, behind the draperies, silently agreed on that point.

"I have someone for you to meet," Geoffrey said, glancing around the room.

Silas molded himself into the wall behind the fabric.

"Silas," Geoffrey called. "Silas?"

"You found them?" Sapphira said. "Oh, Geoffrey, that's wonderful."

Silas heard Geoffrey cross the entrance hall and go out onto the porch, calling his name.

The woman's lighter tread followed. "So where is he? I can't wait to meet him. And the dear girl . . . is she here too?"

"He must have left."

"Why would he do that? He's not a fugitive, is he?"

Silas's heart skipped a beat. Did this person know something?

The footsteps returned to the parlor.

Silas peered out from behind his curtain and saw Sapphira fling aside the drapes from one of the parlor windows.

"I shall have my seamstress prepare new window coverings," Sapphira said. "Red-purple for this room, with white roping and tassels."

She turned toward the entrance hall. "And what about those ugly things in the entrance hall?" She walked to the drape that concealed Silas and stood in front of it, her perfume arriving first.

"We should tear these down and replace them . . . with sheers." Sapphira stood inches from Silas on the other side of the fabric. He tried not to inhale.

Sapphira strode back to the parlor. "I brought you some new clothes, Geoffrey. The latest cut, from the continent. Perfect for this broad chest." She squeezed his shoulders. "And some decent work clothes, since you seem to enjoy playing in the dirt."

"Thank you," Geoffrey said.

"Oh, and some scarves."

Silas grimaced. This woman seemed to know all about Geoffrey. He peered out again.

Geoffrey picked up his cap.

Sapphira snatched it away and sailed it toward the fireplace. "Gentlemen of your stripe do not wear such."

They headed for the front door.

Silas withdrew behind his drape.

"Goodbye for now, my darling."

Had she kissed Geoffrey? Silas could not be sure.

They exited, Geoffrey apparently continuing on to the garden shed.

Sapphira's footsteps returned and bee-lined to Silas's hiding place. The curtain was thrust aside, and a pair of dark eyes raked him from feet to face, where they lingered.

The drape dropped back into place.

A few moments later, her carriage clattered away.

Silas was halfway to the woods when Geoffrey spotted him.

"Silas?"

Silas kept walking. Geoffrey caught him near the edge of the woods.

"Who was that woman?" Silas said.

"Lord Nostromal's daughter, the one who sat with me while I was sick. You saw her?"

"She saw *me*. Recognized me. There must be a new poster."

"Of course she recognized you—she was at our show in Farharven."

"Why would someone from the house of the Lord Chancellor of the Realm attend any show of ours?" Silas asked.

"I don't know. But she has been very helpful."

"I noticed."

Geoffrey felt the scorn in his words. How to explain to Silas that persons of substance like Lady Sapphira and Lord Nostromal might actually see him as more than a carnival sideshow freak?

"She is not to be trusted," Silas said.

"You don't even know her."

"She discovered where I was hiding. She knew you were searching for me. Why didn't she tell you?"

Geoffrey changed the subject. "I think when Damaris sees this place, she will want to live here."

"No."

"Why not?"

"Because this is not Markarian," Silas said. "Because she doesn't quit every time the wind changes."

"This is better than Markarian."

"Geoffrey." Silas waved his arm toward the mansion. "Why would someone hand all this over to you and not expect something in return?"

"I'm the rightful owner of property that was stolen. It's the law."

"*You* live here then," Silas said. "Auldeland is not safe for me."

"As a member of the House of Overlords, I could possibly intervene to help you, maybe get you pardoned."

"Don't be a fool, Geoffrey. The House of Overlords? Who do you think passed the decree calling for the arrest and execution of former Rebels?"

Geoffrey's head was starting to ache.

"If I stay in Auldeland," Silas said, "how long before I end up on a stake, like Rufus?"

"Let's go talk it over with Damaris, see what she says," Geoffrey said.

Silas stopped walking.

"How far is it?" Geoffrey asked.

"You're not going," Silas answered.

"Why not?"

"Because you've lost your senses."

"I'd like to see Damaris."

"Maybe she doesn't want to see *you*."

Geoffrey's heart went wobbly with pain, like a spinning top about to stop. *Could that be true?*

"And maybe I don't want to be impaled." Silas walked into the woods.

After some deep breaths, Geoffrey followed.

Silas turned around and shoved him. Geoffrey, surprised at the force, nearly fell.

Silas walked on.

Geoffrey rejoined him. "At least tell me where you two are staying. I could come tomorrow."

"I would sooner tell a bounty hunter."

Geoffrey continued to follow a few paces behind Silas. The older man turned on Geoffrey and shoved him so hard that he fell backwards and landed painfully on his tailbone.

"Run on back to your castle, Mr. Overlord." Silas trotted away.

Geoffrey leaped to his feet, chased Silas down, and grabbed his shoulders. "Tell me where!" he shouted and slammed Silas against a tree, harder than he meant to.

Silas, eyes closed, didn't move at first. Then he touched the back of his head and regarded the blood on his fingers. For a long moment, he looked at Geoffrey. Then he stumbled off through the trees.

Had there been tears in his stepfather's eyes? Something around Geoffrey's heart began to come undone.

CHAPTER 46

"**D**erina has been asking for you since it happened," Gertie said. Dr. Qwenten followed the housekeeper's flickering candle up the back stairs at Darrowick.

"And Lady Lorica's mother has gone quite out of her wits. Me and Medders are the only servants she hasn't run off, raging about like she is."

Gertie led Qwenten down a narrow servants' hallway that smelled of mothballs.

"But my dear Derina, poor woman, carrying on so." Gertie wiped her eyes with the back of her hand. "I wish you'd come sooner, Dr. Qwenten."

He should have tried to slip past Nostromal's sentries before now; it hadn't been that difficult this evening.

"Derina said the reason you didn't come—she's so bad out of her head, doctor—is because she's a murderer."

"What?" Qwenten wondered if he'd heard correctly.

"Else you would've come right away," Gertie said. "She blames herself for her Lady's death. And now she's locked herself in her room and won't come out."

Gertie stopped in front of a closed door and tapped. "Derina, dearie, I've got the good doctor." She tried the knob. "Be a lamb, now, unlock the door."

"Derina? It's Lucius." Qwenten knocked on the door. No answer.

"She's never locked her door, sir, all these years."

The doctor was still slamming his puny shoulder against the door when Gertie returned with a chunk of firewood and struck the knob off.

Qwenten grabbed Gertie's candle and stepped into the room.

His heart stopped.

Derina sat in a chair, head back, mouth open. Her legs were outstretched, her arms hanging limply at her sides. Blood dripped from her fingertips onto the floor, wetting the shards of a shattered heirloom hand mirror. The mirror's handle—a silver serpent—caught the candlelight and writhed horribly in the red pool.

CHAPTER 47

"What took you so long?"

Damaris hopped to the door and threw her arms around Silas. "I was afraid I was going to have to go out and rescue you again."

Silas forced a laugh.

Damaris studied his face. "I told you Geoffrey was alive. At Castleford, right?"

He nodded.

"Why didn't he come back with you?"

Silas did not reply.

"What's wrong? Is he sick?"

"No."

"Didn't he want to see me?"

Silas chewed his lip. "Geoffrey has a new life."

"What's that supposed to mean?"

"His inheritance has been restored. He is the master of Castleford, with a seat in the House of Overlords."

"Geoffrey . . . an Overlord?"

"They want him there tomorrow, for the Annual Session."

"There's something you're not telling me, Papa."

"Don't be silly," Silas said.

Geoffrey had carried that woman in his arms to the couch, if Rudy's words were to be believed. And she—peculiarly beautiful—had gifted him with new clothes and called him "my darling." Had they kissed too?

"You're not a good liar, Papa."

Silas shrugged.

"So now it is 'Lord Geoffrey, Baron Castleford,'" Damaris said. "A nobleman by birth. A member of the House of Overlords. Wealthy." She looked at Silas. "He can have any woman he wants." She regarded the calluses on her palms. "And what are we, Papa? Poorer than pig mud. You're a fugitive. And I'm the daughter of a scullery maid."

"No, you're not," Silas lied.

Damaris touched his cheek. "It's all right."

Silas looked down, shaking his head.

Damaris broke the silence. "Sandy will probably be here soon."

PART THREE

CHAPTER 48

"Clown Prince Geoffrey is downstairs," Sapphira said. "He has decided to attend the House of Overlords session tomorrow."

Nostromal rose from a chair by the fireplace in his bedroom. "Well done, my dear."

Her father need not know she'd had nothing to do with Geoffrey's decision. "He said you have some papers for him."

Nostromal crossed to a desk and handed her a document. "You could be the next Lady of Castleford."

"With him as Lord?"

"That would be entirely up to you," Nostromal said.

Sapphira smiled and secreted the document under her cape.

Geoffrey paced the entrance hall at Dunnesmore, turning over and over in his mind the encounter with Silas that day—and wishing he had somehow done things differently.

He stopped pacing when Sapphira returned.

"Daddy said he will bring the document down shortly. Do you want to see the library while you wait?"

Geoffrey followed Sapphira down a short hallway. He would show Silas that he could, in fact, take his seat as an informed member of the House of Overlords and make a difference. After all, Nostromal believed in him. And Silas would too before long. He and Damaris would then come and live with him at Castleford—and be proud to do so.

Sapphira, dressed in a sky-blue gown with a black velvet cape off the shoulders—had she expected company?—ushered him into a musty chamber. A candelabrum on a table in the center of the room threw shadows on bookshelves stretching up into blackness.

Sapphira settled herself into a loveseat. When Geoffrey sat on a couch across the room, she rose and sat next to him. Her perfume was a blend of hyacinth and rosewater, but not overpowering as before.

"You must do as Daddy says, you know."

"What do you mean?"

"The House of Overlords—you must vote the way he tells you," Sapphira said. Her black hair, swept up, was shiny in the candlelight. "It will make things so much easier for us . . ."

"Us?"

Sapphira lowered her voice and spoke into his ear. "What kind of silly fool doesn't know"—her long lashes brushed his temple—"when a woman is in love with him?"

Had he heard correctly?

Geoffrey finally formed a reply. "A silly fool might want to know . . . why?"

"Only if he did not know that he was strong. Intelligent. Noble."

"Does she remember those who laughed?"

"I am she who did not laugh." Sapphira touched a forefinger to Geoffrey's lips then slipped her hand under his scarf and traced one of the scars that connected his chin to his collarbone.

Geoffrey waited for her to pull back in disgust. But her hand was on his chest now, caressing.

He jumped to his feet, breaking her touch.

Sapphira stood and faced him, dark eyes level with his. "Damaris," she said.

Geoffrey was puzzled. Where was this going?

"Damaris is exceedingly beautiful, Geoffrey." Sapphira waited, the concern on her face inviting his confidence. "Flawless."

Unlike me. Geoffrey sighed. "I once wished that she really were blind."

"Not pretend, like in your show."

He nodded.

"You must forget her."

Like I could forget my own life.

"She is the same as the others."

"No," Geoffrey said.

"Oh? Damaris has never laughed at you?"

Only that time, right before the farm boy thrashed me . . .

"Or called you a name?"

"You really are a monster . . ." Geoffrey could still hear the abhorrence in Damaris's voice, after his cruel treatment of Sandy.

Sapphira loosed the jeweled comb from her hair; black tresses tumbled down. "I'm different," she said. Her lips were suddenly upon his, her arms coiling their bodies together. Geoffrey's momentary paralysis made the event seem longer than it was. He pushed Sapphira away.

A dark silence, as before a tornado.

Geoffrey finally spoke. "Could we, uh, see if Lord Nostromal has the document yet?"

Sapphira pulled her long hair back into a twist and swept to the door. "Come with me."

———————————

Geoffrey could hear the rhythmic ring of a blacksmith's hammer as he followed Sapphira out to the estate's stable. Odd that someone should be working so late at night—surely not Nostromal.

Sapphira pushed the door open. A charcoal fire blazed up as the blacksmith, perspiration streaming down his naked back, pumped the bellows.

She motioned to Geoffrey to wait and crept up behind the big man.

"Bobo."

The man whirled to face her. Geoffrey started. The blacksmith's face was hideously misshapen, with bulging forehead, close-set pig eyes, and sausage lips.

Bobo's grin exposed snaggle teeth. He grabbed Sapphira and kissed her full on the mouth. She returned the embrace, twirling her finger on his hairy shoulder.

Geoffrey stumbled backwards out through the door.

"Don't you want the document, Geoffrey?" Sapphira called.

"I . . . I'll go find Lord Nostromal."

"He doesn't have it."

Geoffrey re-entered the stable as Sapphira pulled a folded document from her cape. She waved it in his face. "After you meet Homer."

Geoffrey reached for the document, but Bobo's massive paw grabbed his wrist. "After you meet Homer," he growled.

A hard-muscled young man of about eighteen stepped from the shadows. He was holding a pitchfork in one hand; the other arm was missing at the elbow. His nose had been cut off, leaving two gaping holes in the middle of his face—an unnatural specter in the lantern light.

"They cut out his tongue too," Sapphira said.

The boy bobbed his stump up and down like a bird flapping a wing.

"Daddy lets me keep whomever I bring home as long as I can find him a job on the estate. Homer is our stable boy."

Homer jammed his pitchfork into the wooden floor, thrust a finger and thumb into the holes in his face, and honked like a goose.

Sapphira giggled and played her palm over the boy's stump.

Geoffrey tried to edge away, but Bobo blocked him.

"Could your precious Damaris look on Bobo and fall in love with him?" Sapphira said. "Could she gaze at Homer and give him her heart?"

Another man slouched in the shadows behind Homer. He had a hump on his back.

"So you see, little Scar-boy, if you want love, you're stuck with me." She tucked the folded document into the belt at Geoffrey's waist.

Homer yanked his pitchfork out of the floor. Bobo then snatched two red-hot pokers from the fire and tossed one to the hunchback.

"Don't kill him," Sapphira said. "Daddy still needs him. Just a new face—the rest of him is already perfect."

Her laugh crescendoed into a shrill whinny as the three men charged Geoffrey.

CHAPTER 49

"**B**e sure you feed the monkeys and rats twice a day, and make sure they have plenty of fresh water."

"Uh, doctor—"

"Is that clear, Limuel?"

Dr. Qwenten loaded his notebooks into a satchel. He would leave behind the elements from the Gypteziam tombs: it was not his money that had paid for the expedition.

"We had a visitor here last night," Limuel said. "While you were gone."

"Who?"

The door opened. Nostromal strode in carrying a wooden box that resembled a small coffin. Limuel mouthed "him" and scurried out of the room.

Nostromal deposited the box on Qwenten's workbench. "I believe you will find the contents most interesting, doctor."

"I have no further interest in materials you supply." Qwenten scooped up some loose papers, trued them, and placed them in his satchel. "You can sell the monkeys and rats. Limuel will care for them until you do."

"You will not leave these premises," Nostromal said.

"You have no hold over me now." Qwenten picked up the satchel and headed for the open door.

"Please accept my condolences for the untimely demise of your lady friend. I'm given to understand she took her own life."

Qwenten, almost to the door, did not see Nostromal hoist the wooden box and hurl it in his direction. It splintered against the doorpost a foot from Qwenten's head. Something tumbled out onto the floor.

At Qwenten's feet lay the crumpled body of a little girl, perhaps three years old. Her skin was covered with large purple splotches, her neck and face swollen to grotesque proportions.

The satchel dropped from Qwenten's hands; his papers spilled out. He retched, turned away from the girl's corpse, and retched again.

"You . . . have released Scourge?"

"Not yet." Nostromal ran his hand along the top of a monkey cage. "When my sources informed me of your paramour's death, I gave one of your rats our little leech meal and released it near a lone peasant shack five miles from here. Early this morning I returned there to behold a dead family."

Qwenten gnawed on the back of his fist, trying not to scream.

"I burned the shack and the bodies with it, except for this one," Nostromal said.

"And the rat?" Qwenten was shaking all over.

"Dead outside the shack. The old man must have killed it after he got bit."

"You could have unleashed Scourge on the entire continent!" Qwenten shrieked.

Nostromal's voice remained calm. "Thousands of superfluous people foul our land, like barnacles dragging down a great ship. I would rebuild our country with those hardy ones who survive. And with the indebted ones whose lives I save with my serum."

Qwenten ground his forehead into the doorpost.

"When Scourge does strike Auldeland again—and I will decide the proper time—a panicked country will turn to me," Nostromal said. "So we will need a plentiful supply of your new serum, won't we?"

Qwenten edged along the wall to his dissecting table. Behind his back, his hand closed on a scalpel.

"I know you men of the so-called healing profession," Nostromal said. "As the compassionate physician you are, you will do everything in your power to fight the next outbreak. Regardless of your feelings for me."

Qwenten charged Nostromal with the scalpel.

Nostromal struck the instrument away, grabbed Qwenten by the throat, and slammed his head backwards onto the bench top. "And you will do it here, in this cellar."

Qwenten, his neck hyperextended, couldn't breathe. He picked frantically at Nostromal's iron fingers.

Nostromal wiped the bench with the back of Qwenten's head and flung him to the ground. "Many lives are depending on you, *Dr.* Lucius Qwenten."

CHAPTER 50

Geoffrey's back was up against a horse stall gate. He dodged Homer's pitchfork thrust, released the gate latch, and leaped over the gate into the stall. He smacked the horse and raced beside it as it charged out.

He ran for the lane, the blacksmith in pursuit. How could a man that big run so fast? Geoffrey leaped a low stone wall and landed in the formal garden. He heard his pursuer bolt past him and was concealing himself behind a morning glory trellis when the moon slid from behind its cloud cover.

"There he is—the garden!"

Geoffrey darted for a corner of the mansion, crabbed along the wall, and nearly fell into a cellar window well. Feet pounded nearer. He ducked down into the well, slipped through the open window, and fell hard onto a table beneath. Above, a man ran past.

"Check the house!"

Geoffrey stood up on the table, closed the window, and latched it. In the faint light from orange embers at one end of the room, he saw a door. He fumbled for the bolt, slid it home. He became aware of a familiar, terrifying odor. Burning flesh. A low moan.

The moan came again, this time almost a sob. As his eyes grew more accustomed to the dark, he saw a man lying on the floor near the firepit. Geoffrey found a lantern, lit it.

"Dr. Qwenten?" The man was disheveled, eyes bloodshot. "Dr. Qwenten, it's Geoffrey." Geoffrey helped him up, walked him to a stool at one of the tables. "Please forgive my intrusion. I'm sorry if I startled you."

The doctor shuddered violently, like a man shaking off a swarm of bees. A vein on his temple bulged.

Geoffrey dipped some water from a crock, made the doctor drink it. "Are you going to be all right?"

"Don't leave me."

Geoffrey glanced up at the window, shielded the lantern.

"What has happened?"

"Derina is dead," Qwenten said. "It's my fault." He buried his face in his hands, his shoulders shaking.

"Who's Derina?"

"We were going to be married."

"I'm so sorry." Geoffrey climbed onto the table under the window. "Dr. Qwenten, I hate to leave you like this . . ."

"Stay. Please." Tears ran down Dr. Qwenten's cheeks. "The little girl. She was innocent. And I killed her. Just like I killed Derina."

This wasn't the rational man whose medical skills had saved Geoffrey's life. Geoffrey left the window and pulled up a stool.

"I couldn't go to my dear Derina. But how could she know that?" Dr. Qwenten ground his fists into his eyes then looked straight at Geoffrey. "Do you believe you can sell your soul to the Dark One?"

The man wasn't making any sense. *Maybe if I play along.* "Why would anybody do that?"

"To survive a deadly injury. Or fatal disease."

"Uh-huh," Geoffrey said.

"Scourge kills most of its victims. Only a few recover. But how could it live on and on in a man's bloodstream and not kill him?"

Talking, Qwenten's color seemed to be returning. "Go on," Geoffrey said.

"I just burned up a little girl," Qwenten said. He buried his face in his hands.

Geoffrey doubted the gentle physician had ever killed anyone, but the odor of burned flesh was unmistakable. Maybe it was one of the caged animals, related to some experiment. He put his arm around the man's shoulders.

At that moment, a log shifted in the firepit and onto the hearth flipped the charred remains of a small human hand. Geoffrey could see the tiny fingernails even from where he sat across the room. He yanked his arm off the doctor as if he had been burned.

Dr. Qwenten sobbed.

A knock on the door.

Geoffrey vaulted onto the table under the window, opened the latch, pulled himself up into the fresh night air. He crouched in the window well.

The knock came again, and a muffled voice. "Please, doctor, let me in. It's Limuel."

Qwenten shuffled to the door and opened it.

"We gotta get back to work, sir." A young man's voice, shaking. "Or terrible things the master will do to me."

Geoffrey dropped back down into the room. Limuel screamed. Geoffrey grabbed the boy and clamped a hand over his mouth. "Quiet."

When Geoffrey released him, Limuel fell to his knees. "Don't torture me, I beg you, mister, please."

"I'm a friend of Dr. Qwenten's."

"So you never yanked anyone's tongue out?" Limuel blubbered. "Or sliced off their ears and nose and . . . things?"

"No." Geoffrey helped Limuel to his feet. "The doctor's not well right now. Can you look after him?"

Geoffrey and Limuel got Dr. Qwenten onto a bench, covered him with a blanket, pillowed his head. Geoffrey waited until the man was asleep.

"Are you the one they're chasing?" Limuel asked.

Geoffrey ignored the question. "Can you bring Dr. Qwenten some food when he wakes up?"

Limuel nodded.

Geoffrey climbed out of the window well, flattened himself in the damp grass. He waited for the moon to glide into a cloudbank before he ran for the main road.

Geoffrey shuddered as he recalled Sapphira's mouth on his.

How had he not seen the unloveliness in that face? When she smiled, her white teeth were perfect and the corners of her eyes crinkled—but the pupils remained cold.

Approaching the front of his house, Geoffrey heard something under the parlor window.

"Who's there?"

A canary flopped in circles around a steel spike that pinned its wing to the ground.

Geoffrey knelt, cupped his hand over the bird's head; it quieted. He did not see the person on the roof above him, nor the stone pot they balanced.

He pulled the spike out of the ground. *Why would someone—?*

The stone pot fell.

Before Geoffrey's mind could finish the question, his body sprang sideways. The stone pot grazed his shoulder and struck the ground.

He charged into the house and up the grand staircase. Hearing footsteps on the back stairs, he raced down, caught someone running out the back door. He pinned the intruder against the wall of the house. The moonlight over his shoulder lit the face of a middle-aged woman.

"Murderer!" she said.

Geoffrey held her at arm's length.

"Lady Bertraks?"

"Curses upon you."

"Who carried the pot to the roof?"

The woman spat at him.

"Your sons? Jumped me yesterday?"

"Next time they'll kill you."

Geoffrey released her. She ran.

He returned to the front of the house and rolled the stone pot aside. There on the ground, wings outstretched to take flight, was the little yellow bird—crushed.

He searched the mansion but found no one else, including Rudy. The old drunk had apparently cooked some meat in the parlor fireplace before absconding with the last of the brandy.

Geoffrey carefully read the bill entitled "Amendment of Justice" then reread it. He added a log to the fire and pulled his mother's rocking chair close to it. The *creak, creak* as he rocked was a comforting sound from his childhood, and for a few moments Geoffrey was a toddler in the arms of his mother, floating along on the rhythm of the squeaking chair.

Watching the firelight shadows on the ceiling of the room in which his parents had burned to death, Geoffrey soon found himself inside the nightmare that still haunted him. *His mother shrieking, "Run, baby cricket, run!" The torch of Bertraks, hissing and snapping. The screams of his mother and father . . .*

Geoffrey startled awake, falling out of the rocking chair to his knees. His hand closed on his cap on the floor where Sapphira had flung it.

He stumbled out the door and made his way to a wagon near the stable, crawled under it, and curled up on his side. The last of the moonlight glinted on Damaris's locket as Geoffrey turned it over and over in his fingers.

Conk-la-ree, conk-la-ree. Sleep had not yet come when a red-winged blackbird began serenading the first pink strands of daylight.

Geoffrey returned to the house and located the bundle of clothes Sapphira had brought. He donned a white shirt, dark leggings, and leather boots. He skipped the coat but wrapped a black silk scarf around his neck. The ruffled shirtsleeves he tore off, accidentally ripping the fabric to the armpits.

Moments later, the carriage of Lord Nostromal arrived. Probably to convey him to the Palace Presidio. Geoffrey slipped out of sight into the woods behind the house.

He would walk.

CHAPTER 51

Geoffrey stood across the street from the Palace Presidio and watched the elegant carriages of the Overlords arrive, each with its own fancy livery representing the estate from which it hailed.

His stomach was a nervous knot, just as it had been at the debut of their new play not so many days ago. Self-conscious in the unfamiliar attire, he regretted his ripped sleeves and absent coat.

After a quarter hour passed with no further arrivals, Geoffrey forced his feet to move toward the grand building's entrance.

"No one allowed today except Overlords," an official said. "Assembly in session today."

"That's why I'm here," Geoffrey said.

"Who are you?"

"Geoffrey."

The official glanced at the two guards flanking the door then back at Geoffrey.

"I mean, Lord Geoffrey."

"There is no 'Lord Geoffrey.'" Spoken like an obscenity.

"There is now," Geoffrey said, not meaning it the way it sounded.

"Where is your carriage?"

"I don't have one—yet." He started forward; the guards blocked him.

"But I am who I say. Of Castleford."

"Baron Castleford is dead."

Geoffrey tried to go around the guards. An officer on horseback charged up, shouted an order, and Geoffrey was on the ground, spears in his face.

"Take him to Starknell."

Red-beard and the whip. Geoffrey's muscles tensed for an escape attempt.

"You fools."

Lord Nostromal.

"Release this man at once."

"Begging your pardon, your grace," the officer said, "but this man is not—"

"He is the one I instructed you to watch for," Nostromal said. "I should have the lot of you flogged."

The guards pulled Geoffrey to his feet; the official brushed at some dirt on Geoffrey's shirt.

"Very glad to see you, sir," Geoffrey said to Nostromal. "Thank you."

"I had purposed to bring you myself, Castleford being on the way," Nostromal said. "We tried but did not raise you."

The doorkeeper bowed as Nostromal swept into the marble corridor. Geoffrey had to walk fast to keep up. He glanced over his shoulder. Behind him was Captain Axelrad and three of his armed men.

"The Amendment of Justice is the first bill to be addressed, Geoffrey," Nostromal said. "You must rise and say 'content' when your name is called. That is all. Do you understand?"

Geoffrey nodded.

"Wait here." Nostromal left Geoffrey at an arched doorway, the only entrance to the Council Hall.

Geoffrey watched as Nostromal moved into the chamber, weaving through scattered knots of gentlemen.

"Lord Geoffrey?" The white-haired man did not wait for a reply. "I am Mr. Smadgins, Clerk of the House."

Mr. Smadgins led him to a high-backed chair at one end of the front row. There were five curved rows of chairs, each row higher than the one in front.

The paneled walls and high ceiling, adorned with frescoes, proclaimed the Council Hall a place of opulence and prestige. A balcony ran high along the rear wall beneath a dozen skylights. Rectangles of light splashed onto a magnificent tapestry behind the speaker's platform. Geoffrey, recalling Silas's history lessons, tried to puzzle out the name of the ancient battle depicted.

The older man in the chair beside Geoffrey extended his hand.

"Welcome, Lord Geoffrey. My name is Tyrus."

"Thank you, Tyrus. Uh, Lord Tyrus, I mean."

"Tyrus is fine. It's what your father called me."

The bang of a gavel came from the podium.

"We shall have much to discuss," Lord Tyrus said, anticipating Geoffrey's question.

Lord Nostromal took his place on the speaker's platform in front of the tapestry. More than a hundred strong, the rest of the Overlords found their seats in the ascending rows of chairs.

Attendants shut the massive door near the front of the chamber as Axelrad and his men arrayed themselves on either side.

"How did you manage it?"

Geoffrey turned. The eyes of the man sitting behind him seemed to pierce Geoffrey's skin.

"Manage?"

"Having Bertie killed like that."

Geoffrey looked to Lord Tyrus.

"He means Lord Bertraks," Tyrus said.

"Everyone knows it was you," the man said. "How did you do it?"

Tyrus laughed. "Pay no attention to Lord Sour Stockings."

Smadgins, the Clerk, stood at one of two podiums on the speaker's platform and struck a bell. "The House of Overlords now commences session 341, this 217th day of the year 873, Calendar Botan. The first order of business: this assembly shall recognize and seat Geoffrey Lord Davenant, Baron Castleford."

Unused to hearing his full name, Geoffrey froze to his chair. Lord Tyrus motioned for him to stand. Geoffrey rose.

Smadgins approached and addressed him in a loud voice.

"Geoffrey Lord Davenant, son of Wellam Lord Davenant: as the Baron Castleford, with all rights, property, and titles appertaining thereto, you will on this day commence your service ex officio as member of the House of Overlords, Caerdon, Auldeland, until such time as your natural death."

Smadgins now handed Geoffrey a ring. Geoffrey glanced at Tyrus, who lifted his hand slightly to indicate which finger. Geoffrey slid the ring—depicting the rare Fresian sea eagle in bronze relief—onto his right index finger.

Lord Tyrus called out, "Here, here. The rightful heir restored." Several voices assented.

Tyrus reached for Geoffrey's hand. "Congratulations," he said, and pulled him back down.

"On his hands is the blood of Lord Haviwade Bertraks!" came a shout, followed by a chorus of agreement.

The Clerk, having regained his podium, banged his gavel and the chamber quieted.

Geoffrey struggled to maintain focus as minutes were read and administrative business conducted. This was followed by agricultural reports from the various provinces and finally an accounting of revenues raised through taxes, tariffs, and fees.

The mention of the Palace Presidio tax caught his ear. "As duly passed in previous session, a new tax on each subject of the Realm, to pay for amenities and improvements to the Palace Presidio and this chamber, has generated the following revenue by province . . ."

After a list of numbers was read out and the total given, one of the Overlords in the middle of Geoffrey's row stood up.

"This paltry amount will not begin to pay for the refurbishing this edifice needs," he said. "It is disgraceful that we, the Overlords of Auldeland, hold session in such shabby and decrepit quarters."

Geoffrey's eyes moved from the marble floor and columns to the crystal chandeliers gracing the ceiling.

"Lord Jalfry is right," another Overlord said. "I shall be proposing that we increase that tax in this session."

Geoffrey stood. Heads and eyes turned in his direction. "Uh . . . I, uh . . ." His voice locked up.

Mr. Smadgins cleared his throat. "Does the Baron Castleford have a remark he wishes to make?" The official seemed embarrassed to address the inappropriately attired newcomer.

"Uh, that tax has worked a great hardship on me and my companions."

"At two and a half silver bob per year?" Lord Jalfry scoffed. "If that is supposed to be some kind of joke, young man, it is not funny."

Actually, they always charged us more than that. But Geoffrey's thoughts failed to come out as words. His face reddened and he sat down.

The heat in the chamber rose as the Clerk droned on. Geoffrey wiped perspiration off his face with the end of his scarf.

At last came the call for new business.

"After much deliberation during the previous session, the vote on the Amendment of Justice ended in a tie and the measure was tabled," Smadgins said. "The Clerk now yields to the Chancellor, Lord Nostromal, Baron Dunnesmore."

Lord Nostromal rose from his seat on the platform and took the other podium. "My lords, regarding the Amendment of Justice, I hereby move that a vote be taken to test the impasse of our last session. Should deadlock again ensue, debate can recommence."

"All those in favor of such a vote, say aye," the Clerk said.

A chorus of ayes.

"Those opposed?"

The nays were slightly less.

"The ayes carry. The roll call vote, for or against the Amendment of Justice, shall now be taken," Smadgins said. "Each Lord, on his name being called, shall rise and answer 'content' or 'non-content.'"

The Clerk's assistant, wearing a black eyepatch, stood near the Clerk's podium and unrolled a scroll.

"My Lord John, Baron Joratis," the assistant boomed out.

An elderly gentleman, supporting himself with two bony hands on top of a cane, wobbled to his feet. "Content," he said, and swayed back down.

"My Lord Finch, Baron Guernsey."

Lord Finch rose. "Content."

"My Lord Hanoch, Baron Rutherford."

"Non-content."

Geoffrey—expecting to hear his own name called each time Eyepatch opened his mouth—gripped his chair with sweating palms.

"Lord Tyrus, Baron Loridine."

"Non-content." Tyrus nodded at Geoffrey as he sat down, as if assuming they were on the same side of the matter.

"My Lord Nostromal, Baron Dunnesmore."

"Content."

"My Lord Smithson, Baron Villford."

Lord Smithson rose and shouted, "Content."

The chamber was hotter than ever. It seemed to Geoffrey that every member had been called on to vote except himself. Feeling woozy, he loosened his scarf and wondered if he might leave soon.

He was relieved to see Mr. Smadgins and Eyepatch conferring over the scroll.

"Fifty-four votes in favor, fifty-three votes opposed," the Clerk announced. "The Amendment of Justice is hereby passed and at midnight tonight becomes the law of the land."

Nostromal smiled as the prevailing Overlords clapped.

Lord Tyrus rose. "With due respect to the Clerk of the House, I believe there has been an oversight in the roll call. We failed to hear from Lord Geoffrey, Baron Castleford."

A flare of nerves in Geoffrey's brain.

The Clerk huddled with his assistant, who flipped his eyepatch up as though to see better. He squinted over his scroll then flipped his patch back down and pointed to Geoffrey.

"Ah," said Smadgins. "My apologies to you, Lord Geoffrey, and to the body at large." He nodded to Eyepatch. "Please proceed, Mr. Wallers."

"My Lord Geoffrey, Baron Castleford."

Geoffrey felt all eyes boring in on him. He licked the sweat off his upper lip.

"My Lord Geoffrey, Baron Castleford?" Wallers repeated.

Geoffrey knew he should stand up, but something in his body resisted.

"Lord Geoffrey, Baron Castleford," the Clerk said. "Content or non-content?"

Geoffrey rose partway. He suddenly felt the terror of one who fears he might actually jump off a cliff, the edge of which he is peering over.

"I, uh, have some uncertainty regarding . . . the bill."

"There is no debate period," the Clerk said. "You must cast your vote."

Geoffrey glanced at Nostromal, who nodded encouragement.

The Clerk said, "Content or non-content, young man?"

Geoffrey stood all the way up. He swallowed. "Well, then, non-cont—"

"I believe I can help our newest member," Nostromal interrupted. "Inasmuch as he was not present when this bill was debated during the last session."

A low murmur hummed through the chamber as Nostromal left the platform and crossed to Geoffrey.

"No doubt, Lord Geoffrey, you perceive the wisdom in clarifying the jurisdictional prerogatives of this body and its leadership."

"Lord Nostromal." Tyrus rose. "Forgive me, but as we are straying from protocol, perhaps we should hear from Lord Geoffrey himself."

"We have heard quite enough from him this morning," Lord Jalfry said.

"Let the young Overlord speak," Lord Hanoch said. "His vote determines whether the Amendment of Justice becomes the law of the land or remains tabled."

A chorus of approval.

Nostromal gave a slight bow. "Lord Geoffrey?"

Geoffrey pushed a trembling palm across his damp forehead. "The bill seemed like a good idea when Lord Nostromal told me about it. He said it would prevent the kind of thing that happened to my parents." He turned to the assembly. Some of the faces seemed attentive; the shaking in his limbs slowed. "I read the bill last night. I couldn't sleep so I read it again."

"A capital remedy for sleeplessness," someone called out, to scattered laughter.

"I did not understand it at first," Geoffrey said. "It has a lot of legal and linguistic decorations."

Several members nodded.

"Mainly, I am puzzled that this bill gives so much authority to one man. For example, the Lord Chancellor may declare war. He may raise an army—by conscription, if necessary. He may levy new taxes. And all without a vote of this body."

"Perhaps I can help," Nostromal said. "First of all, I am very pleased that you have read the bill—not once but twice. Our members could take an example."

A few chuckles.

"As to your question of strengthening the leadership of our country, you will soon learn that an assembly such as this one is a sluggish vessel, meeting only twice a year. But these difficult times—our foreign enemies rattling their swords and our colonies their chains—call for the prompt action of a resolute and steady hand. Do you not agree?"

"Provided it is a hand such as the present Lord Chancellor's." Geoffrey faced Nostromal. "You have been both generous and just to me."

Nostromal inclined his head to acknowledge the compliment.

"But a man of the stripe who killed my parents and took their property—what if he were to become the Lord Chancellor under this bill one day?" Geoffrey said. "Who would hold him to account?"

"Do you mean to imply, Lord Geoffrey, that this assembly would, in a crass act of poor judgment, elevate a tyrant?" Nostromal said. "Most of us will find that insinuation offensive."

Nostromal's demeanor had changed from fatherly to annoyed. Geoffrey wondered if he should continue.

"Enough already," Lord Finch said. "Get on with the vote."

"No, hear him through," Lord Hanoch said.

Sweat ran down Geoffrey's face. His scarf was completely soaked.

Lord Smithson stood up, pulled a handkerchief from his pocket, and—in an exaggerated motion—wiped his face and wrung out the cloth.

Geoffrey's face reddened as he waited for the laughter to die down.

"Keep going," Lord Tyrus said.

"I have more concerns," Geoffrey said. "But in sum, and in good conscience, I must oppose it."

"Now get on with the vote!" Lord Hanoch bellowed.

"No, open it up for debate!" shouted Lord Finch.

Dozens of shouts rang out. The Clerk banged his gavel, but the commotion only intensified.

Nostromal, now in Geoffrey's face, hissed, "You have a chance to save your life, unlike your father, who also once opposed me."

Geoffrey was confused. Nostromal bent his mouth to Geoffrey's ear. "You heard me. 'Baby Cricket!'"

The last two words his mother ever spoke hammered into Geoffrey's brain like steel spikes.

Baby. Cricket. Had Nostromal been there that terrible night? *The blue roan rider, who had nearly trampled him on the snowy road.*

His breath knocked out of him, Geoffrey swayed and sat down.

The noise in the chamber continued, and several men—now on their feet—argued with one another.

"The necklace of fire awaits your companions at Cliffhaven should you vote against my bill." Nostromal hunched over Geoffrey. "Unlike you, they will not survive . . ."

The shouting continued. The Clerk banged his gavel. "Order, order!"

Nostromal leaped onto the platform, snatched the gavel, and pounded the assembly to silence.

"Order!" Smadgins said. "All Overlords will please be seated." He waited as the members found their seats, then looked to Lord Nostromal.

"Take the vote," the Lord Chancellor said.

"The vote on the Amendment of Justice shall now be concluded," Smadgins said.

"Lord Geoffrey, Baron Castleford, content or non-content?"

Geoffrey was huddled in his seat, staring at his trembling hands.

"Is the gentleman from Castleford abstaining?"

The chamber was now as calm as it had been raucous.

Geoffrey looked up. The black eyes of Nostromal—triumphant—bore in on him, daring him to condemn Silas and Damaris to the same torturous death his parents had suffered. To save them, he need say only one word: "content."

And thus condemn all persons—except the ruling class—to a life even worse than the one they now endured.

Geoffrey's mind cleared, like leaves settling after a whirlwind. He stood up to do what he had been helpless to do for his father and mother.

But when he tried to form the word "content," his tongue became a clumsy block of sand. He tried again; his throat closed up. His jaws worked until, finally, out came a high-pitched squeak.

Peals of laughter rang through the chamber as Geoffrey wilted down into his seat.

CHAPTER 52

"The gentleman from Castleford abstains," the Clerk's voice boomed out. "Duly voted on and passed by this body, on a margin of one vote, the Amendment of Justice becomes now the law of the land, as recorded on this 217th day in the year—"

Geoffrey jumped up and shouted, "NON-CONTENT!"

He bolted across the speaker's platform toward the door. Could he get to Cliffhaven ahead of Axelrad's soldiers?

Nostromal leaped to block Geoffrey's path.

"No one departs this chamber until the session is over," he said. "You are one of us."

"He may have the title of Overlord," Lord Jalfry said. "But he is *not* one of us."

"You're right," Geoffrey said. "I don't belong here." He faced the assembly. "Lord Nostromal restored me for one reason only: to vote for his bill."

The accusation seemed to hang in the stuffy air.

"But I voted against it because it is wrong."

"Are we to be instructed in right and wrong by this young man who talks like he represents the commoner?" Lord Finch said.

"He's certainly not one of us," Nostromal said. "But neither is he a commoner."

Nostromal grabbed the back of Geoffrey's shirt and ripped it off, followed by the scarf.

A collective gasp went up, every eye riveted on something they had never seen before.

Geoffrey fought a desperate urge to cover himself. Then his voice rang out. "I have lived for years under your rules, taxes, laws, restrictions, and harassments—and this bill will make it worse."

"You have lived as a traveling sideshow freak." Nostromal spat out the words. "A monster on exhibit for money." He pointed his finger at Geoffrey and faced the Overlords. "And now he presumes to lecture this august body."

"Hear, hear."

"Two days ago," Geoffrey said, "Lord Nostromal talked about a resurgence of Scourge. He told me this bill will make it easier for him—the Lord Chancellor—to assume power in such a crisis."

"Scourge hasn't been seen for a generation," someone said.

"Scourge?" Lord Finch said. "Where would it come from?"

The leeches on Nostromal's arm . . . Dr. Qwenten sobbing, "How could it live on in a man's bloodstream and not kill him?"

And all at once, Geoffrey knew.

"Nostromal himself carries Scourge!" he shouted.

"Carry Scourge and live?" Lord Smithson said.

"Impossible, by the laws of nature."

"He's healthier than I am."

"If Lord Nostromal's got Scourge, *Lord* Geoffrey, what cankerous rot have you got?"

Laughter.

"I'm telling the truth. I know it sounds—"

"Farcical?" Nostromal said. "Gentlemen, are we to stand by while this mountebank makes a mockery of our proceedings?"

"Get him out!"

More shouts. A book struck Geoffrey on the chest. The din increased as a scroll, shoe, riding crop, and more rained down on him. He stood, a pillar in the gale, making no effort to protect himself.

A roar went up when an inkwell, thrown like a rock, struck Geoffrey in the forehead, glass bottle shattering. Dazed, he dropped to his knees, then to all fours. He shook his head, tried to clear the blinding pain.

Geoffrey slowly got to his feet. Ink and blood flowed down his scarred body in rivulets of black and crimson.

The shouts died away; planned projectiles dropped.

Geoffrey, feeling a ferocity he had never known before, glared out at the now-silent assembly, moving his eyes from face to face. And then his voice—steady and clear— reverberated throughout the chamber.

"This man—Nostromal, the Lord Chancellor—murdered my parents, Wellam and Marsilla Davenant, Lord and Lady of Castleford. And since that day I, Geoffrey Davenant, their son—" He turned to face Nostromal. "Have born the marks of your attempt to murder a six-year-old boy."

Geoffrey picked up his torn shirt and pulled it on. "And you call me monster . . ."

He started toward the door.

"A treasonous accusation against the Lord Chancellor of the Realm!"

"Arrest him!" Nostromal barked to Axelrad and his soldiers.

Surrounded, Geoffrey had no room to run. A dagger sailed at him from somewhere above and stuck in the tapestry behind him.

He dove for the dagger, missed, and pulled a soldier down with him. Wresting the man's spear away, he rolled to his feet, brandished the weapon.

"Drop it," Axelrad said.

The soldiers backed Geoffrey against the tapestry.

"Cabbagehead, Lord Geoffrey!" a voice called out.

A blur of motion followed as someone on a chandelier rope swung down from the balcony and slammed Axelrad to the ground.

Silas snatched up Axelrad's sword and sprinted for the balcony staircase, Geoffrey right behind. With spear and sword, they fought the soldiers, backpedaling up the stairs.

At the top, they sprinted across the narrow balcony to a skylight. Silas shattered the glass with his sword, laced his hands, and boosted Geoffrey up. Geoffrey locked wrists with Silas and pulled him up onto the roof.

They scrambled to the edge of the tile roof and slid down a pipe to a ledge.

Axelrad raced out of the building. "Corporal!" he shouted at the officer on horseback. He pointed up at Geoffrey and Silas. "Bring them down."

The corporal barked at his men.

"Crossbows, ready, fire!"

As one, Silas and Geoffrey leaped from the ledge, a hail of arrows hitting the building behind them. Geoffrey, landing on the corporal, unhorsed the man and scrambled onto the animal, Silas jumping on behind.

As they galloped up the street, Geoffrey heard a sickening impact and felt Silas's chest slam against his back.

Order returned to the Council Hall.

"I have a motion that this session be adjourned until the morrow," the Clerk said.

The motion was seconded and approved. Some of the Overlords left the hall, but most remained, talking in small groups.

Axelrad returned to the chamber.

"Where is he?" Nostromal demanded.

"I have ordered pursuit."

"You let him escape?"

"The old man is hit," Axelrad said. "They won't get far."

"They may head for Castleford—proceed there at once," Nostromal said.

"But the girl's at Cliffhaven."

Edging close enough to overhear—as Nostromal dropped expletives and orders on Captain Axelrad—was Lord Tyrus.

CHAPTER 53

"Limuel, try to remember. When you last counted the rats, how many did we have?"

"I don't know."

Dr. Qwenten, going cage by cage, counted the rats again. Forty-one. But shouldn't there be forty-three, not counting the one Nostromal had taken the previous night?

Qwenten grabbed the boy by the shoulders, shook him, shouted in his face. "Was it forty-one or forty-three?"

"I never counted 'em for a month." He twisted away from Qwenten. "There, I admit it. I just wrote down the same number every time. What difference does it make?"

"Nostromal—he's infected at least one rat, maybe more," Qwenten said.

He found Rigdin in the front hall. "It is urgent that I speak with Lord Nostromal."

"Lord Nostromal departed for Assembly a short while ago," the butler said.

"Did he have a rat cage with him, or a small sack?"

"A rat cage?" Rigdin looked at Qwenten as if he were a lunatic.

"Was he going directly to the Palace Presidio? It is urgent that I find him."

"For what reason?"

Qwenten pulled a thumb-sized vial of red-brown liquid from his pocket. "He forgot this. It is part of his daily regimen."

"What has that to do with a rat cage?"

"I am the Lord Nostromal's personal physician. When he returns, shall I tell him of your obstruction?"

Rigdin scowled. "Castleford first, then the Palace Presidio."

CHAPTER 54

When the town was several miles behind them, Geoffrey guided the horse into a wood. He followed the sloping ground to the bottom of a swale, lifted Silas from the horse, and laid him on his side in the moss, hidden among the roots of a massive oak where it gripped the bank.

The arrow protruded from Silas's back near his right shoulder blade. Geoffrey gingerly grasped the shaft and was surprised when it came away in his hand. But the projectile was not attached. He opened Silas's shirt. There was no exit wound, just a dusky, palm-sized bulge on Silas's chest below his collarbone.

Silas grimaced, took in a sudden breath. The wound on his back made a sucking sound; a gush of blood came out.

"Silas, try not to move," Geoffrey said.

He found a blanket in the saddlebag, ripped it into strips, and bound the wound as best he could. He then laid Silas on his back, folded the remainder of the blanket, and placed it under his head.

"You saved my life," Geoffrey said.

From the direction of Caerdon came the faint baying of a hound.

"It's not saved yet."

"Silas, I . . . I should have listened to you. "I'm sorry."

Silas did not respond. His breathing was slow, each breath rattling in his throat, the sucking sound still audible despite the bandage.

Geoffrey had never known Silas to be ill, injured, or even fatigued. His face was pale, brow creased in pain, mouth open as he sought air. Something inside Geoffrey crumbled; he was unable to speak.

After a long minute, Silas said, "Tobacco . . ."

"You . . . want to smoke?"

Silas shook his head.

"Oh, like we talked about," Geoffrey said. "Tobacco will be our first crop in Markarian, of course."

Silas nodded. He extracted something from his pocket, folded it into Geoffrey's hand. A silversmith's mandrel, worn shiny by his fingers.

"Take Damaris with you . . ."

"We're all going, Silas. You're going to be all right." Geoffrey's voice trailed off. He hung his head.

A hound bayed, closer.

Geoffrey felt Silas's knuckles rub weakly against his scalp, saw his arm drop, saw his eyelids slowly close. Then, like water calming after ripples from a stone, Silas's face relaxed.

"Silas?"

Geoffrey's eyes blurred. He clutched up Silas's hand, rubbed the limp knuckles against his scalp, tears spilling down his cheeks.

"Papa . . ."

Geoffrey heard the bark before he saw the dog, heard the shout before he saw the horseman.

CHAPTER 55

Running until his lungs burned, then walking until he could run again, Dr. Qwenten got to Castleford as fast as he could.

As he climbed the front steps, an arrow slammed into the door. He threw himself to the ground. Another arrow hit the door an inch above his head.

"It's Dr. Qwenten," he yelled.

The crunch of boots. Captain Axelrad.

Qwenten stood up.

"You could have killed me."

"Could have. But didn't."

"I seek Nostromal," Qwenten said.

"Why?"

"He, uh, forgot his serum. Where is he?"

"Cliffhaven, by now."

Qwenten turned to go.

Axelrad fitted another shaft into the crossbow, notched the string, and leveled the weapon at Qwenten's midsection.

"You're staying here."

"What about the serum?"

"Lord Nostromal has a vial with him. As you know."

"Where's Lord Geoffrey?"

"If he comes here instead of Cliffhaven, you're the hostage."

In the parlor a few minutes later, Axelrad reclined on a stuffed chair. He leaned his loaded crossbow, stock resting on the floor, against the cushion near his leg.

Qwenten sat in a side chair across the room and wondered what exactly he might have done had he been able to find Nostromal. Especially if the man had already released a Scourge-infected rat or two. He contemplated the crossbow.

When Axelrad dozed, the doctor crawled to the crossbow. He wrapped his fingers around the stock—

Axelrad startled awake, grabbed the crossbow with one hand, and punched at Qwenten's face with the other. Qwenten kept his grip on the stock and lunged for the trigger lever with his other hand.

Qwenten saw Axelrad's eyes go wild as the man swallowed convulsively against the steel in his throat. Then he clutched the shaft with both hands and jerked the arrow out in a gush of blood, shortening his life by several minutes.

CHAPTER 56

Geoffrey leaped up, roared the battle cry Silas had taught him, and charged the horse at a full run.

It reared and threw the rider. The horse's front hooves crashed down onto the dog, killing it.

Geoffrey jumped astride the mount as three foot soldiers scrambled into the swale.

The spooked horse ran at the soldiers, scattering them. Geoffrey gained the reins, turned the animal in the opposite direction, kicked it to a gallop as the soldiers raised their crossbows.

The horse—hit twice—buckled and went down. Geoffrey freed the sword from the saddle scabbard and scrambled into a thicket of wild rosebushes. He crawled on his belly to the other side of the bushes and attacked the soldiers from behind.

He stabbed the nearest soldier in the leg and disarmed the second with a slash to the wrist. The third man hurled his spear at Geoffrey, missed, and fled.

Geoffrey slid behind a tree and waited for more soldiers to appear. None did.

"The necklace of fire awaits your companions at Cliffhaven."

Silas had mentioned a leg injury, which meant Damaris would likely be with Dr. Avery, the physician Geoffrey had seen as a youngster for his burns.

Could he get there in time?

CHAPTER 57

Damaris rested in a rocking chair by the fireplace, her leg propped on a stool. She sang a nursery rhyme to herself and tried to imagine Silas and Geoffrey returning together in a happy homecoming. Silas would have a funny story to tell about how he sneaked into the Palace Presidio. Geoffrey wouldn't have needed any help, of course, but she had thought, just in case . . .

A horse galloping up to the porch, a knock on the door.

Damaris froze in mid-verse. The knock came again—more like a pounding—and despite Dr. Avery's admonition to admit no one, she limped to the door.

"Who is there?"

"Lord Tyrus, Baron Loridine. I am a friend of Lord Geoffrey, Baron Castleford."

Damaris opened the door.

"Forgive me, my lady," Tyrus said. "But you may be in grave danger."

"Who are you?"

"I served with Geoffrey's father, in the House of Overlords." Tyrus tried to catch his breath.

"You know Geoffrey?"

"Yes, my lady."

"Is he all right?"

"When I saw him last, he was, uh, managing."

"How about Papa—Silas—have you seen him?"

"He was with Geoffrey."

"Where are they now?"

"Lord Nostromal's men are pursuing them. They intend to capture—and probably kill—Lord Geoffrey."

The sandcastles of reassurance Damaris had built for herself swirled away.

"Is Dr. Avery not home?" Tyrus said.

"He and his wife went to Comstoke to help the miners' families."

"I believe you are not safe here," Tyrus said. "We must leave at once."

"Why do they want to kill Geoffrey?"

"Nostromal tried to use Geoffrey to further his ambitions, but Geoffrey did not cooperate."

The story rang true—especially the part about Geoffrey not cooperating—but Damaris was not sure about leaving with Tyrus.

"Why are you doing this?"

"Because I, who have sat these many years in silence and in shame, watched a young man stand up today and speak truth," Tyrus said.

Damaris got her shawl and started with him out the door then stopped.

"Wait. Does Geoffrey know of your mission? Did he send you?"

"No."

"Then he and Silas might be on their way here," Damaris said. "If Nostromal gets here first, they'll be walking into a trap."

"If Nostromal gets here first, he will probably kill you."

"I'm not leaving."

"Please, miss."

Damaris folded her arms across her chest.

Tyrus sighed. "There are some men who might help us, miss. I shall return with them as fast as I can."

Tyrus listened for Damaris to drop the latch.

The Gerber brothers, who lived nearby, might be willing to assist—Nostromal had orchestrated the false imprisonment of their father.

But in his haste Tyrus had failed to tie his horse when he arrived at Dr. Avery's. The animal was gone. On foot, the fastest way to the Gerber house was through the woods beside the mill pond. He followed the millstream, which flowed near Dr. Avery's house.

A squirrel scolded from high up in a tree then fell silent—as did the birds and bullfrogs.

Tyrus did not notice.

"Lord Tyrus."

The voice came from behind a willow tree. Tyrus saw sunlight flash on the dagger blade, gasped as the point pierced his navel. Nostromal yanked the weapon free, and Tyrus felt his body falling toward the glassy surface of the pond.

Tyrus wondered why he heard no splash, although he had distinctly heard the little ripping sound as the fabric of his shirt split for the dagger point.

Damaris was wishing she and Tyrus had arranged a special knock when the door crashed open.

A man charged in and grabbed her face.

Fingers digging into her cheek, a thumb hooked behind her jaw, pain shooting into her scalp.

The man kept his grip on Damaris as he made a quick inspection of the two-room cottage, then hurled her to the floor. "Attempt escape and I will kill you."

Nostromal.

She watched, her stomach a knot of fear, as he cleared the furniture from the center of the room.

Setting a trap.

Nostromal drew his sword and began pacing from window to window, looking out.

Tyrus and his men should be here any minute.

A sound outside. Nostromal sprang to Damaris and clamped his hand over her mouth before she could cry out a warning.

A knock on the door and a child's whine: "I don't wanna see the doctor."

"Shut up, Gentry," came a woman's voice. Another knock, long moments, then footsteps shuffling away.

The hand came off her face. Nostromal ordered her to sit on the floor in the corner then resumed his vigil, window to window. From where she sat, Damaris could not see outside.

"Don't move," Nostromal said abruptly, walked to the door, and opened it to leave.

He is going to set an ambush outside. She would not be able to warn Geoffrey.

"Lord Nostromal, do not leave yet." Damaris's voice was quiet. She stood.

He turned around and seemed to see her for the first time. "How curious that a girl from a carnival sideshow should be more comely than most of those who are brought to me."

Nostromal closed the door and strode back in. He grabbed both her wrists in one hand.

Damaris fought the iron grip, realized her bones would crush like eggshells, stopped.

The man drew his dagger and put the point at the hollow of her throat.

"I heard Nostromal only killed with a kiss." She had meant to scorn, but her voice sounded small to her.

Nostromal re-sheathed the weapon. He forced her hands down in front of her and grasped a handful of her hair. She couldn't move her head, so tight were his knuckles against the back of her scalp.

His mouth moved toward hers. Damaris smelled the perfumed oil in his beard, felt the breath of his nostrils on her chin. She screamed before his lips could touch hers.

"That ought to bring Sir Idiot, Lord Geoffrey, to your rescue." Nostromal released her, but Damaris forced her feet to remain planted, facing him. She forced her hands to remain at her sides, fists clenched in balls of terror. She kept her eyes on his face.

Nostromal inclined his head toward her and almost smiled. "Aren't you the brave one?"

They were in a game of sorts, each wondering how far she would go in her efforts to delay him.

Where is Tyrus?

Nostromal touched his fingertips to the skin below her ear. She jerked her head sideways then steadied herself. The fingertips returned with light strokes, index and third finger walking in place on the side of her neck. The urge to flee nearly mastered her as she fought her body into rigidity.

Tyrus and his men will arrive any second, kill this beast, and Geoffrey will be saved.

Nostromal's fingers trailed down to her collarbone. But when his hand crept lower, Damaris's leg muscles exploded and she ran for the door, forgetting her injured leg. Nostromal grabbed her before she could open it. He propelled her to the center of the room, yanked off her shawl, and looped it over an upper beam. He tied the shawl corners to her wrists and stretched her arms high above her head.

Nostromal strode back to the door, opened it a crack, peered out. Closed it quickly.

The man drew his sword and pressed himself out of sight on the opposite side of the fireplace.

As Damaris formed the words to warn Geoffrey—she would call out calmly, so that he would not charge in—Nostromal suddenly had her face clamped between both his hands and was driving his mouth toward hers.

Don't scream . . .

Qwenten kicked himself for fleeing Castleford without Axelrad's crossbow, somehow forgetting his inexperience with such a device.

As he scurried along toward Havencliff, he tried to convince himself that Limuel was in error, that Nostromal had surely taken no additional rats, or if he had, there was still time to stop him. Stop him how? His mind circled back to the crossbow.

He also told himself that the reason he saw almost no one else on the road was because of the time of day, or the day of the week, or the weather, or . . . well, any number of reasons. *But surely not because people now thought they had reason to fear Scourge . . .*

The door burst open.

"Geoffrey!" Damaris screamed. "It's a trap!"

Nostromal charged out from beside the chimney. Geoffrey parried the first blow, but the next opened a cut on his cheek.

He counterattacked and landed a glancing hit on Nostromal's chest.

The two combatants circled each other. Nostromal maneuvered himself toward Damaris, hanging by her arms in the center of the room. He raked the tip of his dagger across her bare shoulder.

Geoffrey attacked in a fury. Jabbing, thrusting, slashing, he drove the man away from Damaris.

Nostromal defended himself with seeming ease.

Geoffrey saw that the cut on Damaris's shoulder was superficial— rubies forming on a red thread.

He drove his opponent against the kitchen table, but Nostromal vaulted over it to Damaris and this time scratched a line from her armpit to her elbow. Blood ran.

Geoffrey sprang at Nostromal, spun sideways, shoved him away from Damaris.

"Geoffrey, he is using me to defeat you!"

Geoffrey kept his back to Damaris as Nostromal circled him, striking high, thrusting low, Geoffrey with no room to maneuver, his arm tiring against the relentless blows.

"Geoffrey," Damaris said, "I am already killed . . ."

Her neck was swollen and bruised-looking. *Maybe Nostromal tried to strangle her.*

Geoffrey lunged, but Nostromal jammed him with a kitchen chair. He jabbed the legs at Geoffrey's face, blocking his vision.

Nostromal hurled the chair at Geoffrey then thrust his sword at Damaris. Geoffrey struck Nostromal's sword away just before it could pierce her, lost his balance, and landed on his back.

Nostromal was on Geoffrey in a rush, aiming a thrust at his chest. Geoffrey rolled clear and regained his feet.

They squared off, Nostromal fresh, Geoffrey breathing hard.

Nostromal slashed, Geoffrey ducked. Again and again, the blade closer each time.

"Geoffrey, save yourself." Damaris's voice was weak. "I have Scourge . . ."

"No," Geoffrey said. He did not, would not, believe that.

"Your little friend's attempt to delay me was pathetic, her sacrifice wasted," Nostromal mocked. "But her mouth was . . . delectable."

In a leap of fury, Geoffrey closed the gap and punched his fist at the leering face, but Nostromal sprang away. Geoffrey saw—too late to dodge—the flash of steel arcing toward his head. At that instant Damaris arched her back, shot forward on her tethered arms, and smashed her feet into Nostromal's back like a trapeze artist landing on her platform.

Jolted off balance, Nostromal missed his aim. Geoffrey drove his sword forward into the big man with both hands, twisted it.

Nostromal collapsed to his knees. His hand went to the darkening patch on his midsection.

"You cannot kill me . . . you freak son of a traitor." He crumpled onto his face. "I am Nostromal, the Lord High Chancellor," he said through clenched jaws. "No one even knows your name."

Nostromal slowly rolled to his back. "Your father had a message for you . . . the night he died." He continued in a whisper, but the words were unintelligible.

A message from father . . . Geoffrey strained forward to hear, thought better of it even before Nostromal drew his blood-soiled dagger from his waistband and lunged up. Geoffrey sprang back. Nostromal sprawled facedown, his dagger clattering across the floor.

Geoffrey watched for breathing movements. None. He prodded Nostromal's neck with his sword tip. Nothing.

That's when Geoffrey noticed a damp patch at his waistline. He pulled his shirt away.

A two-inch cut.

Damaris sagged, hanging by her arms tied to the overhead beam.

"Oh, Dee."

He untied her, carried her outside.

Geoffrey placed Damaris on her back in a grassy patch of sunlight beside the millstream, not far from the cottage. He took both her hands in his as he knelt beside her.

"You are all right, Geoffrey?"

He did not answer.

"Geoffrey?"

"Just a little cut, it's nothing."

"Scourge blood," she said.

His silence confirmed it. Tears spilled from Damaris's eyes.

She touched Geoffrey's face, studied him.

"You are a beautiful man . . ."

She clasped her hands around his neck. By old habit, Geoffrey sought to remove them lest she find his scars. But Damaris held on.

"You are a beautiful man," she repeated. "And I love you," she whispered. "All of you."

All of you. Something in Geoffrey, after so many years of shame, believed her. He enfolded her in his arms, and they clung to one another.

"Where is Papa?"

"He is . . ." Geoffrey's voice broke.

Damaris sobbed. At last she spoke. "How?"

"Saving my life."

Damaris nodded. "And in a little while we shall all see one another again."

CHAPTER 58

When Dr. Qwenten arrived at the cottage in Cliffhaven, he saw Geoffrey and Damaris lying motionless together in the sunlight beside the millstream, like fairy-tale lovers who had fallen asleep in each other's arms.

"Lord Geoffrey? Miss?"

Geoffrey lifted his head. "Dr. Qwenten, please help her."

Qwenten's heart sank when he saw the unconscious girl. A purple rash extended from her closed eyelids to her swollen neck. Her breathing was labored.

He knelt, felt a faint pulse in her wrist. He pulled a vial from his pocket. "This may be enough, if she is recently infected. Was it a rat?"

"Nostromal," Geoffrey said.

"Where is he now?"

"In the house. Dead."

"Dead? Are you sure?"

"Yes."

"Geoffrey," Qwenten said, "was Nostromal carrying any rats, in a cage or sack?"

"I don't know."

"Miss," the doctor said, touching Damaris's cheek, "I need you to take some medicine."

Damaris drew in a wheezing breath. Geoffrey cradled her head in his lap.

"Please, Damaris, wake up. The doctor has something for you."

Dr. Qwenten uncorked the vial and put it to the fevered lips. Her eyelids fluttered open. She pushed the vial away. "Geoffrey is stricken too."

Dr. Qwenten looked a question at Geoffrey, who did not meet his eyes. "I have only enough for one of you," Qwenten said.

"Give it to Geoffrey."

"No," Geoffrey said. "Damaris must have it."

"Geoffrey," Qwenten said. "Nostromal had a vial—his dose for tonight—it should be with him."

Geoffrey ran into the house. Nostromal lay facedown where he had fallen. Geoffrey rolled him onto his side, retrieved the vial from an inside pocket, and ran back outside. He had not noticed one of Nostromal's eyes coming slowly open . . .

Geoffrey knelt again beside Damaris and Dr. Qwenten. "Got it."

Damaris's hands dropped as she fainted again. Geoffrey took them in his.

"Doctor, what are you waiting for?"

"Nostromal's vial was empty, wasn't it?"

"Please save her, doctor."

Qwenten thought the better plan was to treat the one who was not yet symptomatic, rather than see them both die.

"I fear she is too far gone, Geoffrey. But you—"

Geoffrey snatched the vial from the doctor's hand and began dripping the fluid into Damaris's mouth.

A protest rose to Qwenten's lips before he realized that he would have done the same for his beloved Derina. He helped support Damaris's head until Geoffrey had given her all the serum.

A sudden black blur at the edge of Qwenten's vision, a sword thrust at Geoffrey, and Qwenten arching his own little body up to block it.

Geoffrey leaped to his feet as Nostromal attacked again. He dodged a slash, glanced about for a weapon, spun away from the second thrust, yanked Silas's mandrel from his pocket. When Nostromal raised his sword again, Geoffrey charged forward and stabbed the mandrel into the hollow of Nostromal's wrist, wrenched, felt a snap, and grabbed the sword as it dropped from Nostromal's hand. He swung the sword and struck Nostromal across the throat, cutting through windpipe and arteries. The man toppled into the grass, head partially severed from his body.

Geoffrey knelt beside Damaris, helped her sit up. She looked much better. His heart lifted.

Dr. Qwenten lay on his side, hugging his knees against his chest. That's when Geoffrey realized the little man had been stabbed.

"Dr. Qwenten?" Geoffrey started to roll him onto his back.

"No," Qwenten said. "I will bleed out if you move me." He moaned then looked at Damaris. The rash was fading from her cheeks; her breathing was no longer wheezy. He managed a smile.

"Geoffrey," Damaris said. "You drank the other vial, right?"

Geoffrey shook his head. "But I feel all right."

"Then you survived Scourge as a youngster," Qwenten said. "You will live."

"He's never had Scourge," Damaris said.

"Let me see the wound, Geoffrey." Pink froth drooled from the corner of Qwenten's mouth. "Quickly."

Geoffrey lay down on his side, his abdomen a few feet from the doctor's face, and pulled up his shirt.

"Damaris, hurry, get the sharpest kitchen knife you can find."

She hobbled to the cottage, tripped on Nostromal's leg, sprawled onto the doorstep, got up.

"Geoffrey," Qwenten said, "on your back. Then don't move, not a muscle."

Damaris returned, paring knife in hand.

"Get on the other side of him," Qwenten ordered. "You must be my hands."

Damaris was unsure. "Doctor . . ."

"Damaris, your hand. Place it on his stomach, over the cut. That is how much you must remove."

"But—"

"Blood flow in scar tissue is slow. The Scourge element may not yet be in his system. We must cut that tissue out, like cutting out a snake bite before the venom spreads. Quickly! We may have only seconds to save him."

"I can't cut into Geoffrey like a piece of meat." Damaris was near tears.

"He will die then."

"Geffy?" Damaris looked at his face. He nodded.

She put the knifepoint against his skin near Nostromal's cut.

"Push the blade in," Qwenten said.

She pressed down. "It won't go in."

"You are cutting into scar tissue. It's like gristle."

Damaris stabbed the blade in. Geoffrey flinched. She jerked back.

"Be still, Geoffrey," Qwenten said.

"Sorry," Geoffrey said.

"Again, my dear. Keep pushing in, about the thickness of your finger, until you feel no resistance."

"I can't." Damaris looked to Geoffrey.

"It's all right, Dee." Geoffrey managed a smile. "But I'm regretting that night I tied your braids to the water pail while you slept."

"Damaris." Qwenten's voice was pleading.

She again put the knife into position against Geoffrey's skin.

Geoffrey clenched his hands into fists as Damaris pushed the blade in again. She stopped when the point was buried about a finger-thickness.

"Forgive me, Geoffrey," she said.

"Keep pushing," Qwenten said.

She did so; the resistance suddenly gave way.

"You're at the fat layer. Cut at that depth, the size of your hand. Three sides."

Sweat beads popped out on Geoffrey's face. He bit through his lip, tried to focus on the salty taste in his mouth.

"Hurry," Qwenten said.

Damaris could feel the warm blood, sticky, between her fingers as she cut. She forced her blurring eyes to stay on the task and off Geoffrey's face.

"Done," she said.

But Qwenten's eyes were closed, his breathing shallow.

"Doctor?"

"Push your fingertips under the flap you made." The doctor's teeth were chattering.

"Work it free from the underlying muscle. Then cut across the base of the flap."

The flap of tissue was as thick as a man's hand and so slippery she had trouble gripping it as she cut. At last the lump of flesh came loose. Blood everywhere.

"What now?"

Dr. Qwenten did not reply. Damaris reached across Geoffrey, now unconscious, and thumped the doctor's shoulder.

"What about the bleeding?"

Qwenten opened his eyes, tried to focus. Blood pumped from Geoffrey's wound. *Possibly a branch of the mesenteric artery, or . . .* His eyes closed again.

"Doctor!" Damaris tried to stuff the bottom of Geoffrey's shirt into the hole in his side. The fabric was quickly soaked. "He'll bleed to death!"

"Cauterize . . ." Qwenten managed to whisper.

Damaris raced into the house, dropped on her knees in front of the fireplace. With the tongs, she grasped a large chunk of burning wood.

Outside, Qwenten reached a feeble hand to press at the wound.

Geoffrey opened his eyes.

"Here, Geoffrey, hard as you can, both hands."

Geoffrey pushed his shirt edge into his bleeding wound, but the flow was unstaunched.

"My laboratory," Qwenten rasped. "You must destroy every creature—leeches, rats, monkeys . . . burn them. Promise me."

Geoffrey nodded. "Yes."

"My journal . . . you must . . . you . . ."

Dr. Qwenten died with his eyes open and his lips puckered in mid-word.

Damaris returned and knelt beside Geoffrey, the flaming chunk of wood in her tongs.

Geoffrey felt the heat, saw the flames hiss and snap like a living beast. *Bertraks's torch.*

"Don't touch me!"

"Dr. Qwenten said cauterize."

"No."

"You'll bleed to death."

"Get away from me!" He guarded his abdomen with both hands.

"Geffy, there's no choice!" Damaris thrust his hands aside and plunged the fire in.

Geoffrey had not cried out when the carnival toughs clubbed him, nor when he was whipped in prison, nor when Damaris hacked the tissue out of his abdomen. But as the burning coal devoured his raw flesh, a scream burst forth from his lungs like nothing Damaris had ever heard.

Tears streaming down her face, she ground the coal in, searing each side of the wound in turn, each thrust eliciting a fresh scream from Geoffrey. Not until the sizzling ceased did she extract the tongs.

Damaris had heard Geoffrey weep only once, when he was a boy, after the farm punk beat him so badly. He cried now, in a child's voice— the voice of the little boy who had read to her, teased her, laughed with her. The voice that had animated their puppets and whispered stories about life together someday in Markarian.

At last he fell into residual sobs, like an infant who continues, even though there are some things that tears can never finish.

Damaris let these sounds blend into the soft babble of the stream, until finally they ceased.

She washed her hands and arms in the flowing water, then her face.

Geoffrey did not resist as Damaris tenderly washed him, cleansing the blood away. She retrieved some of Dr. Avery's bandages from the cottage and dressed his wound. She splashed a plume of water from the millstream into Geoffrey's face.

"Hey . . ."

Damaris giggled, splashed him some more, then gently log-rolled him into the stream.

Geoffrey was on his back in the shallow water. Damaris stretched out on top of him, smoothed the wet hair from his brow, looked into his eyes.

"I love you, Damaris," Geoffrey said.

Their first kiss.

CHAPTER 59

They had not been long together in the soothing stream when Damaris saw a red swirl in the water above Geoffrey's shoulder. Was he still bleeding? She looked up and shrieked.

Drifting down the millstream, almost upon them, was a corpse.

"Geoffrey!" Damaris splashed to her feet. "Get up!"

Geoffrey was first to recognize the dead man. "Lord Tyrus."

"Oh, no," Damaris said.

"You knew him?"

"He tried to help me."

A jagged gash in the man's stomach drained water and blood as Geoffrey dragged the sodden body onto the stream bank. When a severed loop of intestine flopped out, an awful thought hit Damaris. What if she had cut too deeply on Geoffrey? She could have killed him. Nauseated, she began to tremble.

But Geoffrey seemed strong as he laid Tyrus's body next to Dr. Qwenten's. Nostromal's corpse lay a few yards away, nearer the cottage.

Damaris, recovering herself, explained to Geoffrey about Lord Tyrus's earlier visit. They guessed Nostromal as the man's murderer.

"We must bury Nostromal," Geoffrey said. "If they find his body . . ."

"You'll be wanted for the murder of the Lord Chancellor of the Realm," Damaris said.

"Yes."

"And if they try to embalm him . . ."

Damaris shuddered. "Could that start a Scourge outbreak?"

"I'm not sure."

They looked up—the sound of tramping feet.

"Soldiers?" Geoffrey said. "Hurry." He lifted Damaris in his arms.

"No," she said. "You might start bleeding again."

"What about your leg?"

"I'm fine."

They held onto one another for support and quickly made their way to the edge of the woods where the millstream flowed forth. Peering from the trees, they watched a small phalanx of soldiers march by, shields and spears catching the last of the day's sunlight. As they waited for the troops to pass, Damaris nudged Geoffrey and pointed. Upstream was Lord Tyrus's horse, still saddled, reins dragging in the water.

"Could we take it and . . . retrieve Papa?"

Geoffrey nodded. "Maybe the rose garden."

Damaris looked puzzled.

"I mean, we could bury Silas at Castleford," Geoffrey said, his voice hoarse.

Damaris assented, tears welling.

But although they approached the horse slowly, the animal moved farther upstream. They pursued, the horse skittering away each time they closed in. At last the horse trotted out of the woods and onto the road, where they decided not to follow.

In the deepening dusk, Geoffrey and Damaris retraced their path through the woods along the millstream. The brook babbled and chattered, dumb to the violence wrought beside it that day. As they emerged from the woods onto the grass, they stopped, Geoffrey motioning silence with a finger to his lips. Something was amiss. Were they being watched?

Geoffrey and Damaris noticed it at the same time: Nostromal's body was gone. The other two bodies—Lord Tyrus and Dr. Qwenten—lay undisturbed.

"Maybe dogs dragged him off?" Damaris suggested.

"I'll check downstream," Geoffrey said.

Damaris moved cautiously across the grass toward the cottage, noting items that seemed untouched: the kitchen knife, the fireplace tongs, the chunk of wood.

The cottage door was still open. She peered in, but the murky twilight revealed nothing but dim window squares. She stepped inside for a better look, waiting for her eyes to adjust. No corpse. As she turned to leave, a convulsion hit her stomach. Looming dark in the doorway was a man. Damaris backed away, tripped over a stool, went down with a clatter.

"Who's there?"

The voice was familiar to her. "Dr. Avery?"

A flint was struck and a lantern blazed up.

"My dear, are you all right?" Dr. Avery helped Damaris to her feet.

Geoffrey appeared in the doorway. "What happened?"

CHAPTER 60

After Dr. Avery had rekindled the fire and put the teakettle on—and explained that Mrs. Avery was still in Comstoke to assist the midwife—Geoffrey and Damaris relayed their tale, concluding with the death of Lord Nostromal.

"That explains why the roads are full of soldiers," Dr. Avery said. "You must flee Auldeland at once, both of you. Book passage at dawn."

"With what means?" Damaris said.

"I know not," the doctor said.

"We'll sell off the furnishings from Castleford," Geoffrey said.

"Is there time for that?" Damaris felt a spark of hope.

"No. Troops at Castleford await you even now," Dr. Avery said. "And Geoffrey, by tomorrow evening, wanted posters with your name on it will be more numerous than ever Silas could boast of."

Back to the beginning. A weight settled on Damaris's heart.

Dr. Avery rose abruptly, grabbed the lantern, and marched outside. Geoffrey and Damaris followed.

The doctor was beside the millstream riffling through the pockets of Lord Tyrus's corpse.

He pulled out the man's purse. Damaris expected him to check Dr. Qwenten's pockets next. As if reading her thoughts, Dr. Avery said, "I'll wager he's got less money than I. Which is nothing or you'd already have it."

Dr. Avery looked in Tyrus's purse. "This should be sufficient. Find a cargo vessel—they will be watching the passenger ships."

"We can't take money from a dead man," Geoffrey said.

"You'll wind up dead yourselves then."

"Geoffrey, Lord Tyrus told me that in the Overlords meeting, you stood up for truth," Damaris said. "Something he wished he would have done. He wanted to help us."

Dr. Avery handed Tyrus's purse to Geoffrey. "If you do escape—by no means a certainty—then Lord Tyrus will have saved your lives."

Back inside the cottage, Dr. Avery promised to learn what he could about Silas's remains and effect a proper burial, if possible. He would also apprise relatives, if any, of the demise of Lord Tyrus and Dr. Qwenten and see that their remains were taken care of as well. But Dr. Avery seemed far more concerned about Nostromal's Scourge-ridden body.

"Who has taken it? Why? What have they done with it?"

"I just realized," Damaris said, "Nostromal's sword and dagger are gone too."

"The corpse and everything with it should have been burned," Dr. Avery said. "Very troubling."

Geoffrey jumped up, recalling his promise to Dr. Qwenten about his journal and laboratory animals. By now it was after midnight.

"I'm going with you," Damaris stated.

"It's not safe," Geoffrey said.

"Then we shall die together."

"No."

"We are not going to be separated again, Geoffrey."

Geoffrey appealed to Dr. Avery. "Doctor, please tell her."

"Geoffrey. If you leave and she's made up her mind to follow you, do you think I could stop her?" Dr. Avery chuckled. "You forget—I've known Damaris as long as I've known you."

A pounding on the door jarred them out of the argument. Dr. Avery pointed at the back window. "Go!" he hissed.

CHAPTER 61

The night began to pour rain, shrouding the moon and shifting the guards at Castle Dunnesmore to shelter under the balconies. With Damaris hunkered down in the window well keeping watch, Geoffrey slipped into Dr. Qwenten's cellar laboratory. He found Limuel asleep under a bench. He shared with the boy the sad news of the doctor's death.

"They were here, Mr. Lord Geoffrey," Limuel said. "Looking for you."

"Who?"

"From the Realm."

"How do you know?"

"The pennant and scimitar." Limuel tapped his chest, indicating the emblem position. "Did you really kill Lord Nostromal?"

Geoffrey ignored the question and instead explained Dr. Qwenten's last request.

"I already packed up the mold trays and journals," Limuel said. He pointed to a satchel and a small crate.

"Why?"

"Lady Sapphira's orders. She's sending a man to get them in the morning."

"I think not. Where are the animals?"

"I turned them all loose."

Geoffrey was dismayed. "What if—"

"I would have known if any were infected."

"I need you to come with me, Limuel." Geoffrey surmised that the boy's knowledge of Dr. Qwenten's methods might be helpful to whomever received the journal and materials.

Limuel was excited, but terrified of Sapphira should he be caught.

Damaris called down from the window well. "Hurry up, Geoffrey. The rain has stopped."

"Limuel, grab the satchel." Geoffrey boosted the boy up through the window then passed the crate up to him.

By the time the trio had fled the castle grounds, slogged through muddy fields, and twice hidden in the woods to avoid soldiers, it was almost dawn when they reached Dr. Avery's cottage. A brief perusal of Dr. Qwenten's journal left Dr. Avery astonished and excited. He insisted that Limuel accompany him that very day to the town of a physician whom he knew had an interest in Scourge studies. Limuel got the surprise of his young life when they arrived in Marmet Crossing at Dr. Rudolph Tarrold's practice and found Musette, his blossoming young apprentice.

CHAPTER 62

"If the money is not sufficient," Geoffrey said, "we can also work."

"As I told you, the *Peregrine* takes no passengers," said the captain of the four-masted grain ship. He handed the money purse back to Geoffrey. "Besides, it's sore treacherous weather to be sailing with landlubbers aboard."

Geoffrey and Damaris exchanged a glance. The morning sun, sparkling off the buildings of Caerdon, was already climbing a cloudless sky.

"Weigh lines!" the captain barked. "Haul the squares!" He fixed a glare on Geoffrey and Damaris. "Step ashore or be thrown."

"Captain Joppert, please reconsider," Geoffrey said.

"Are we running from justice, mayhap?"

"No." Geoffrey beckoned the man closer and—sharing a confidence—showed him the bronze ring on his right index finger, recently bestowed by Mr. Smadgins at the Palace Presidio. The effect of the Fresian sea eagle, marking Geoffrey as a member of the House of Overlords, was immediate.

"Forgive me, my lord," Captain Joppert said.

"Lord Geoffrey, Baron Qwenten, at your service, captain." Geoffrey was surprised that the gambit had worked. "And may I present to you the Lady Damaris, Princess of Avery."

"I could not have known, my lord." The captain seemed defensive. "The garb of commoners, and without a retinue?"

"The House of Overlords dispatched me—clandestinely—to determine possible foreign connection in the assassination of Lord Nostromal, High Chancellor of the Realm," Geoffrey said in a low voice. "You have heard the news?"

"I do not concern myself with politics," Captain Joppert said. "We have been engaged in refitting the ship. The owner will brook no more delays."

"I would be pleased if this mission remain our secret, captain." Geoffrey slipped the patrician ring off his finger and pocketed it. "No one else is to know."

"Of course, my lord."

The wind filled the sails as the ship eased away from the wharf into the blue waters of the harbor.

"One more request, Captain Joppert, if I may." Geoffrey took both of Damaris's hands in his and looked into her eyes. "What is the customary offering to perform a wedding at sea?"

Damaris's eyes were shining.

"For my lord and lady, not a penny," the captain said. "'Twill be my honor. At sunrise, weather permitting?"

"Perfect," Geoffrey said. "Thank you, captain."

Captain Joppert gave a slight bow and strode aft. "See to the spanker! Lively, now!"

Damaris, hair streaming in the ocean breeze, threw her arms around Geoffrey and kissed him.

Geoffrey lifted his face to the bluest sky he had ever seen, closed his eyes, and savored the salt air.

THE END

ACKNOWLEDGMENTS

I wish to thank David Hancock and his amazing team at Morgan James Publishing, including Jim Howard, Bethany Marshall, Bonnie Rauch, Nickcole Watkins, Taylor Chaffer, Amber Parrott, Lauren Howard, Heidi Nickerson, and Jessica Burton-Moran. Also instrumental in the publication of *Scourge* were Crystal Miller, Terry Whalin, and Angie Kiesling. To Tyler, Myles, Lucas, Lauren, Ashley, Charles, Sue, Pete and Andrew—thank you. Finally, I have been greatly blessed by the encouragement and support of my wife, Tacy.

ABOUT THE AUTHOR

Terry Weston Marsh brings *Scourge* to life both as a practicing physician dealing with contagious diseases and as a practiced storyteller in the world of film. Terry's writings have garnered numerous regional Emmy nominations as well as an Aurora award. He was also tapped by iconic artist Bob Ross to write the children's TV program "Bob's World" prior to Bob's untimely passing. Terry and his wife, Tacy, reside in Mooreland, Indiana,  near their three sons and their families. To learn more about Terry and his current projects, visit FeatherwindProductions.com.

CPSIA information can be obtained
at www.ICGtesting.com
Printed in the USA
BVHW072143240321
603057BV00002BA/11